Tales

MW00882567

Starbrite Motel

By Scott J. Ginsburg

An almost true Southern romance set against a fading, small town mom & pop motel and it's assortment of 'by the week' renters, who's dramas, traumas and conflicts with their momma's play out in the rapidly changing landscape of Youngstown, NC.

Tales from the Starbrite Motel

Preface

Before we get started, I want y'all to promise me, pinky swear, that you won't get your under-britches in a knot over any part the story I'm about to tell. I especially don't want to hurt the feelings of any of our Yankee friends. Lord knows, we've got plenty of y'all in North Carolina these days. I think it has a lot to do with New York and New Jersey having a 'no returns' policy, which I can fully appreciate. I do love Yankees even though y'all talk funny and always insist on telling us slow witted Southerners how you did things correctly back home. You should know that when we listen politely and respond with a 'How nice!' we mean something else entirely.

Everything I'm going to tell you is somewhere close to the truth or at least a reasonable lie. As God is my witness, it's all meant in good fun, except for the sad parts. I recommend having a box of your favorite tissues handy, just in case. I write very emotional stories.

I will try my level best not to have any, or at least not very many, cuss words in this book. So rather than be offensive, I will substitute *** for the missing letters of the bad words, should any be necessary to the story. I suspect you'll get my drift.

My sons sometimes call me RandomMan and my loving wife says that I occasionally digress in my writing, wandering off in all sorts of odd directions. If that should be the case, I want y'all to feel free to write me with any of your concerns. I'll take them under consideration and get back to you at my earliest possible convenience. Don't be real surprised if I just say 'How nice!'

Chapter 1 – U.S. 1

There are a lot of folks who claim that Route 66 is America's Mother Road, but I respectfully beg to differ.

U.S. 1 flows southward for 2328 miles from Ft. Kent, Maine to Key West, Florida. Before 1925, when the Federal government began numbering roads, it was The Atlantic Highway and had been around since the time of George Washington, connecting the thirteen original colonies that became the God-blessed United States of America. No need to stand, unless you feel particularly patriotic today.

Since it was the mother of all roads in this country, I think it deserves the proper recognition. Those Route 66 guys will probably argue the point, since they had a television show back in the 60's and all.

Dotted along U.S. 1 are big cities like New York, Philadelphia, Baltimore, Washington and Miami, but more importantly, at least to this story, are the villages and small towns that are commonly referred to as "Rural America," though most folks I know consider those wide spots along the highway to be the "Real America."

The Village of Youngstown, NC is a tiny dot on the U.S. 1 map at the halfway point between Raleigh and the Virginia border. Founded in 1754 by Jewish merchant, Isaac Rabinowitz, who established a trading post for local tobacco farmers, the village hasn't changed much over the years. Well, one thing that did change was that Isaac's youngest son married a Baptist sharecropper's daughter and converted. Just a little local history. I thought it might add some to the story.

Longleaf Tobacco has been the big cash crop in the area for over 200 years. During the Civil War (known to locals as the Northern War of Aggression), Union soldiers (known to locals as Blue Shirted Devils) felt the town wasn't worth the effort to loot or burn, so just kept marching south toward Raleigh. Remember, you pinky-swore not to take any offense.

About the time that The Atlantic Road became U.S. 1, the Youngstown General Store and Blacksmith Shop, located on the northbound side of the road, began selling Aycock Gasoline and Oil and doing some auto repairs. It can be noted with a great deal of local pride, that they had first electric gasoline pump in Quincy County. OK, maybe it was a lot bigger deal back then.

Eustace Camber and Willa Mae Nichols grew up in Youngstown, attending the one-room schoolhouse that served first grade through twelfth grade pupils. They were members of the graduating class of six students in May of 1934.

At that point in the history of Youngstown, it was home to about 1200 North Carolinians. A tiny branch of the Quincy Farmer's Bank and Trust and a café had been built on the south side of the road where Holden St., which runs east and west, intersected with U.S. 1. On the northwest corner of Youngstown a Free Will Evangelic Fundamentalist Church had been constructed facing U.S. 1, with its cemetery behind the building. Holden Street was where the tobacco auction warehouse and feed store were located as well as the majority of homes. There were also a half-dozen dirt streets that comprised the balance of the town. On the far eastern edge of the village, the C&O Railroad tracks ran parallel to U.S. 1. The black residents of Youngstown lived east of the tracks back in those segregated days, and had their own small general store, schoolhouse and AME (African Methodist Episcopal) church.

After graduation, Eustace divided his time between his parent's tobacco farm and a part time job at the General Store. Smart as a whip with numbers, Willa Mae was hired as the junior teller at the bank. Both socked away every penny they could, in hopes of being able to afford getting married in the near future. When Willa Mae got wind of an upcoming bank foreclosure sale on forty acres of land just to the south of town, she convinced Eustace to combine their savings and try to buy the property.

During the Great Depression, times were especially tough in rural North Carolina and even though the acreage coming up for auction was decent farmland, there were few if any takers with the cash to make a purchase. The property included eight acres that faced U.S. 1, was five acres deep and about a quarter mile south of where Holden St. made the Youngstown four corners.

The auction was held on a cold, rainy Saturday afternoon in mid-November with only two bidders in attendance, Eustace and a land speculator from Raleigh. Shortly after making the first bid at $7.50 per acre, the land speculator began feeling the ill effects of the country ham and red eye gravy breakfast he'd eaten in Wake Forest, while on his way to Youngstown, and headed full steam for the outhouse behind the General Store. Eustace was able to purchase the property for $8 per acre, which was just about the entire total of his and Willa Mae's combined savings.

During the winter months, Eustace cleared the remaining pine timber from the land, selling most of it to the lumber mill in Franklinville and keeping enough back to build a four room farmhouse on the property. Instead of spending money on indoor plumbing or electricity, he and Willa Mae used the remaining funds to get married in March of 1935, just before Eustace planted the first tobacco seeds in the red dirt of their farm. Both of them continued their paying jobs as well as spending all their spare time working on their crop of longleaf tobacco.

During World War II, the local draft board gave Eustace a farmer's exemption on the condition that he convert his fields to soy beans and corn, to help feed the country. He was happy to oblige.

After the war, in the early 50's Youngstown really expanded with a Rexall pharmacy and an IGA grocery store. The old general store was replaced with a shiny white ESSO three pump gas station and a small building was constructed as the Village Hall and Post Office on the southbound side of the road. With U.S. 1 as its single-stoplight Main Street, Youngstown grew like so many of the neighboring communities.

It wasn't long after that the town of Wake Forest, just to the south of Youngstown, lost the college that shared the name of the community. It moved on to Winston-Salem, becoming Wake Forest University. Over the years, this has caused considerable confusion for folks. Today they even sell shirts that say "Wake Forest, NC.....where the University ISN'T!" If you're interested, you can buy one down on South Wait Street. After a while, the Southeastern Baptist Theological Seminary took over the old college campus and has turned out hundreds of fine preachers in the years since.

A probably true fact is that the Arnold Palmer drink was invented in Wake Forest. Arnold Palmer was a student at Wake Forest College and a regular patron at a local lunch counter. He used to ask them to mix up half a glass of sweet tea with half a glass of lemonade. Once he became famous, they named the drink after him. Now you know the probably true story! Remember it the next time you order an Arnold Palmer.

Am I digressing? You've got to tell me when I start going off track.

Eustace and Willa Mae were in their forties and dead tired of the back-breaking labor associated with farming tobacco. One night, after a particularly low-paying tobacco auction, they decided to sell off all but the eight acres of their farm that faced U.S. 1 and start a new business venture. It was here that they constructed their motel in the summer of 1958.

The plan was for Eustace to run the motel until it was profitable enough for Willa Mae to quit her job at the bank and join him in running the place.

Sitting on the front porch of the old farmhouse that was to be sold with the acreage, enjoying a clear Carolina summer night, Eustace

8

told Willa Mae that she should come up with a name for the new motel.

"Star light, star-bright first star I see tonight, wish I may, wish I might have the wish I wish tonight," she said aloud, repeating a rhythm from childhood. "Starbrite! I want to call the new place the Starbrite Motel," Willa Mae declared. Having no better (or worse) names in his head, Eustace quickly agreed with her decision.

While Willa Mae was a financial ace, the only thing the Cambers knew about being innkeepers came from their two night honeymoon stay at the Wigwam Village Motor Court, near Richmond. That limited experience didn't stop them from constructing a 12 unit, single story motel made of concrete blocks with a front to back sloping roof. Each modern room featured air conditioning, an electric heater and a small three piece bathroom. Eustace felt that having air conditioning for every room might be too expensive, but Willa Mae insisted and since Eustace almost never won when he tried to change her mind, he gave in. There was no point in offering TVs in the rooms, since they were a real luxury back then and the reception from the two Raleigh stations was fuzzy at best. There was a General Telephone booth in the gravel parking lot, so there was no need for in-room phones either. The Starbrite had a neon sign on the roof, facing U.S. 1, with a red 'no' that could be turned on or off before the word 'vacancy.' The Cambers built a single story, two bedroom home next door that served as their residence as well the motel office.

It took only a couple of weeks before the Camber's figured out that if they didn't turn on the 'no vacancy' sign at bedtime, some crazy Yankee yahoo would want to rent a room at two in the morning.

"Can you believe that folks stay up 'til all hours of the night?" Eustace said to Willa Mae after one such rude awakening.

The September 12th edition of the Quincy County Weekly Tribune carried the story of the Starbrite's grand opening on their front page, along with a photo of Eustace and Willa Mae standing in front of the motel. Willa Mae had convinced Eustace to change from his bib overalls into his Sunday suit for the picture and to "git that darned toothpick out of your mouth." Billed as the only motel on U.S. 1 between Raleigh and Henderson, the Starbrite's comfortable rooms rented for $4.00 per night and offered a roll-away bed or crib for the young'uns for fifty cents more.

It took very little time for the Camber's to understand the ins and outs of running a small motel. Willa Mae had always been a fussy housekeeper; so, the rooms were spotlessly clean and the bathrooms sparkled. A traveling salesman who sold motel supplies stopped by the office shortly after the Starbrite opened and sold Eustace a six month supply of 'sanitized for your protection' paper ribbons to put on the toilet seats and a bunch of little bars of Ivory soap, wrapped up in wax paper. He even convinced him to buy large black numbered plastic tags for the room keys.

Having far less property to manage than when he was farming tobacco, Eustace kept the motel lawn mowed and trimmed in fine fashion and even raked the gravel parking lot on a daily basis.

Being located on the southbound side of U.S. 1 seemed to benefit the Starbrite, since so many people from New York drove down to Miami, rather than taking a train. Back then it typically took three full days to make the trip and Youngstown was a good 'first night' stop for snowbirds headed south for the winter.

"Them New York folks are strange," Eustace told Willa Mae shortly after the motel opened. "The feller that checked in last night asked me if the café served beagles. Can you imagine?! I told him that we use our beagles for huntin' rabbits. He gave me the oddest look."

Eustace and Willa Mae ran a no-nonsense motel and insisted on keeping the Starbrite a highly respectable lodging facility. Couples were expected to check-in together, with both signing the motel registration cards. Willa Mae had no hesitation in asking questions if she didn't see wedding rings or if she saw any signs of hanky-panky going on. A sign behind the registration desk stated '**Only married couples, members of the same immediate family or a single individual may occupy rooms at the Starbrite Motel**.'

"This ain't some sleazy No Tell Motel," Eustace would say with a big grin.

The other thing that the Cambers were insistent on was that blacks (colored people back then) could stay at the Starbrite. In those days, well before the Civil Rights Act of 1964, segregation was still alive and well with 'whites only' establishments all across the south. Eustace and Willa Mae would have none of that and felt that anyone who could afford the $4.00 per night room rental was welcome to stay at their motel.

That didn't sit too well with some of the white hooded boys from nearby Johnson County, who initially sent Eustace and Willa Mae a letter calling them a bunch of "ni**er-lovers" and other such terms of endearment. When the letter was ignored and the Starbrite continued renting to blacks, four Knights of the Invisible Order decided to pay the Cambers a visit one evening in the late summer of 1959, with plans to light up a cross in the motel parking lot.

If you grew up anywhere near Youngstown, you knew better than to try butting heads with Willa Mae Camber. Apparently her reputation for dealing with fools hadn't ever spread as far as Johnson County.

When the boys started getting out of their car, two of them with axe handles in hand, Willa Mae realized what was about to happen and greeted them with the sawed-off double-barreled 12 gauge shotgun that she kept behind the registration desk.

"Just so's you boys know, ol' Betsey is loaded with slugs, not birdshot nor rock salt. I'd advise you to git the hell back under whatever rock you crawled out from and go mind your own business," she said.

11

Initially thinking that the owners of the Starbrite would cower in fear and immediately apologize for their abhorrent ways, Willa Mae's greeting took them more than a little off guard.

Hearing the commotion, Eustace grabbed his thirty-ought-six hunting rifle and came around the motel to the back of the group, pointing it directly at the four hooded knights. His cousin, Are Dee Camber was a sheriff's deputy who lived next door to the motel. When he was born, Are Dee's momma wanted to just name him 'R.D.' but the doctor insisted that he have a first and middle name for the birth certificate, so she named him Are Dee.

Are Dee was sittin' on his front steps when he saw the carload of Klansmen roll into parking lot. Figuring they weren't there to rent a room, he grabbed his .38 Police Special and his badge and walked over to the Starbrite.

"Boys, I am the LAW around here and I want y'all to know that you're fixing to sh*t in your own mess kit," he said with a mouthful of Redman chewing tobacco. "If I was you, I'd git down the road before my cousin's wife kills the four of you and he and I have to dispose of the evidence."

It was a hot, humid North Carolina summer evening and the four knights immediately came to the conclusion that a cold beer back in Smithville beat getting a gut full of lead in Youngstown.

"We'll be back! You can count on it!" yelled one of the Klansmen as they loaded back into their '56 Plymouth.

"I got your license plate number, so's we'll know just who to expect," was Are Dee's reply.

After they left, Are Dee called a hunting buddy who was a deputy on the Johnson County Sheriff's department. Convincing him that his cousin's wife was bat-crap crazy and meaner than a coiled rattlesnake, the word got out about Willa Mae and there were no further incidents at the Starbrite.

As a thank you, Willa Mae baked Are Dee one of her famous pecan (pronounced locally as pee-CAN) pies, though at 320 pounds, he probably could have done without it.

While the Cambers didn't have any children of their own, they did take-in Willa Mae's four year old nephew Franklin Delworth, when his parents were killed in a car accident in 1963. Willa Mae's only sibling, Viola, was eight years her junior, but closer than close to her older sister. Folks around Youngstown always felt that her name fit her perfect since Viola was shaped like a viola.....smaller at the top, wider at the bottom. Ok, a whole lot wider.

After graduating from Bushy Fork Bible College (BFBC) and becoming an ordained minister, Philo Delworth couldn't find a church or denomination that would hire him. For those of you who may be unfamiliar with North Carolina geography, Bushy Fork is located between Frogs Hollow and Hurdle's Mill, up by Roxboro.

Feeling strongly that, under the circumstances, the Almighty would want him to form his own church, Philo took his life savings of $126, and rented an empty store building not far from Youngstown, in nearby Franklinville. While a student at BFBC, he'd heard tell about all the sinning going on in Franklinville and felt that it was his personal obligation to save as many souls as possible in that tiny community. Slowly building up followers, it took about six months before Philo had a congregation of nearly 60 good folks. Viola had heard about his preaching and attended one of the Wednesday night services. Seeing her in the congregation, Philo was immediately taken with Viola. After the service, while shaking his hand, her heart melted when he asked her to pray in private with him that very evening. With the help of a half bottle of Mogen-David sacramental wine, their courtship began and he asked for her hand in Holy Matrimony only a month later.

Viola moved into the back of the store building where Philo stayed and prayed, sharing an old mattress with her new husband. After only a month of marriage, Philo found out that Viola was with child

13

and declared it a miracle, immediately promising his congregation that if the baby was a boy, he'd name him Franklin, after the place where he was conceived, though his name could have just as easily been Former Western Auto.

In the four years that followed, Philo's congregation grew to over 200 loyal followers, and the church was relocated to a large metal Quonset building out on U.S. 1. With the success of his church, he could afford to rent a small house in Youngstown, so that Viola could be nearer to her big sister.

In one of the few times when Eustace laid down the law to Willa Mae, he insisted that they not abandon their church for Philo's.

"Add religion or politics to any family and something's bound to sour pretty quick," he said.

While returning from preaching at the funeral for a member of his congregation and with Viola in the car, Philo's '55 Chevy stalled in the middle of the NC98 and was hit broadside by a logging truck. It took the undertaker most of a day to pull him and Viola out of the wreck and put 'em back together. Probably more information than you wanted to know, right?

Though nearer to the age of grandparents, Willa Mae and Eustace did their level best to raise Franklin in a loving home, providing well for the child and eventually sending him off to North Carolina State University in Raleigh.

An inherently good natured kid, as he grew up Franklin readily pitched in with chores at the Starbrite, cleaning guest rooms, tending to the property and nudging his aunt and uncle to add amenities to keep competitive with other motels in the area, especially as I-95 began siphoning-off traffic from U.S. 1.

When he arrived to live at the Camber's home, Franklin was a light haired, freckle faced, skinny-as-a rail little kid. By the time he graduated from Youngstown High School, he was a handsome 18 year old man, five-eleven in height, with a thin 150 pound frame and deep brown eyes to match his thick, dark hair. Willa Mae would often tear up when seeing Franklin because his face reminded her so much of his mother, her dear, departed younger sister.

After earning his college degree in Electrical Engineering and getting a job in Raleigh, Franklin continued living at the Starbrite, helping his aging aunt and uncle to keep the place running.

In 1982, Eustace was diagnosed with terminal lung cancer, which came as a surprise to almost nobody, since he'd smoked at least two packs of unfiltered cigarettes daily since his mid-teens. Knowing his time on this earth was quickly drawing to a close, and being completely bedridden in his final days, he asked Franklin to come to his bedroom.

"How did you get so big, boy? You weren't but a little squirt when you came to live with Willa Mae and me," Eustace said.

"Yes, sir," was all Franklin could say.

"I don't know as I ever told you this, but I hope you always knew, I love you Franklin....love you like the son you've always been to me. And I couldn't be prouder of you in a hundred years," Eustace said, his voice cracking along the way.

"Yes, sir," Franklin said, as tears flowed down his cheeks. "And I love you too, Daddy."

"You ain't never called me that before, son."

"Figured I'd best start while I still had the chance," he replied.

"I don't know that the angels in heaven could make a sound that would mean more to me," Eustace said softly.

Franklin leaned over, placing his head on Eustace's chest, sobbing as quiet as he could. Eustace patted him gently on his head.

"Call me that name just one more time before Jesus comes to take me home," Eustace whispered.

Still laying against his chest, Franklin whispered, "Daddy..... Daddy, I love you."

With one soft, final breath Eustace was gone. Willa Mae, watching from the doorway came over and held Eustace's hand in hers, reaching over to Franklin with her other hand.

"You meant the world to him, Franklin, and to me, too. The world."

(Y'all can stop and get a tissue, blow your nose and wipe your eyes now. Try not to get anything on the pages. Remember, we're still only in the first chapter.)

Willa Mae died eighteen months later of a heart attack in her sleep, just the way most of us want to go. When she hadn't gotten up by 9:00 a.m. on a Saturday morning, Franklin thought something might be wrong and knocked on her door. When she didn't answer, he opened it and found her with a bible in her hands and a gentle smile on her face. She was with Eustace again.

Willa Mae left the motel and everything else to Franklin, as you'd have expected. Out of respect for his aunt and uncle and because it had been his home since early childhood, he resisted any urge to sell it, instead converting the Starbrite to 'by the week' efficiency apartments, often rented by those who were down on their luck. Franklin remodeled the house he'd lived in with the Cambers and continued his 85 mile daily round trip to work at the Esterhouse Electrical Manufacturing plant on Capital Blvd. (U.S. 1) in Raleigh.

Renting the 12 rooms by the week made great sense to Franklin, since he worked during the day and there was no one available to check renters in or out of the motel. It was 1983 and the Starbrite no longer shined as it once did. There were newer, fancier places to stay in Raleigh and Henderson, with color TVs, in-room telephones and swimming pools. The Starbrite had become just another 'mom & pop' motel along U.S 1, dying a slow and miserable death at the hands of progress and potential customers who now preferred cookie cutter, chain motels along the Interstate.

Because he rented by the week, Franklin had to be around on Saturday afternoons to collect the $35 per-room weekly rent, hear any tenant complaints or concerns and keep the place going. Daily room cleaning was eliminated and replaced with fresh bed linens and towels, available at the office when the guests paid their rent. A shared vacuum cleaner was also available to borrow from Franklin.

Each room was equipped with a double bed, small dresser, a chrome rack attached to the wall for hanging clothes, a small microwave oven and an old TV, most of 'em black and white. Guests also received a 40 quart ice chest that they could keep filled from the ice maker that was located just outside the office. Dishwashing and all other cleaning had to be done in the shower or bathroom sink. Far from the Ritz, the Starbrite was much closer to a stale soda cracker.

Renters paid for a week in advance, with no refunds if they left earlier. Because of this policy, any renter who came up short of cash on Saturday was usually evicted, regardless of the sob story they may have offered. Franklin also insisted on a maximum of two people to a room. Like his aunt before him, they had to be either a married couple or members of the same immediate family. As it turned out, nearly all the rooms were occupied by single tenants.

Renters were a mixture of recently divorced men, people working short-term jobs in the area, retirees who were trying to live on just Social Security and the occasional down-and-outer. Often members of the latter group would only stay for a week or two, prior to running out of money. The common thread for all the Starbrite renters was that it was often the final stop before becoming homeless.

To no small extent, Franklin lived a double life, working as an up-and-coming engineer during the week and reverting to his landlord role on the weekends. Further complicating his life was his serious crush on Lisa Ann Prescott, a 21 year old smokin'-hot secretary at the Esterhouse plant where he worked. She was a New York native who'd moved to Raleigh with her parents at the start of her senior year of high school. Along with the face of an angel and a nearly perfect body, came a vocabulary that could make a longshoreman blush.

While she did a great job keeping the 'f-word' at bay during working hours, Lisa Ann was a true potty-mouth once she got away from the factory and had sucked down a beer or two. Even when he was a student at NC State, Franklin had seldom heard the multi-syllabic cuss words that came out of her beautiful mouth. It was at a Friday after-work Happy Hour with Franklin and a group of other coworkers, when she'd referred to a recently fired manager as a "low life, motherf*cking, coc*sucking, son of a bi*ch!" Franklin nearly chocked his complementary meat ball and mini smoked sausage hors d'oeuvres! His Aunt Willa Mae would never have allowed such language in her house and it ran completely contrary to his conservative upbringing. With her short skirts, phenomenal legs and habit of wearing blouses with the top two buttons undone, Franklin was positively amazed when Lisa Ann finally agreed to go out on a date with him. Even more astounding to him was the fact that she'd accepted a second and even a third date, as they slowly got to know each other during the late summer and early fall of 1984.

Franklin knew in his heart of hearts that he could help her to mend her ways, find religion and perhaps even become his wife. All that right after he got the chance to fu*k her brains out, more or less. Ok, probably more. I'm not digressing again, am I?

Chapter 2 – Are Dee and Brenda Camber

Are Dee Camber was a deputy on the Quincy County Sheriff's Department for over 27 years prior to taking an early retirement as a result of a gunshot wound to his left knee. It happened when he was asked to assist in weapons training for three new recruits to the department. One of them was fidgeting with the safety on his service revolver when it went off. The bullet struck the concrete wall of the Sheriff's Department basement training room before ricocheting and nailing Are Dee's knee. Had he been younger and in better shape, he might have fully recovered and returned to the job. Instead, he walked with a slight limp. Because the new deputy who shot him also happened to be the son of the Quincy County Commission's Chairman, the decision was made to offer Are Dee an early out, with his full pension.

There are some people who are just big boned and there are some folks who are fat. Are Dee was both. He was six foot four and built like a 320 pound side-by-side refrigerator. The few strands of his still black hair were slicked straight back from his forehead to partially cover the large bald region that began developing in his 40s. Now in his 50's, he didn't hide his age or weight particularly well and seemed to always be red faced, out of breath and slightly sweaty. Most folks thought he was a heart attack waiting to happen.

Are Dee was a genuinely kind, compassionate person who knew almost all the good people he'd protected during his career and never hesitated to give one of them the benefit of a doubt when he was on the job. He was respected and appreciated by those same folks.

During his career, he was mostly assigned to the Youngstown area. While he may have looked like a stereotypical overweight Southern lawman, to the best of my knowledge he never in his life said, "You in a heap of trouble, boy."

As Eustace Camber's first cousin, next door neighbor and closest friend, he took it upon himself to make sure that young Franklin had plenty of playmates as a kid, including Are Dee's own three children. Because Eustace and Willa Mae were older, it was Are Dee who took Franklin hunting and fishing, making sure the he had the chance to experience the things other kids were doing at his age.

When Eustace, and later, Willa Mae, passed, Are Dee and his wife Brenda stayed close to Franklin and became yet another set of parents to him.

"No matter what the problem is, you know you can always come to us," Are Dee told him on the day of Willa Mae's funeral.

With the continuing growth of Youngstown, in the fall of 1983 the Village Council felt that the time had come to establish a police department. The timing was near perfect, since Are Dee had been retired for almost six months, was bored out of his mind and was driving Brenda stark raving mad by constantly hanging around the house. Overlooking his knee injury for his extensive experience and given his willingness to accept the meager salary they offered, he and the Village Council reached agreement that he'd come out of retirement to become the Chief of Police. While they had the funds to pay him, purchase a used Ford cruiser from the NC Highway Patrol and give him an office in the Town Hall, his back-up would have to be deputies from the Sheriff's Department, most of whom had previously worked with Are Dee.

Are Dee took his new responsibilities seriously and wanted to show the Village Council that the Police Department could be self-funding. To that end, he developed a system for enforcing the speed limit in Youngstown, especially for out of town drivers who disregarded the signs along U.S. 1 that reduced speed from 55 miles per hour to 45 and finally 30 before reaching the stoplight at the main four corners of town.

Fearing that Youngstown could get a reputation as being a speed trap, he limited himself to no more than three or four stops per hour, generally targeting higher end cars with out of state license plates. He gave friendly verbal warnings to drivers that were five to ten miles per hour over the speed limit and invited them to spend some time in Youngstown, try the Carolina Country Café or fill up with gasoline and stretch their legs. It was warm southern hospitality at its best and it worked like a charm to generate more sales for the local businesses and plenty of goodwill for the village.

"What da fu*k do you think of dat, Bernice? Barney F-ing Fife just let us off with a warning!" a Yankee driver might say to his wife.

"Let's get out of dah cah and see if day got a gift shop in town, I gotta to pee like a race horse," his Yankee wife might respond.

Drivers disobeying the speed limit by more than ten but less than fifteen miles per hour were ticketed with a simple $25 'first offense – pay on the spot fine, cash, VISA and MasterCard accepted' ticket.

Drivers going more than fifteen but less than twenty miles per hour over the limit paid a $100 fine.

Few, if any, drivers asked to plead not guilty, since doing so would require returning to the Youngstown Village Hall for a trial with the Magistrate that was always inconveniently set for six to eight weeks after the violation.

With the added revenue, the Youngstown Police Department was soon able to obtain a second used patrol car and hire another officer to assist Are Dee.

Marcus Lorenzo Cooper was the first person to apply to be the second officer on the Youngstown Police Department. He was 23 years old, a Youngstown native, fresh out of the Army with some MP training and was about as big Are Dee. At six feet, five inches tall and 260 pounds of solid muscle, he was intimidating, even when he was smiling, especially when he was smiling. Marcus was a very dark skinned black man. He also had some of the biggest, whitest teeth you've ever seen. When he gave a big smile, the contrast in colors was amazing and could be somewhat intimidating, if you didn't know what a gentle man he was.

He and Are Dee had also some history, when the Quincy County Sheriff's Department assisted the Feds in arresting Marcus' daddy, George Washington Cooper, for cooking up some first class whiskey on his farm just outside of Youngstown. It would be insulting to call George a moonshiner. He was a distiller of fine, locally produced spirits, aged in genuine plastic barrels for a minimum of five days and available for the discerning palettes of his customers. Marcus was 15 when the Feds swooped down on his daddy's business. The Sheriff's Department was on hand as back-up, though none was really needed. It was Are Dee who pulled Marcus away from the goings-on, explained what was happening and kept him from being implicated in the illegal distilling and sales.

While George was sentenced to a three to five year term in the Federal slammer, Marcus was free to finish high school and decided to enlist in the Army.

Are Dee knew he wanted to hire him from the minute he saw his application, but still went through the motions of interviewing eight other candidates, none of whom were worth a tinker's darn. He held Marcus' interview until last.

"I'll bet you don't remember me," Are Dee said to him at the start of the interview.

"I most certainly do, Chief Camber. You kept me out of that mess when they raided my Daddy's still. I don't know as I ever thanked you for that or for checking up on my family after he was arrested. You didn't have to do none of that stuff."

"Whatever became of your daddy after he served his time?"

"He and Momma moved to Kentucky and he got a job with a distillery in Loretto. He works in quality control at their main still and helps make some truly fine bourbon!"

"Somehow, that just seems right," Are Dee said thoughtfully. "Marcus, why on earth do you want to become a Youngstown police officer?"

"Actually, sir, you're the reason. I've seen how you treat folks. It don't matter who they are or what color they are. You treat 'em decent, like they're human beings. I saw a lot of that in the Army. Respect, you know what I mean? I'd really like to work for you. Besides all that, Youngstown is my home, I know almost as many folks around here as you do."

"A lot of what you'd be doing is boring stuff....traffic stops and such."

"That's OK. At least people won't be shooting at me."

"Probably not," said Are Dee as he felt a tinge of pain in his knee, "hopefully not."

After fully vetting Marcus' military records and confirming that he had been honorably discharged at the end of his hitch, Are Dee made his recommendation to the Village Council and got their approval to hire him.

The following Saturday afternoon, Are Dee walked over to the Starbrite to speak with Franklin. After knocking on the screen door and letting himself in, he walked straight to the refrigerator and helped himself to a cold Dr. Pepper.

"You got any empty rooms this week Franklin? If you do, I need a favor."

"Don't tell that Brenda threw you out after all these years?" Franklin asked with a smile.

"Women don't get rid of a stud like me, boy," Are Dee said straight faced. "You may not know it, 'cause Brenda don't like to brag, but I am a 57-year-old love machine!"

"Good to know. I've got two empty rooms this week, if you want to borrow one for a couple of hours, Mr. Love Machine," Franklin replied.

"I just hired a new officer for the department. Nice kid, just out of the Army and he needs a place to stay. You may know him....Marcus Cooper. I was hoping that you'd rent him a room at the family discount rate, since we ain't paying him much."

"Marcus was two years behind me in school. Wasn't his daddy a moonshiner?" asked Franklin.

"Yup, one of the best. Served his time and moved out of state," Are Dee replied.

"I had some of his 'shine once, when I was about 14. Eustace bought it home in a Mason jar and asked me if I wanted to give it a try. As I recall, it singed my eyebrows," Franklin said with a laugh. "Do you think Marcus can afford thirty bucks a week?"

"That should work. I'll let him know."

"Just one thing, Are Dee, please have him leave his patrol car at your office. If people see one parked at the Starbrite, they might get the wrong idea," Franklin added.

And that's how Marcus Cooper landed in Number 6 at the Starbrite Motel in March of 1984.

"You got it! I certainly wouldn't want to tarnish your image," Are Dee said smiling. "You want to have Sunday supper with us? Brenda's going to fry up a mess of chicken and we've got fresh collards, too."

"Is she gonna make banana pudding for dessert?" Franklin asked.

"If that's what it takes to get you to come to supper, I'll see that she does!" Are Dee replied.

The following Monday, Marcus became a sworn officer in the Youngstown Police Department, though he wouldn't have uniforms for a week or so since they had to be special ordered from a shop in Charlotte, given his size and all.

Are Dee did equip him with a badge, gun, holster and walkie-talkie radio. Wanting to make sure that he handled traffic stops properly, he and Marcus did several role playing exercises. As Marcus walked up to Are Dee's car, he rolled down his window and turned to look directly at the belt buckle of the new officer.

"License and registration, sir" Marcus said in an all-business manner.

"No!" said Are Dee. "I want you to lean in, so's they see your face and smile that big friendly smile of yours. And I want you to always say 'please' when you ask for their license and 'thank you' when they hand it over. As long as you're polite, most of 'em will be polite back. If they say something ugly, I want you to smile back and say 'Excuse me, but I'm sure I didn't hear you correctly.' Ok, let's try it again."

"License and registration, please, sir," Marcus said smiling.

"Much better!" said Are Dee. "Now, go f**k yourself, boy!" he added.

"Excuse me, but I'm sure I didn't hear you correctly," Marcus said.

"Perfect! Now stand up straight so's they can see how big you are and place your right hand on the butt of your gun and your left hand on the handle of the car door, like you're gunna open it up and yank 'em out by their nuts," Are Dee instructed. "That will generally make them think twice or just crap their britches. Either way, you'll get their full attention."

"One more thing," Are Dee added, "if they say anything else you don't like, look 'em in the eye and tell 'em that you was discharged from the Marine Corps for using excessive violence and that they are starting to stir up some of them ugly feelings in you.....and say it with a real big smile."

"But I was in the Army!" Marcus protested.

"Work with me on this one, Marcus, it's just play-acting" Are Dee pleaded. "Work with me!"

As the day wore on, Are Dee continued the detailed instructions.

"Don't get greedy," he warned the new officer. "We're a friendly town and want to keep that reputation."

In his crisp new uniform, Marcus went on official patrol duty the following Tuesday. Are Dee took him to all nine of the local businesses and introduced him to the owners. They also visited Youngstown High School, where Marcus had graduated, met with the two local church pastors and the manager of the Quincy Farmer's Bank branch. There was no doubt that Are Dee was showing off his new officer to folks in Youngstown!

Having an assistant to keep the cash cow producing, Are Dee started looking at crime in the general area, since other than traffic violations, there was virtually none in Youngstown. I-95 had become the cocaine corridor between Miami and New York, with regular drug busts resulting in millions of dollars of cash and white powder being confiscated.

"I wonder if some of those folks might be taking an alternate route to New York?" he asked Marcus.

Are Dee asked his assistant officer to be on the lookout for cargo vans coming through town with Florida or New York license plates.

"If they're speeding, even three miles over the limit, stop 'em and call me for back-up. Be careful and don't let your guard down. I don't want you to approach the vehicle until I get there. These ain't going to be like the old folks drivin' Cadillacs," he instructed.

It took nearly two weeks to hook the first fish, but it was a monster. Marcus stopped a high-cube Econoline van loaded to the ceiling with bails of marijuana. It had New York plates and the driver was going ten miles per hour over the posted speed limit. With a street value of well over a million dollars, the drug bust made the Raleigh and Charlotte newspapers.

Are Dee turned the case over to the NC Highway Patrol, if for no reason other than having no place to store the confiscated pot. He and Marcus would be key witnesses at the trial of the driver and his passenger, who swore they were told they'd only be transporting landscaping materials.

Upon hearing their explanation, Are Dee said to Marcus, "They must think we came to town on the back of a turnip truck!"

Just six months after establishing a Police Department in Youngstown, it not only was self-funding but also had scored a major drug bust and had even received a letter of commendation from Governor Hunt!

Because the Youngstown Police Department was housed in the tiny Village Hall, it was limited to one small office. The most recent arrest pointed out the critical need for more space.

The Starbrite Motel sat on the north end of the eight acres of land owned by Franklin. The property had been annexed into Youngstown in the early 70's as the community had expanded. This gave Are Dee an idea that he needed to discuss with Franklin during the coming weekend.

Are Dee walked over to Franklin's house on Saturday morning, carrying a coconut cream pie, freshly baked by Brenda. After knocking on the door and not getting an answer, Are Dee let himself in.

"I'll be right back Honey, I promise," he heard Franklin say.

As Franklin opened his bedroom door, wearing only his boxer shorts, Are Dee could see a pretty blond girl in his bed, pulling the sheets up to cover herself as he came out of the room.

Are Dee let out a low, slow whistle and said quietly, "Lordy, Lordy! Franklin Delworth, playboy motel owner! Just wait until I tell Brenda about this! Your poor old Aunt Willa Mae must be rollin' in her grave to know the carryin' on's in her old bedroom."

"You will do no such thing, Are Dee!" a red-faced Franklin pleaded. "This needs to stay between you and me."

"What about the girl? Ain't she in on this too?" Are Dee teased. "I just come over to talk some business with you, but since you're so deep into monkey business, it can wait until you're more appropriately dressed for the occasion. I was going to leave you this pie to eat, but by the looks of things I'm guessing you've already had a piece this mornin'. Come see me when you get the chance. Oh, and next time, lock your door."

Are Dee left the coconut cream pie on Franklin's kitchen table, letting himself out and walked back home grinning ear to ear.

It was just a little before 5:00 that afternoon when Franklin walked over to Are Dee and Brenda's house. Are Dee was sitting on the front porch, sipping a cold beer and listening to the end of the UNC football game on a transistor radio. Not saying a word, Franklin sat down in the wooden rocking chair next to him and grabbed a beer for himself from the iced bucket next to Are Dee.

"You'd think that a college that wins national championships in basketball could turn out a decent football team ever once in a while?! They just lost to Boston College, 52 to 20! If Dean Smith could coach football, they'd be in the danged Rose Bowl," Are Dee said with some disgust, as he turned off the radio.

"It 'peers to me like you've been sowing some wild oats, Mr. Delworth," Are Dee said, grinning widely. "I can only hope that you have crop failure within the next month or so."

"Are Dee, I am a twenty-five year old man. I have needs," Franklin said.

"I'd say them needs are getting taken care of pretty good these days," Are Dee said. "I really don't want to talk about your love life, unless you need some pointers. What I wanted to discuss is a business deal that could help the village and you." Hearing Franklin's voice on the front porch, Brenda came out to give him a hug.

Brenda Camber was five-one in any given direction, with short brown hair and eyes to match. She and Are Dee had raised three children. Their two sons, Robert Dee, who was three years older than Franklin and Richard Lee, who was in his class throughout school, had been hellions growing up. By the grace of God, they had managed to stay out of jail (it helps when your daddy's a Sheriff's Deputy), graduate from high school, get jobs at the textile factory in Wake Forest, and avoid producing any illegitimate grandchildren for Brenda, at least to the best of her knowledge and as of this writing.

Her "angel" was her baby daughter, Patrice, who never caused a lick of trouble for her parents until she went off to UNC Wilmington (otherwise known as Surfboard Tech), got hooked up with an exchange student from Uruguay and eloped to South America to live on his parents coffee plantation at age 19. At least she sent pretty post cards every month or so.

"Can you stay for supper Franklin? I'm making pot roast and there's plenty. I can set another plate," she suggested.

"Thanks! I wish I could, but I've got a date in Raleigh tonight," he replied.

"Are Dee told me you've got a new girlfriend. Says she's real sweet on you! You know she's always welcome to come to supper, too."

The thought of having Lisa Ann Prescott and her extensive vocabulary sharing a meal with Are Dee and Brenda was far more than Franklin was prepared to deal with at that point.

"I appreciate the offer, but I'm taking her to the Shorthorn Barn tonight."

"The Shorthorn Barn?! My gracious, she must be special!" Brenda said.

"Oh, she is," said Are Dee, taking great pleasure it torturing Franklin.

Brenda gave Franklin a kiss on the cheek and returned to the house.

"Have you ever thought about subdividing your land and selling off the extra property? My guess is that the Starbrite and your house take up somewhere close to three acres, even with the parking lot. You could break up the other piece into four or five lots and generate some income for yourself," Are Dee suggested.

"Uncle Eustace told me that he'd laid out the land so that he and Willa Mae could eventually add a restaurant and maybe a filling station, south of the motel. With the interstate getting built, and them getting older, none of that ever happened. What do you suppose I could get for a piece of property like that?" Franklin asked.

"What you could do is negotiate a deal with the Village Council for one of the lots so's they could build a new police station, in exchange for them not charging you property taxes on the rest of the land for some period of time. That way, the town wouldn't have to lay out any cash and you could lower your expenses," Are Dee offered.

"I didn't know Youngstown needed a new police station? Other than your big drug bust, is there really that much crime around here?" Franklin asked.

"Franklin, for as smart as you are, you ain't much of a visionary. Look at how Raleigh is growing, moving out in all directions, and Wake Forest, too. As the area expands, I think Youngstown could eventually become a suburb, like Cary or Apex."

"Seriously?! We're forty miles from Raleigh. There aren't many fools like me, willing to make that drive every day," Franklin said. "If it weren't for the Starbrite, I'd be livin' a lot closer to work."

After a few more minutes of conversation with Are Dee, Franklin excused himself and headed into Raleigh to pick up Lisa Ann at the apartment she shared with her roommate. Lisa Ann was ready to go when he arrived and they drove the short distance to one of the best known restaurants in the area.

It was nearly ten o'clock when they'd finished their dinner and returned to her apartment. Lisa Ann invited Franklin inside and casually mentioned that Marie, her roommate, was out of town for the weekend. With the lights turned down, they began some intense smooching, with Franklin feeling increasing confident about his relationship with Lisa Ann.

Franklin was already seriously worked up when Lisa Ann flashed her beautiful blue eyes at him and asked, "Do you like to play games Franklin?"

Franklin didn't quite know what to think and wondered if she meant board games or some of those new electronic ones, so he innocently asked, "What kind of games?"

Lisa Ann leaned into him real close and ran her tongue around the rim of his ear before whispering, "Bedroom games."

Franklin immediately got the drift.

In the interest of not offending any of you readers and keeping this story available for public libraries, I'll skip any of the sordid details of what went on between the two of them during the balance of the night, the early hours of the morning and one more time, just before lunch. Sufficed to say, Franklin didn't make it to church on Sunday.

It wasn't like him to miss church unless he was deathly ill, Brenda thought. As he was growing up, Willa Mae and Eustace made sure that he was properly baptized (full emersion), attended Sunday school and at age 13 became a member of the Youngstown Free Will Evangelic Fundamentalist Church where Brenda, Are Dee and their three children also worshipped.

Since Are Dee was snoring through the Washington Redskins game on TV, Brenda took it upon herself to walk over to Franklin's house shortly after she'd seen his car pull into the parking lot.

Franklin wanted only to take a long nap and rest-up some that afternoon, when Brenda knocked on his door. Being as she and Are Dee had always been like second parents to him, he suspected that her visit wasn't to borrow a cup of sugar, especially since he'd missed church. Greeting her with a hug, he let her in and offered Brenda a Coke.

"No thank you, Franklin," she said. "I came here because Are Dee and I love you so very much, just like you was one of our own children. We promised Eustace and Willa Mae that we'd always look out for you."

"I know, Brenda, and I can't tell you how much you and the rest of the family mean to me, just knowin' you're there," Franklin said in hopes of defusing what he was expecting next.

"We missed you at church this morning," Brenda started. "The Lord missed you, too! He looked down at his precious flock in our little church and wondered 'Where is my Franklin? Did he get into an **otto** accident in Raleigh last night? Did his appendix burst? Or was he caught-up in sinning? Lusting? Doing before marriage what you're only supposed to do after marriage?"

"Yes, ma'am," responded Franklin, thinking back to Are Dee and Brenda's younger son, Richard Lee and the fact that he'd succeed in bedding nearly half the girls in their Senior class, even some of the pretty ones.

"Yes ma'am to which part?" Brenda asked, slightly puzzled.

It has been my experience that guilt is part of every culture and religion in the world. My personal preference is Catholic guilt, since you can visit a priest, confess your sins, and say a bunch of Hail Mary's and such and then drive on.

Jewish guilt is more like carrying a twenty pound gunny sack of potatoes with you for the rest of your life. Once a Jewish momma lays guilt on one of her young'uns, it sticks with them long after she's gone to the great delicatessen in the sky.

I know for a fact that there's also Muslim and Hindu guilt, though I doubt that those godless atheists have any.

One thing I do know for sure is that Brenda Camber Guilt (BCG) has a world-class standing of its own, well above all the others. When her two wild boys begged to have their daddy give 'em a royal whoppin' over having their momma lay some BCG on 'em, you know it had to be serious stuff.

"I was only agreeing that I should have told you that Lisa Ann and me would be praying together in Raleigh," Franklin said.

Brenda gave him an odd look.

It was at that exact moment that the preacher spirit of his late daddy, Philo Delworth, channeled itself through Franklin's body and he spoke with the same charisma that had so enchanted his momma twenty five years previous.

"We are sinners, Lisa Ann and me, and we know it in our hearts. Last evening about midnight, I got down on my knees with Lisa Ann and we spent hours trying to touch heaven! Trying to reach that place where mortals like ourselves become one with Him. We both spoke in tongues, uttering sounds not heard before by either of us. It wasn't until after dawn that we'd come together to find the path of righteousness," Franklin said with as much sincerity as he could muster.

Pausing to wipe away a tear, Brenda looked directly at Franklin and said, "You are as full of sh*t as a Christmas goose, Franklin Delworth! And you should be absolutely ashamed of your behavior and your pale attempt to hide it in such a….." she was searching for the right word, "sacrilegious, there I said it…..sacrilegious manner. May the good Lord forgive you!"

For the second time in less than twenty-four hours, Franklin knew he was screwed.

"Are Dee and I will expect you and…..what's her name….Lisa Ann to have supper with us next Saturday night and I most sincerely hope you'll both attend church with us next Sunday morning. What you do in-between those two events shall be the subject of prayer on my part. As your substitute momma, I want to get to know this young lady and make sure you aren't going down a path that could lead to eternal damnation! Do you understand me, Franklin?"

"Yes, ma'am," was his only response, now filled with BCG.

"Now give me a big hug and plant some sugar on my cheek," Brenda said before heading for the door.

Chapter 3 – Lashaya Bryan

Lashaya Bryan became Franklin's first weekly tenant in the late summer of 1983, when he started switching the Starbrite from daily rentals. It was a call from Reverend Hubert Carter at the Youngstown AME (African Methodist Episcopal) Church that prompted him to rent her Number 5 at $35 per week.

"Lashaya's gets $362 on the third of the month from Social Security," Reverend Carter said. "Her landlord just raised the rent on her house to $250 a month. On top of that, she's got a bank loan on her car and spends nearly $80 a month on medicine. When she came to me for advice, I told her that she needed to find a less expensive place to live."

"Why doesn't she just get a roommate and stay where she's at?" Franklin asked.

After taking a long pause, Reverend Carter answered, "The truth is Franklin, Lashaya is getting evicted."

Lashaya and her late husband William had moved to Youngstown from Richmond, shortly after WWII. William got work at the lumber mill in Franklinville and Lashaya was a short-order cook at the café. With the help of a VA loan, they were able to buy a small house on the east side of town. In those days, the C&O railroad tracks were the dividing line between whites, west of 'em and blacks, east of 'em. Black children attended the old one-room schoolhouse where Eustace and Willa Mae had gone, while white kids went to the new school built in 1947.

They were both hard working people of deep faith, who raised smart, beautiful twin daughters. Both of their girls were in the first integrated graduating class at Youngstown High School in 1961. Obtaining a second mortgage on their house, Lashaya and William sent the girls to Kitwell College, just north of Youngstown, where they studied to be teachers, with both graduating in 1965. Their daddy and momma couldn't have been prouder!

After William was killed in an accident at the lumber mill in 1969, Lashaya tried her best to keep up with the payments on their house and car, but even with his life insurance, it still wasn't quite enough. Being an extremely proud woman and not wanting help from her daughters, she sold the house and moved into a smaller rental home, this time west of the railroad tracks.

Lashaya retired from the café in 1981, having cooked there for thirty-five years under three different owners. With her retirement, the biscuits and sawmill gravy were never quite the same! Her knees were shot from all those years of standing at the grill for ten hours a day and with other ailments associated with aging, Lashaya started to become difficult for folks to deal with. With a short temper and an increasing number of nasty outbursts, she even had to be counseled several times by Reverend Carter about her behavior in church. While her daughters wanted to help, neither was willing to have Lashaya live with them. As things got worse, even their visits and those of her grandchildren became more infrequent. So, Lashaya spent her days sitting in front of the TV with the volume cranked up to compensate for her hearing loss, often watching that television preacher out of Charlotte, The Price is Right or soap operas. She went to the IGA every Wednesday to purchase groceries, including two bottles of wine, and to church on Sunday. She filled the gas tank of her car on the third of the month, after getting her Social Security check and spent the balance of her time complaining to anyone who'd listen.

Wanting to update the house she was renting and tired of her constant barrage of nasty phone calls, her landlord raised the rent in hopes of convincing her to move. When Lashaya accused him of being a raciest, he'd reached his breaking point and gave her an eviction notice.

"And now you think I should rent to her by the week at the Starbrite?" Franklin said to Reverend Carter.

"I'm asking you this as a favor. She's a good person and a devout Christian. I think all she needs is a change or two and she can get her life back on track," he said.

As he was growing up, Franklin had been aware of numerous instances where Eustace and Willa Mae let people stay at the Starbrite for free or at greatly reduced rates when one of the local preachers had interceded on their behalf.

Thinking about Lashaya's situation, Franklin could almost hear Willa Mae saying, "We've been so blessed in our lives! It's only right that we reach out a helping hand to someone in need."

Knowing what his late Aunt and Uncle would do under similar circumstances, Franklin told Reverend Carter that she could move in on a trial basis and to send her over. Franklin, strongly suspecting that no good deed ever goes unpunished, found that it took less than twenty-four hours before he was proven painfully correct.

"Mr. Franklin," as Lashaya called him, "I'll need you to empty the room of all that cheap furniture. I've got my own things."

"The room comes furnished, Miz Bryan," he said. "We've got no place to store extra furniture."

"As shabby as that furniture is, maybe you should just take it to the dump," Lashaya suggested.

"The room comes as it is, at $35 per week. If you'd prefer to have an empty room, I'll rent it to you for $45 a week," Franklin responded.

"Is that how you was raised to treat people? I'll bet your dear Aunt and Uncle taught you better?"

"The room comes furnished," he repeated.

"Do you have a special rate for retirees?" she asked.

"Miz Bryan, I've been renting rooms for $8 a night since I took over the Starbrite. $35 a week is a special rate."

"Well, I suppose if that's the best you can do. I'd like to look over the other rooms that are available and before I make my selection."

"Room 5 is what's available. I'm in the process of converting the others for weekly rentals."

"So, I'm receiving a newly renovated room?"

"Absolutely."

"In that case, I'll take it. You did say the retiree rate was $32.50 a week, right?"

"No ma'am. What I said is that the room comes as is for $35 per week," Franklin repeated, already regretting his offer to help her. "It's a take it or leave it kind of situation."

"There is no need to be disrespectful, young man! I was hard at work in this town when you were still messing in your diapers!"

"Not a problem, Miz Bryan. If you'd prefer not to rent at the Starbrite, I'll certainly understand."

"In spite of your attitude, Mr. Franklin, I will take the room on a one week trial basis."

After concluding the conversation, Franklin called Reverend Carter, as he had requested.

"How did it go, Franklin?" he asked.

"I need you to pray for me tonight and every night that she's a tenant," he responded.

"That good, eh?"

"Yup."

"You're a good man to do this, Franklin. I know how proud Eustace and Willa Mae would be of the decision you made."

(For those of you who skimmed past my digression on the different types of guilt, it's back in Chapter 2. Y'all might want to re-read it.)

To show his appreciation for Franklin's good deed, Reverend Carter recommended the Starbrite to several other far less difficult folks, most of them trying to get by on just Social Security. By the middle of November and just a few months after Willa Mae's passing, he had fully converted the motel to by-the-week rentals with nine of the twelve rooms occupied.

Unfortunately, it didn't take nearly that long before Franklin started receiving a list of demands along with Lashaya's weekly rent payment.

After living at the Starbrite only two weeks, Lashaya came to the office on Saturday to pay her rent and looked around to see if there'd be an audience when she started in on Franklin. Seeing that she was the only other person there seemed to disappoint her.

"Mr. Franklin, do I not pay my rent promptly?" she asked.

"Yes ma'am, you do," he said, accepting her thirty-five dollars and writing out a receipt.

"Would you consider me to be a good tenant?" she asked.

"Yes ma'am, so far."

"Then why must I have the only room with an old black and white TV that barely works?"

"Because all the rooms have old TV's, Miz Bryan."

"I think you should replace mine with a color TV, preferably a new one."

"I don't think so, Miz Bryan," Franklin said. "If I did that, I'd have to raise your rent to cover the expense. Am I safe in assuming that you'd prefer I not do so?

"So it's your desire to be a slumlord, Mr. Franklin?"

"No more so that it's your desire to be evicted," he responded.

After a number of weeks and after consulting with Reverend Carter on how best to deal with Lashaya's demands, things had reached a stalemate.

It was only after Marcus Cooper moved in to Number 6, next door to Lashaya in March of 1984, that things started heating up again.

"I have been informed that you give preferential rates to others living here, when I've been your longest tenant," Lashaya started.

"What makes you say that?" Franklin asked.

"I have been told by a person, who shall remain anonymous, that he is paying five dollars a week less than me. I believe I am due a refund and a reduction in my rent!" she demanded.

"Miz Bryan, I was asked by my cousin, the Chief of Police, to grant a special rate to Marcus Cooper out of respect for the fact that he places his life on the line every day to protect the citizens of Youngstown."

"Writing speeding tickets don't seem very risky to me! What about showing proper respect to senior citizens?" she asked.

"Miz Bryan, I am not lowering your rent and I am not giving you a refund."

"I should at least get a color TV," Lashaya said.

"Thank you for your payment. I'll see you next week."

Unable to get Franklin to give in on any of her demands, she tried a new approach three weeks later.

"Mr. Franklin, I am respectfully refusing to pay my rent until the following situations are rectified. First, I want a new color TV. Second, I demand a five-dollar per week reduction in my rent. Third, I want a telephone installed in my room. As a senior citizen, I might someday need urgent medical care and without a phone to call for help, I could easily die. Fourth, I am concerned about quality of the folks you rent to."

Franklin stopped her in her tracks.

"Miz Bryan, you live next door to a police officer!" he said. "I've heard everything you've said and want you to know that you can either pay your rent now or I will evict you, immediately. Those are your options. One more thing, these ridiculous complaints will stop today. If you don't like living here, then you should move elsewhere."

"Is that how your Aunt and Uncle would have treated a senior citizen?"

"No. Aunt Willa Mae would have pulled out her shotgun and walked you off the property several months ago."

"Are you threaten' me, Mr. Franklin?"

"Only with eviction, Miz Bryan," Franklin said, though the idea of using the shotgun was gaining momentum in his mind.

Lashaya kept up her steady campaign for a color TV and came banging on Franklin's door just before 9:00 on a Tuesday night.

"That old TV in my room has exploded!" she hollered. "Between the sparks and smoke, I could have lost my life. It's only because the Lord was watchin' over me that Mr. Collins (Number 4) came runnin' over and unplugged it or I would surely have perished. Now, you've got to do something about it!"

Franklin walked down to Number 5. There were several other tenants standing outside of the room and the door had been left open to let the smoke clear. As he looked at the old black and white TV with a large hole in the picture tube, he noticed almost no broken glass on the floor. He also noticed that there was a ballpeen hammer sticking out from under the bed.

"Seems to me that if the TV had exploded, the floor would have glass all over," he said to no one in particular. "Now, if something hit the picture tube then 'most all the glass would be inside. What do you think?" he asked.

Mr. Collins nodded in agreement.

"What are you sayin', Mr. Franklin?" Lashaya asked.

Franklin smiled at her. "I was just thinking out loud," he said. "I'll bring you a TV after work tomorrow."

"Can't you do something about it tonight?"

"Sure," said Franklin, "I can get this mess out of your room."

On his way home from work in Raleigh the following afternoon, Franklin stopped at the Cash Now Pawn Shop just north of Spring Forest Road.

Knocking on the door of Number 5, Lashaya answered immediately.

"Got you a color TV," Franklin said.

"It's about time! Bring it in."

With that, Franklin rolled in an ancient cabinet-style television with a badly scratched simulated maple finish. He attached it to the shared tower antenna and plugged it in, waiting for the tubes to heat up. Within thirty seconds, it came to life showing Charlie Gaddy anchoring the Channel 5 evening news.

"No remote control?" Lashaya asked.

"No remote control Miz Bryan," Franklin said.

"Is this old thing the best you can do?"

"Yup, unless I raise your rent to cover a newer one. They had several others at the pawn shop."

Not long after, Lashaya came barreling into the motel office on a Saturday afternoon with a full head of steam.

"Mr. Franklin, I want to put you on notice that we are forming a Tenants Union to address our ongoing complaints and your lack of responsiveness as our landlord, or should I say slumlord! All of our demands are listed right here on this piece of paper," she said, shoving it at him.

"Who are the members of the Tenants Union?" he asked.

There was a long pause.

"We'll me, so far, but I'll get everybody who's staying here to sign-up."

Franklin reached into his drawer and pulled out a 3 x 5 card, dialing the phone number written on it.

"Miz Sanderson? This is Franklin Delworth at the Starbrite Motel in Youngstown."

"You got no business calling my daughter in Greensboro!" Lashaya said angrily.

"Yes, ma'am, you told me to call you if there were any more problems. No, she's alright. She's standin' right here and has just announced that she's formin' a Tenant's Union. I am fixin' to give her an eviction notice as soon as we get off the phone. No ma'am, I don't know if they have any beds available at the Henderson Retirement Home, but I can give you their number. Yes, ma'am, I'll give her the phone right now."

With that Franklin handed Lashaya the telephone receiver and stepped out of the room. About five minutes later she called him back in and said that her daughter wanted to speak with him.

"I'm not sure I can do that, Miz Sanderson. This has become far more of a problem than you can imagine. Honestly, I'd rather let the room sit empty than continue like this. No, ma'am, I do understand, but that's really none of my concern. I suppose I could, but only until you can make other arrangements. Their number in Henderson is 919-555-8681. Yes, ma'am, I'll wait to hear back from you. Thanks."

Grabbing back the paper she'd thrown at Franklin, Lashaya quickly tore it in half.

"It appears that you've won, Mr. Franklin," she said.

"This isn't a contest, Miz Bryan and the Starbrite Motel isn't a daycare center. Once your daughter finds a place for you, you'll be moving-on voluntarily or otherwise. I'll bring the eviction notice down in a few minutes."

Lashaya stormed out of the office, slamming the door behind her. It only took about 15 minutes before he saw Reverend Carter's car pull into the parking lot, in front of Number 5. After a bit, Reverend Carter knocked on Franklin's door and was invited inside.

"Her daughter called me from Greensboro," Reverend Carter said.

"I figured as much," Franklin responded.

"I'm guessing that I'm out of favors with you Franklin," he said smiling.

"Depends on what you're asking for," he responded.

"Is there any remote possibility that you'd give Lashaya another chance?"

"Could I donate a kidney instead?"

"I'm serious, son. If you don't let her stay, her daughter will place her in a retirement home."

"Are you sure that wouldn't be the best thing for her?"

"If she were still alive, would you do that to your momma?"

Danged if he didn't play the guilt card again, and poor old Franklin was so poorly equipped to deal with it.

"If I could have her daughter send you the rent by check every month, so that you didn't have to deal directly with Lashaya and if I could get her to promise to behave, would you give her another chance?" he said, negotiating as best he could.

"If the rent is paid by the month, I'd have to give her a month's notice if I was gonna evict her. That I won't do, Reverend Carter. If we continue by the week and I didn't have to deal directly with her, we could try it for a while longer, I guess."

"Thank you, Franklin. You are such a blessing to the community."

(There went the guilt card again! I'm just sayin'.)

"If I have to bring you her rent myself every Saturday, I will. I'm going back to speak with Lashaya and I'll call her daughter this evening. You are a good man, Franklin. Your aunt and uncle raised a truly good man!"

And the crowd at Reynolds Coliseum went wild, as Reverend Hubert Carter hit a three-point shot from mid-court for Team Guilt! So it was that Lashaya Bryan continued to be a resident at the Starbrite until the End of Days, or at least the end of Franklin's Patience-of-a-Saint. Sorry, no disrespect or blasphemy meant. Honest.

Chapter 4 – Lisa Ann Prescott

Lisa Ann Prescott was born in Astoria (Queens), NY on April 2nd, 1963, the only child of Norman and Phyllis Prescott. Her daddy was a Korean War veteran who had studied under the GI Bill at NYU and was in the process of working his way up the corporate ladder at Northern Telecom, when she was born. Her momma was a third-grade elementary school teacher, a woman with a backbone of pure titanium and with Hudson River ice water running in her veins.

Lisa Ann grew up in a quiet neighborhood of row houses, just a short train ride from the heart of Manhattan. By anybody's standards, but especially her parents, she was a strikingly beautiful child, with long blonde hair, bright blue eyes and nearly perfect skin.

At almost every turn, Phyllis pushed…drop-kicked would be more accurate….Lisa Ann into almost any new challenge that she herself had failed at as a child. Whether it was tap dancing, ballet, cheer leading, drama club or the debate team, Phyllis made sure Lisa Ann not only tried, but succeeded at whatever she attempted, no matter how much misery it may have caused her daughter.

She also pushed her every bit as hard to be a straight-A student from first grade until the end of her junior year in high school; a model child in almost every way. Lisa Ann had a close circle of friends who referred to her mother as The Stepford Wife, an unfeeling robot who worked tirelessly to create a perfect world for her husband and expected nothing less from her daughter.

As a result, Lisa Ann quietly revolted in the few ways should could. When she was safely within the presence of her friends, she quickly transformed from Dr. Jekyll into Ms. Hyde, using the roughest language she could come up with and trying her best to shock her peers in any way she could. In ninth grade, she obtained a copy of "The Joy of Sex" and began reading it after her parents were asleep, sharing the explicit details with her friends at the first possible opportunity.

Since Phyllis wanted her to focus entirely on her studies and other after school activities, Lisa Ann had no social life beyond her closest friends. There was little doubt that she was leading a life of quiet desperation. (OK, I borrowed the last line from that Thoreau feller, but it still describes her situation.) Misery and frustration might also be included.

It was in early May of 1980 that Norman Prescott sat down for dinner with his wife and daughter to deliver the biggest news of his career. "I've just accepted a promotion to Director Level," he proudly announced to Lisa Ann and Phyllis.

"That's wonderful, dear," his wife said. "Does that mean you'll be traveling more?" she asked, hoping that he'd be spending more time away from home.

"That's the best part," he responded, "I should be home almost every night. There is just one thing," he added, hoping to slide it in under the door without nobody noticing, "We'll be moving to Raleigh, North Carolina."

That was when the mashed 'taters hit the fan.

"Raleigh, North Carolina!" Lisa Ann cried. "Isn't that where Opie and Goober live? You've got to be kidding, right?! Do you really want to completely destroy my life and leave the center of the universe for the dark side of the moon? No fu*king way!"

Without the benefit of an air raid siren the F-bomb had been dropped in the middle of the Prescott dinner table in Astoria (Queens)!

The dead silence of her parents and the shocked expression on their faces told the whole story. Never, ever, in their house had that word been spoken by anyone, let alone the pure-as-the driven snow Lisa Ann.

Trying to pretend they hadn't heard what they'd definitely just heard, her father said, "Princess, you shouldn't judge things until we fly down there for a visit. It's a lovely community! There are lots of New Yorkers relocating to North Carolina. Plus they've got three major universities, all within a few miles of each other and Raleigh. With the promotion, we'll be able to afford a nice home, maybe even with a pool."

Phyllis stood up, walked around the table and grabbed Lisa Ann's head in both her hands, looking down at her daughter. For a brief second, Norman wondered if she was planning to yank the girls head clean off her body, but decided, as he usually did, not to interfere.

Gathering all the stern, composed authority that made her who (or what) she was, she looked at Lisa Ann and said, "We will go there and check things out. We will love it. Do you understand me? Love it. And we'll support your father in every way we can. We'll find a good high school for you to attend and you will work your spoiled, godda*ned ass off to get into a quality college. Do you understand me? And you will never, **ever** use such horrid language in our presence again, young lady!"

As she turned to walk away, she gave things another thought, whipped around and slapped Lisa Ann right across her beautiful face.

"Phyllis!" hollered Norman, but the deed had been done.

After she returned to her seat at the table, there was total silence for several minutes. Lisa Ann looked down at her lap but never let out a whimper or shed a single tear. Finally, raising her head and looking directly at her momma with eyes that could kill on contact, she smiled and said, "Of course, Mother, whatever you say."

"That's better. Do not disappoint me!" said Phyllis with all the maternal warmth of a Carolina Copperhead.

Willingly or otherwise, but mostly otherwise, Lisa Ann moved with her parents to a beautiful thirty-five hundred square foot, five bedroom home in North Raleigh. She was enrolled in the leading private school in the area and continued to earn straight-A's during her senior year, applying to Duke, UNC Chapel Hill and Meredith College, all of which were willing to accept her for the following fall term. Her mother selected Duke on Lisa Ann's behalf. Without any fight, Lisa Ann agreed. As to her social life, it could best be described as nonexistent.

Sometimes divine providence intercedes in folk's lives, and that was the case for Lisa Ann Prescott. Just a week before her high school graduation, her daddy came home with news that changed her eventual path by a whole bunch.

Sitting on the new furniture in their professionally decorated living room, he gathered Phyllis and Lisa Ann together to share the big news.

"I know we've only been in Raleigh for a year, but the company has been extremely pleased with my performance and they now want me to move to the corporate headquarters in Ottawa! I'll be a Vice President!" Norman proudly announced.

"How soon do you have to let them know? When would we have to move?" asked Phyllis.

Looking just a bit sheepish, Norman responded, "Well, to tell the truth, I've already accepted the job and they want us to move within the next sixty days."

Both Norman and Phyllis turned to look at Lisa Ann, who had said nothing up to this point.

"It's OK, Dad," she said. "I'm going to start school in late August. I can stay here until the house sells. I know how much you've sacrificed to get me into Duke, so I really think it best that I stay in North Carolina."

Phyllis was smiling at the maturity and wisdom of her daughter's response. "Of course, you'll need a car to get around. Dad and I will leave you my Buick."

While that might have seemed like a generous offer, Phyllis was already thinking ahead about the new Mercedes she'd have Norman buy for her as appropriate transportation for the wife of a Vice President.

"I'll be coming back regularly to check on the Raleigh facility, so we'll be able to spend time together," her father reassured her.

Phyllis avoided the subject of travelling back, only saying "And we'll see you at Christmas, of course."

She had considered boarding school for Lisa Ann at several points during her childhood, but Norman couldn't swing the costs back then. This was an entirely different and wonderful development, she thought.

Lisa Ann just smiled at them and said, "I'll be just fine. Really I will."

In late June, a 'For Sale' sign was placed in the Prescott's front lawn and the movers arrived to haul their belongings to Canada. Lisa Ann opted to send her bedroom furniture on with her parents, living for a couple of months out of her new suitcases and using a sleeping bag and air mattress for a bed.

She established a local checking account so that her father could transfer funds to cover her college and living expenses and he had given her a credit card with the bill sent to directly to him for payment.

An offer was received on the Prescott's home less than a month after the listing and the closing was to be held the week after Lisa Ann moved in to her dorm room at Duke. The timing was near perfect!

"Are you OK with getting settled at college by yourself, Princess?" her daddy asked by phone from Canada. "We can fly down for a few days, if you need us."

"I've got it handled, Dad," Lisa Ann responded.

As soon as she'd heard the news about her parent's move to Ottawa, Lisa Ann's mind began churning. She knew that the opportunity had finally come to escape the iron fist of her mother and have a life of her own, but also knew that she had to handle things skillfully.

On move-in day at Duke, she met her roommate, the daughter of a mechanic from Wrightsville Beach, who was attending on a full-boat academic scholarship. Common sense would tell you that placing two academically gifted and motivated students together would result in a nearly total focus on studying, and that was certainly the case for her roommate. Lisa Ann, on the other hand, was ready to experience life at a level previously denied to her. To say that she wanted to break the freshman record for cutting classes and partying would be an understatement.

Lisa Ann was also intent on losing her virginity, but only to the right guy. She found him in Raj Patel, a senior in the pre-med program, who she met during a freshman orientation tour. Not only was he a patient and understanding lover during the course of their three week fling, but he was also an avid student of the Kama Sutra. (Y'all need to look up that one, 'cause there is simply no way I'm going to cover those details here.)

Lisa Ann delivered the bad news that she'd flunked out of Duke during a call she made to Norman and Phyllis a few days after the end of Fall Term. Her grade point average was so low, that there was no consideration of probation or other options. She done spit into the wind, as they say in Youngstown.

Speaking from the motel where she had moved temporarily, her tearful apology at disappointing them and her promise to make amends was swallowed whole-hog by her daddy. Her momma would have none of it!

"You will pack your things, get into your car and drive yourself up here immediately," Phyllis demanded, "or you'll be cut off without a cent! You can damn well count on us dealing with this issue the instant you get here, too!"

"That was more than a bit severe," Norman protested later to his wife.

"Bull sh*t! She did that deliberately just to spite me! I didn't work all those years to see her life go to Hell in a handbasket," Phyllis shouted.

You know that old saying, for every action there is an equal but opposite reaction? After considering her options for a couple of days, Lisa Ann called her daddy at his office.

"I'm not coming to Canada, Dad," she said. "I messed-up here, I'm going to make things right here. I've found an apartment to share with another girl and I'm starting community college classes right after the first of the year. If you and mom want to cut me off financially or otherwise, that's your decision. I'm prepared to get a job and pay my own way if I have to. I'm prepared to get on with my life, living like an orphan, if that's the way you want it."

Unbeknown to Norman and Phyllis was that for several years Lisa Ann had been scrimping and saving every penny she could and now had nearly $3000 in her war chest, should it be needed.

"You know that's not what I want, Princess. I admire your sprite and determination, but you can count on your mother having a major hemorrhage over this," her daddy said.

"That's why I called you," she said. "I need you to run interference for me just this one time. Please, Daddy, I'm begging you. If you don't, I don't know what I'll do. Maybe I'll enlist in the Army or enter a convent!" she pleaded, even though they were Presbyterians.

Calling Norman "Daddy" was the ultimate deal closer for Lisa Ann. She'd worked him to the absolute best of her ability, playing her version of the guilt card to its fullest.

"OK, I'll try to handle your mother, but you've got six months to get things together or I'm coming down there to bring you home myself. I mean it Lisa Ann!" Norman said.

Calling Lisa Ann by her first and middle name was the ultimate deal closer for Norman. He knew that she would know that he **absolutely meant business**; no compromise under any circumstances, unless Phyllis demanded otherwise, of course.

"Will you at least come home for Christmas?" Norman asked.

"I can't. I just can't face you and mom as a failure," she said before completely breaking down in tears.

Hearing the pathetic crying of his only child at the other end of the phone line was more than Norman could bear. Digging deep into his Fruit of the Looms for the pair of cojones that had been in hiding all those years, he promised himself that he would make Phyllis back-off on this one, so help him!

In thinking back on it some, I've got to admit that Phyllis forcing Lisa Ann to participate in the high school drama club had finally yielded positive results for the girl, just as her momma had predicted.

It cost Norman two round-trip first class tickets to San Juan and an 8-day Caribbean cruise over Christmas, to get Phyllis all calmed down, but that was the price of peace, I reckon.

Seriously, don't you find family dynamics interesting? It wouldn't take much for me to go off on a six or seven paragraph digression if it weren't for wanting to get on with the story.

The following don't count as a digression, it's purely a clarification, since Duke is my favorite college basketball team. Duke is a very prestigious and acclaimed university turning out many fine national leaders, and Richard Nixon, too. They make every possible effort to ensure the success of incoming freshman. I read that part in one of their brochures. Some of you plotline fanatics are wondering why Lisa Ann's parents weren't notified about her sinking status before the boat was at the bottom of the lake? There are two explanations, you can take your pick. First, this is a fictional story, so I can write any durned plot twists that suite my needs. How do you like that Mr. On-line, Smarty-pants Critic?! Second, the school did send several written notices to the Prescott's, except they were never received, because the university had never gotten an updated contact address from Lisa Ann. Can you imagine that?

Lisa Ann found a suitable roommate in Marie McKay, a flight attendant for Piedmont Airlines. They shared a small, furnished, two bedroom apartment in Morrisville, just southwest of Raleigh, near the airport, and Lisa Ann drove over to Raleigh Community College three or four times a week to take classes and study. Her new curriculum was training to be a secretary, with the program title of Administrative Assistant Technology.

At the end of Spring term, she sent her folks a copy of her grades, which were back to straight-A's and a note saying that she was going to take summer classes and push forward with a two-year degree. All that still didn't settle well with Phyllis, but at least she could tell her snooty new Ottawa friends that her daughter was making 'splendid' progress studying at a college in North Carolina. In the interests of being polite, we'll call that 'natural organic fertilizer.'

Lisa Ann saw her daddy from time to time when he came down to Raleigh on business, and even cooked him supper at her apartment once, though her culinary skills were something less than good. Phyllis could never seem to find the time to come down for a visit and Lisa Ann didn't have much desire to see Ottawa, either.

She graduated at the end of summer term in 1983 and was hired as a secretary at Esterhouse Electrical Manufacturing, early that fall. That's where she met Franklin a year later. As smart and beautiful as she was, Lisa Ann had no shortage of male suiters, most of whom were 'one-and-done' dates. Having little patience for drooling fools, and seeing an abundance of them while studying at the community college and later at the plant where she worked, she allowed only one date to determine her level of interest in any given guy. Figuring that Franklin was probably going to be yet another 'one-and-done,' she agreed to go out with him after having a few beers at the Friday after-work Happy Hour held at the Holiday Inn lounge, near the factory.

As it turned out, Franklin was different from the other guys she'd been seeing. First, he treated her with respect. He was polite and kind, too. He listened to what she had to say, only wincing when she let an F-bomb fly. He was a little goofy, but in a good-natured, funny kind of way. And he was smart, far more so than you might think from his slow southern drawl. He was handsome, maybe even sexy in an innocent sort of way. While she didn't want him to think she was falling for him, she was surely headed in that direction, in spite of herself.

They'd been dating for several weeks when one thing led to another and she found herself in his bed for the first time. While Lisa Ann sensed that Franklin might be a little inexperienced, he more than made up for it with his gentleness and his desire to please her. She was warm and comfortable with him, until Are Dee spoiled the moment that first Saturday morning.

In the weeks she'd known him, Franklin had told her lots about his late Aunt and Uncle, remembering only bits and pieces about his momma and daddy. He spoke fondly about Are Dee, Brenda and their kids and how much he'd leaned on them after Willa Mae passed. In spite of all the sadness in his life, Lisa Ann was envious of the overwhelming sense of family that was such a critical part of Franklin Delworth.

So, it was with more than curiosity or obligation that Lisa Ann agreed to accept Brenda's invitation for Saturday night supper. Understanding the traditional values of the Camber family, without him saying anything to her, she promised Franklin that she'd carefully control her New York language and show them the respect they deserved.

Driving from Raleigh out to Youngstown, Franklin told Lisa Ann that they were going to make a short visit at the Free Will Evangelic Fundamentalist Cemetery, located behind the church.

Pulling up to the small group of plots surrounded by an iron fence, Franklin opened the car door for Lisa Ann and held her hand as they walked over to the graves of his parents and those of Eustace and Willa Mae.

"They were some pretty incredible people," Franklin said quietly. "My parents gave me life. I've always felt their love, especially when I come here. Eustace and Willa Mae gave me a place to live, kept me fed and clothed, took care of me when I was sick. They got me an education. Most of all, Lisa Ann, they loved me and I loved them, too. Aunt Willa Mae always told me that all she ever wanted was for me to grow up to be a better person then her or Eustace. I wonder if she knew how impossible that would be?"

Deeply moved, Lisa Ann couldn't find any words so just squeezed Franklin's hand all the more tightly.

"If they was here in person, I know how much they'd like you," he said. "This is the next best thing, since they were surely looking down on me from heaven the day we met."

Thinking that people from Astoria (Queens) didn't say or do things like this, she looked over at Franklin, like she was sizing him up. He just smiled at her.

"You are really something, Franklin Delworth," she said warmly.

"Something good or something bad?" he asked.

"Something special, like nobody I've ever known before."

Before they left the cemetery, Franklin knelt down by the graves of his family and offered a quiet prayer.

"Dear Lord," he said, "please hold my daddy and momma, Uncle Eustace and Aunt Willa Mae gently in the palm of your hand until the day when we can all be together again in the Kingdom of Heaven. A-men."

"A-men," said Lisa Ann in a whisper.

With big 'ol lump in her throat, she gave Franklin a hug and a gentle kiss on the cheek before they got back in his car, driving over to the motel and leaving it in the Starbrite parking lot.

(You will recall, that in the preface I advised you to have a box of tissues handy for certain parts of this story. Blow your nose real good. There, now do it again and keep on reading, please.)

During the prior week, Lisa Ann had thought ahead and had asked Franklin if he knew what Brenda's favorite dessert might be. That was an easy one.

"Chocolate brownies," he replied. "The real gooey kind."

Reaching Brenda and Are Dee's front door a few minutes later, Lisa Ann presented them with a plate of homemade brownies, assuming that you count Betty Crocker as homemade. After exchanging 'pleasantries,' that's another Astoria (Queens) word, Brenda called everyone to the table.

When it came time for Are Dee to say the blessing over supper, all four of them joined hands and bowed their heads in prayer, something that was never done in Lisa Ann's parent's house.

For dinner, Brenda had cooked-up Eastern North Carolina pulled pork barbeque in a spicy vinaigrette sauce, with creamy coleslaw to put on top, boiled redskin potatoes and fresh green beans seasoned with fatback. There was a basket of warm "cat's head" biscuits sitting on the table, too, along with a bottle of blackstrap molasses and a tub of Imperial margarine. Brenda was trying to cut back on Are Dee's intake of saturated fats.

(Out of courtesy to you readers, I will resist the urge to digress into a discussion about the differences between Eastern North Carolina barbeque, vinegar based and Western North Carolina barbeque, tomato based, at least for the moment.)

"Lisa Ann, would you like some sweet tea?" Are Dee offered.

"Thank you," she replied, politely.

While fully intending to put Lisa Ann through the Brenda Camber version of the Spanish Inquisition, as she so often did with Robert Dee and Richard Lee's girlfriends, there was something different about this girl that Brenda liked a whole lot, though she couldn't quite put her finger on it. As a result, the supper-table conversation primarily focused on the upcoming college basketball season, the horrible Raleigh traffic and Lisa Ann and Franklin's jobs at the Esterhouse Electrical plant.

"Are your parents coming down for Thanksgiving or are you going up to Canada?" Brenda asked.

"Neither," Lisa Ann replied.

"I guess you'll get together with them at Christmas?" she said.

"No, we haven't spent any holidays together since they moved up to Ottawa," Lisa Ann replied.

Those answers stuck out like a sore thumb to Brenda, signaling her that things weren't exactly all warm and fuzzy between Lisa Ann and her parents.

"You are welcome to spend Thanksgiving with us," she said, even though she'd just met Lisa Ann. "We invite all the folks who live at the Starbrite to come too, since most of 'em don't have any kin in the area. I bake a big ol' turkey and Are Dee deep fries another one, outside. There's always plenty to eat and lots of people to share it with!"

"Lisa Ann and I would love to do that!" Franklin answered as he looked over at her.

"I don't recall that we invited you, Franklin," Are Dee said with a big laugh.

"Don't pay any attention to him!" Brenda said, stepping in. "Franklin has spent most all the holiday's with us since he was just a little guy. He's family, and family don't ever need an invitation to our table."

"You heard her, boy," Are Dee said to Franklin. "I've been overruled again," he added as he patted Franklin on the back.

As they finished dinner, Lisa Ann immediately pitched-in to clear the table and offered to help wash the dishes.

"Do people from New York actually do that?" Brenda wondered to herself.

"That's very sweet," Brenda said, "but I made Are Dee buy me a dishwasher after our two boys got into a fight at the sink and broke nearly half our good plates."

As the evening drew to a close, Brenda asked Franklin and Lisa Ann if she'd see them in church the following morning.

"Yes, ma'am," was Lisa Ann's smiling response.

Thanking Brenda and Are Dee for the wonderful supper, Lisa Ann and Franklin made the short walk back to his house at the Starbrite.

"What happened to the Hellfire and brimstone sermonette that you was fixin' to give those two on premarital foolin' around?" Are Dee asked, after Franklin and Lisa Ann had left. "I saw you rehearsing it whilst you was cookin' this afternoon. Have you gone soft? On top of that, you invited her to Thanksgiving supper!"

"Hush up, Are Dee," she said, "that girl is as sweet as sugar. What those two do ain't none of our business. It's all between them and the Lord. Hate the sin, love the sinner."

"Did that girl put something in your brownies, Brenda?" Are Dee suggested, more than a little amazed at her response to him. "If that'd been one of Robert Dee or Richard Lee's girlfriends, you'd been on 'em like stink on poop!"

"As much as I love those two boys of ours and as good hearted as they can be, ain't neither of 'em got enough common sense to come in out of a hurricane, plus they never brought home a nice girl like Lisa Ann."

"I will give you that," Are Dee said. "Their choices in women always seem to range from bad to worse. They sure didn't get that from me."

"After 32 years of marriage, you'd best say that!"

As Franklin's steady girlfriend Lisa Ann was the newest inductee in Brenda Camber's extended family. That started with Thanksgiving 1984.

The day was forecast to be warm for November, near 70 degrees with plenty of Carolina sunshine. Brenda had enlisted Robert Dee and Richard Lee along with Franklin, to set-up 4 x 8 sheets of plywood on the sawhorses that Are Dee kept in the garage. When they were done, the dining table was twenty-four feet long and the buffet table was sixteen feet. The boys then covered the tables with white paper that came off a big roll, using a staple gun to secure it. Brenda had borrowed three dozen folding chairs from the church and everything was set-up in the Camber's back yard.

Lisa Ann had spent the night with Franklin and was up at 6:00 to help Brenda stuff a twenty-three pound turkey and get it in the oven. Are Dee would start deep frying a second one at about 11:00.

True to her word, Brenda invited all the folks who lived at the Starbrite to share Thanksgiving with her family. Some had family or church commitments, but four of Franklin's renters came to dinner including Lashaya Bryan and Mr. Collins. Richard Lee and Robert Dee both brought their current girlfriends, who were dressed a little too trashy by Brenda's standards. One of 'em even had a tattoo on her wrist! With a few stray cousins, their kids and a couple of aging aunts and uncles, the boys set up exactly thirty-two chairs around the table. Marcus came over in his uniform, since he was on duty and could only stay long enough to eat. Brenda understood.

Standing next to Franklin, Lisa Ann had never seen anything like Thanksgiving at the Camber's and was delighted to be part of it, even though she'd cut her finger chopping up celery for the stuffing. Here were a bunch of folks tied together through blood, marriage, friendship and the Starbrite, all having a wonderful meal in the truest spirit of the holiday.

Are Dee gathered everyone in a big circle and asked them to join hands.

"Heavenly Father, we thank you so much for the blessing of this beautiful November day and for the wonderful folks we are sharing it with. We are mindful of those who are missing from our circle this year and hope that you'll watch over them. We humbly ask for your blessing over this nourishment for our bodies and this fellowship for our souls, in the name of Jesus Christ, our Lord. A-men."

"A-men," everyone repeated.

"That was real nice Are Dee" Brenda said. "Now carve up them turkeys and let's feed these hungry people."

As much as it bothered her, Brenda had to use paper plates and plastic utensils for a crowd this size. Lisa Ann was especially impressed when Robert Dee, Richard Lee, Marcus and Franklin all helped the elderly folks through the buffet line first and carried their plates to the table for 'em. While there may be Thanksgiving dinners in Astoria (Queens), in Lisa Ann's opinion none of 'em were anything like the meal the Camber's served that afternoon.

Christmas was much quieter, with just Are Dee and Brenda's immediate family, including Franklin, of course. Lisa Ann was the only outsider invited and Brenda wasn't going to have it any other way. Unlike Christmas with Lisa Ann parents which always centered on the presents, the Camber's focused on 'the reason for the season' and celebrated the birth of their Savior. They all went to Christmas morning services at the Free Will Evangelic Fundamentalist Church, where they sang, prayed and thanked God for the gift of his only son, Jesus.

Franklin took Lisa Ann to Wrightsville Beach for New Year's Eve, staying at the Blockade Runner hotel and eating a fine meal at the Oceanic Restaurant.

Doing something she'd never done before on New Year's Eve, they walked along the beach that evening holding hands, stopping to warm-up at the many bonfires along the way and being offered some holiday cheer from total strangers. Even with temperatures in the fifties and the cold breeze coming off the Atlantic, it was a wonderful, magical night.

"You know there's a tradition around here of goin' skinny dippin' in the ocean at midnight on New Year's Eve," Franklin said to her.

"Seriously?! Are you going to do it?" she asked.

"Only if you do," he challenged her.

"How 'bout we just dip our toes in the water instead?" she offered.

"You sure?" Franklin asked.

"Positive."

At the stroke of midnight people started shooting fireworks off over the Atlantic. Lisa Ann thought they were breathtaking. (That's another one of them Astoria (Queens) words.)

Chapter 5 – The Village Council Meeting

In the three months since Are Dee had approached Franklin about the possibility of trading some of his property to the Village of Youngstown for a new police station, he had done a whole bunch of research on the legality of bartering land for tax breaks. He'd even talked with a State attorney to make sure the process could move forward, if it got approved. Are Dee wanted to have all his bases covered before sharing his idea with the Village Council.

A few days before the December 15th Council Meeting, Are Dee contacted Mayor Weber and asked to speak during the closed door portion of their session.

The monthly meetings were held in the lobby of the Village Hall, since they didn't have the space for a conference room. The shades were pulled down and the meeting came to order. The first item on the agenda was always the Citizen's Forum, and since, as usual, there was nobody present to complain about anything, the Council moved immediately into Closed Door Session to discuss the more pressing issues, like whether or not they should fill the pothole on Elm Street now or wait until spring, and other such high level matters.

As Chief of Police for Youngstown, Are Dee always attended the meetings and was allowed to stay for the Closed Door part, as long as they weren't talking about his salary. After the Council got through the other business at the December meeting, he was given a chance to say his piece.

"Everybody in this room knows that Youngstown outgrew this building 'bout twenty years ago. We've been stuffing eight pounds of onions into a five pound bag, just waiting for the bottom to fall out." There were nods of agreement in the room.

"Franklin Delworth owns an eight acre plot of land where his house and the Starbrite Motel sit, about a block south of Holden Street, on the southwest side of U.S. 1. Just to keep everything above board, I am stating for the record that he's my cousin, but y'all already knew that."

"A couple of months ago, I approached Franklin about swapping two or three acres of his land for an equivalent value in property tax relief, paid out over several years. He is receptive to the idea, assuming a fair value for the land can be reached."

"Once we have the property, with no direct cash outlay, I'm thinking we should build a new Village Hall and a new police station."

The Mayor and Village Council members just looked at each other. It was finally Mayor Weber who spoke.

"Are Dee, we're going to share a confidential piece of information with you that you can't discuss with anyone until after its made public. Do you understand?"

"Of course," said Are Dee, wondering if the Feds were going to plant a nuke missile site in town.

"Shortly after the first of the year, the Department of Transportation is going to unveil their three year plan for 1985 through 1988. One of the key items will be the widening of U.S. 1 to four lanes from the I-85 split all the way to Wake Forest. To add two additional lanes with a median strip will require the purchase of land or sixty-foot right-of-ways along the route. As the current plan stands, most of the buildings on the west side of U.S. 1, as it runs through Youngstown, will have to be torn down. Unless the plan changes, the DOT will have to negotiate a purchase for most of the land that Franklin owns and tear down the Starbrite."

Are Dee let out a low, slow whistle. "I suppose they'll want my house, too?"

65

"I'm afraid it's on the list of properties that will have to be obtained."

"What are they planning to do about the Free Will Evangelic Fundamentalist Church and cemetery?" Are Dee asked.

"The church is on the list of buildings that will have to be razed. The cemetery sits far enough back off the highway that it should be OK. With the money we'll get from the sale of land owned by the village and a grant from the state, we'll be able to build a nice City Hall and Police Station. That's the other thing, we're going to incorporate the village as the City of Youngstown."

"That does change things, now don't it?" Are Dee said. "When do you think they'll start on Youngstown?"

"Some of that depends on government funding, but it'll probably be toward the end of the project, with them doing the widening north and south of town first," Mayor Weber said. "Our best guess is that it will take at least a year before all the property can be secured. The DOT already owns right-of-ways for some of it. After that, probably another year or so for all the road construction."

"So, somewhere in early '88, give or take," Are Dee said.

"Sounds about right," said the Mayor.

As he left the meeting, Are Dee's first thoughts were of how Brenda would take the news about their house and what he'd say if she asked him if he knew ahead about the plans. He also hoped that Franklin had forgotten about their conversation. If not, he'd have to tell him that the Village Council wasn't interested in the project at this time, which would be pretty close to the truth.

(I'll bet y'all didn't know that North Carolina is known as "The Good Road" state. Just think about all the useful information you're getting from reading this story!)

On the seventh of January the DOT made public their three-year plan for improving North Carolina roads, including the decision to widen U.S. 1 to four lanes. The announcement made the front page of the Quincy County Weekly Tribune and resulted in two very different groups of people wanting their own way in the matter.

The first group were the 'No-Way' folks. Most of them were fine with the road getting bigger as long as that didn't involve tearing down the farmhouse that had been in their family for six generations or paving over their family cemetery. They soon learned a new term; eminent domain, which means that the government can take your property for the greater good of the citizenry if they can't convince you to sell it at a reasonable price and let a court settle it.

As you might expect, there were folks who didn't want to sell at any price, since their land or home meant far more to them than getting the offer the DOT was making. It was reasonable to figure that the DOT wasn't going to make a big curve to go around these places, so after trying to cut a deal for a piece of time, they just seized the property and let a court settle the amount they'd pay.

The second group were the 'Cash-In' folks. Most of them figured they could cut a fat hog with the DOT for the land needed to expand the highway. They went in early, bought pieces of land as cheap as they could and planned to re-sell it to the state at an inflated price. Apparently they'd never heard of eminent domain or thought the DOT was just joshin'. It wasn't.

Are Dee had fully expected Brenda to hit the roof when she heard that the DOT was fixing to put a highway through their house. He was wrong about that.

"As long as they pay us a fair price for the house and land, I'm ready to do something different," Brenda said.

"But this is the house where we raised our kids," Are Dee said.

"You can't stop progress and the fact is the kids are grown up and they ain't movin' back home. Is this house really where you want to live in your old age?" she asked.

"I guess not," he said, still shocked by Brenda's reaction.

"I'd like something brand new, maybe in that subdivision they're building off of Holden Street. You might consider retiring again and we could build a place up on Lake Gaston. Something made just for us, with a screen porch in back and a bigger garage. Wouldn't that be something?"

"I reckon it would be," Are Dee said.

Are Dee hadn't ever said anything more about the deal with the village that he's proposed and Franklin didn't ask about it either. After the announcement was made, there was a bunch of Youngstown folks wondering about how the road widening was going to affect them. That included the tenants at the Starbrite.

Franklin looked into the matter as best he could and took a 'wait and see' attitude.

"A whole lot of things could change before they get to Youngstown," he told folks who were concerned. "Let's not worry about it until they finalize the plans. It could be three or four years before anything happens."

Franklin may have been trying to calm everybody, but in his heart he knew that the clock was winding down for the Starbrite Motel. Like so many others, he had to start looking at his future and where he wanted to live.

Thinking ahead, as he so often did, Franklin decided to slowly start clearing out some of the boxes of Eustace and Willa Mae's stuff that he didn't have the heart to deal with after their deaths. While going through the attic, he came across their files of Starbrite Guest Registration Cards, organized by year, month and day from the time the motel opened in 1958 up to his aunt's passing.

He was fascinated by the names and addresses of the many people who'd stayed there over the years.

Looking through the cards, he could see how things had changed once I-95 had opened and people found the faster route from New York to Florida. Originally planning to throw the cards into a dumpster, he hesitated, thinking about all the history they contained and the great story they told about the Starbrite Motel.

Chapter 6 – Mr. Bazelski

As Franklin returned from work and pulled into the Starbrite parking lot on the Friday afternoon following New Year's, he saw a slightly rusted Ford Pinto with a Washington D.C. license plate sitting in front of the office, with an older man snoozing at the wheel. The moment that Franklin opened the door of his house, the man woke up, got out of his car and walked over to knock.

With gray hair sticking out from under a Baltimore Orioles baseball cap, a matching short gray beard and green eyes, he was wearing a Navy Peacoat and jeans and had a pair of Converse sneakers on his feet. Thin and slightly scraggly, he stood about five feet, eight inches tall.

"What can I do for you?" Franklin asked the stranger.

Saying nothing, the man held out a piece of paper with a note written on it.

My name is Myron Bazelski. I can hear just fine, so say what you need to say and I'll understand. Do you have a room to rent? If so, what do you charge?

Franklin smiled warmly at the man, immediately assuming from the note that he was mute. He said, "Number 12 is vacant. We charge thirty-five dollars a week, paid in advance."

With that, Mr. Bazelski nodded, reached into his pocket and peeled off seven twenty dollar bills.

"So you want to pay for four weeks?" Franklin assumed.

Mr. Bazelski nodded his head up and down again and Franklin wrote him out a receipt for the rent before handing him the key and walking the short distance to Number 12 with him. Once inside, Myron immediately noticed the slightly worn white bedspread and

70

clean towels stacked on the nightstand. There was an old seventeen inch black and white TV in the corner that was connected to the tower antenna shared by all the rooms. The bathroom looked like it had been recently repainted with a glossy white finish. The 50's era plumbing fixtures were clean and bright, though some of the metal was pitted. Franklin showed him the microwave and the cooler, inviting him to fill it from the office ice maker anytime he needed to.

"Do you have any questions, Mr. Bazelski?" asked Franklin, correctly pronouncing his last name.

Mr. Bazelski turned his head back and forth, indicating a "no," and with that Franklin said, "Hope you enjoy your stay at the Starbrite."

While it was hard to say if most of the Starbrite's tenants actually enjoyed their stay, Aunt Willa Mae had always taught Franklin to offer those good wishes whenever he showed renters to their rooms, in hopes that it might come true. I wish I may, I wish I might.

And that's how Myron Bazelski landed at the Starbrite Motel in January of 1985.

During the following month, Mr. Bazelski proved to be a good tenant, keeping to himself, seldom leaving the motel and almost never having any interaction with the other renters. Coming home from work one afternoon, Franklin noticed that Mr. Bazelski had sanded and repainted the rust spots on his Pinto.

"Looks a lot better," Franklin thought to himself.

When Marcus Cooper came by to pay his rent, he casually mentioned that the new tenant seemed to spend a lot of time working under the hood of the car, which tended to puff some blue smoke.

"Is he a mechanic?" Marcus asked. "They could sure use one at the gas station."

"He didn't say," replied Franklin.

When his rent next came due, Mr. Bazelski handed Franklin seven more twenty dollar bills and a note.

This place needs some work! The faucet in my room drips, you've got a half dozen torn screens on the other rooms. The parking lot has pot holes that need filling and the roof has loose shingles. I'm a pretty good handyman. Are you interested in swapping some of my work for the rent?

With Franklin spending an increasing amount of time in Raleigh with Lisa Ann, he had to admit to himself that he had let the maintenance slide at the Starbrite. The fact was, he hadn't done any repairs recently, saving all his strength and energy for Lisa Ann's ever expanding variety of games.

"A man's got to have his priorities," he justified to himself with a slight grin, wondering how on earth she ever came up with all the new stuff they were trying together.

Handing the cash back to Mr. Bazelski, Franklin said, "You do the work on this list and we'll call it even for the month. If you need supplies, just bring me the receipts and I'll reimburse you."

The arrangement couldn't have worked much better. Coming home from work on Monday, Franklin noticed that the parking lot had been smoothed and that Mr. Bazelski had found the ladder stored behind the motel and was working on the roof.

Walking over to the ladder to complement him on the job he'd done, Franklin apparently startled Mr. Bazelski and he smacked his thumb with a hammer.

"SH*T!" he said, before realizing that Franklin had heard him.

In the weeks that followed, Mr. B as he came to be known, was appointed as the official handyman at the Starbrite. Franklin even posted a notice to all the other tenants that they were to contact Mr.

B whenever there was a repair or maintenance issue. This freed up Franklin to do nothing more than collect the rent on Saturday afternoons, pay the bills and occasionally handle any new or departing renters. In exchange for being the on-call repair guy, Mr. B no longer had to pay rent.

While reimbursing him for the supplies he'd purchased the previous week, Franklin said, "The place hasn't looked this good since my Uncle Eustace was alive. I really appreciate what you're doing."

Mr. B nodded, acknowledging the complement. With that he offered Mr. B a cold drink from the refrigerator, which he accepted.

"I don't want to pry," Franklin said, "but I've heard you cuss a few times when you've been working. I assume that you can say other stuff?"

Mr. B nodded his head up and down, took a long pull from his beer, and looked directly at Franklin, "I choose not to talk. I had a wife who did all the talking for both of us. She's dead now and I got nothing more to say."

"I'll be sure to respect that," Franklin responded, figuring that the rest of the story wasn't any of his business.

Sharing the story with Lisa Ann, she said, "I wonder if he might have murdered his wife and is on the lam? Maybe he stuffed her in the trunk of his car and wanted to bury her behind the motel?"

"Not likely," responded Franklin, "his car is a hatchback."

"You should ask Are Dee to check him out, anyway" she suggested to Franklin.

"You really think so?" Franklin asked. "He seems pretty harmless."

"So did Ted Bundy," she responded.

It wasn't more than a couple of days later when Mr. B handed Franklin another note.

Is it OK if I hang a shortwave radio antenna on the TV tower? It won't interfere with the reception. It's pretty good now, since I fixed the distribution panel.

Without him asking, Mr. B had taken it upon himself to repair the TV antenna tower that had never really gotten a good signal since Uncle Eustace had it installed. They now received all the channels from Raleigh, Durham and even the UHF station in Fayetteville. Since Franklin could see no harm in Mr. B adding a shortwave antenna to the tower and since he appeared to know what he was doing, Franklin said yes to the request.

When he arrived home the next afternoon, Franklin saw that a long, vertical metal rod had been attached to the tower with a cable running in the direction of Number 12. Smiling to himself, he figured that Mr. B had already purchased the antenna before checking with him.

While walking down to Number 5 to talk with Lashaya Bryan about the noise complaints he gotten from the tenants in Number 4 and Number 6, Franklin heard a soft but steady tapping coming from Mr. B's room.

Dit-dah-dit, dah-dah-dit, dit-dit-dah. Franklin immediately recognized the sounds as Morse code being sent or received. He tried learning it as a Boy Scout, but could never quite get up to speed.

"Probably coming from his shortwave set-up," Franklin thought to himself. "If you don't want to talk, that would be a good way to communicate."

Waking up at two-thirty the next morning to use the bathroom, Franklin glanced out his window to check on the motel, as was his habit. The only light that was on at that hour came from Number 12.

One of the few tasks that Franklin continued to do at the Starbrite was to sort and distribute mail to the tenants. Everything came to the big mailbox next to his house. Each evening, Franklin would sort the incoming mail by room number and walk down the length of the motel, knocking if he thought the tenant was home or leaving it in the small plastic tray attached to each unit's door. It wasn't a big deal, just something that required attention. The upside was that it gave him an opportunity to check on the place once each day.

During their regular Saturday afternoon "State of the Starbrite" meeting, which usually lasted about three minutes and was followed by having a beer together, Mr. B handed Franklin another note.

People are complaining about how late they get their mail. I can handle passing it out, if it will help.

Not thinking much about it, Franklin quickly agreed, though he wondered to himself it Mr. B's offer had anything to do with the number of small packages that he was now receiving regularly. At first, Franklin thought that maybe his handyman was getting some adult-oriented literature or video tapes, but the shape of the boxes didn't seem to line up with either of those things.

The other thing he noticed was where the packages were coming from. The postage stamps and return addresses were from as far away at Thailand and Singapore or Norway and even Greenland. In the end, he wrote it all off to Mr. B's ham radio activities, but he still had to wonder.

Before heading to Raleigh to pick-up Lisa Ann for their regular Saturday night date, Franklin walked over to Are Dee's house and told him everything he knew about Mr. B. Hesitating just a bit, he also included Lisa Ann's concerns, laughing off the remote chance that Mr. B might have murdered his wife.

"Sounds like someone just trying to put their past behind 'em," said Are Dee optimistically. "Ain't no crime in that. I 'spect that there's lots of folks who'd like doin' just the same. I'll run his license plate, do a little diggin' and let you know what we find," Are Dee added.

The following weekend, after returning from church on Sunday, Are Dee walked over and knocked on Franklin's door.

Dressed in jeans and a sweatshirt, Lisa Ann answered, giving him a hug as she let him in.

"Brenda said she saw you and Franklin at Wednesday night services. That sure beats getting up early on a Sunday morning," he said warmly.

"Franklin is cooking breakfast," she said. "Would you like some coffee?"

"Sure," said Are Dee sitting down at the table. "Breakfast at one in the afternoon! Nothing like young love."

Franklin brought two plates of fried eggs and bacon to the table and offered to make some for Are Dee.

"Brenda's got lunch cooking, so I'll take a raincheck," he said. "I do have some news for you regarding your Mr. B, though. He appears to be clean as a whistle. He served for twenty years in the Navy, working in a classified job, near as I can tell, in the intelligence area. After he was discharged, he became a government employee in Langley, Virginia. Absolutely no details available, which leads me to believe that it might have been an extension of his Navy work. He and his wife lived in D.C. for most of that time. No kids. His wife died three years ago. Lisa Ann, you don't have to worry her being in the back of his car anymore. There was an autopsy that confirmed she passed from a stroke. Mr. Bazelski retired shortly after that and it appears that he's just sort of drifted since then, collectin' both a Navy and a government pension. He still owns a house in D.C., but it's rented out."

"Langley, Virginia," Lee Ann said, "Isn't that where the CIA is headquartered?"

"Sure is," responded Are Dee. "I 'spect that's why there was so little information about his background. One thing's for sure, he's got no criminal record, not even a speeding ticket,"

"So, why would he claim to be a handyman and why would he want to live at the Starbrite?" Franklin wondered.

"That MacGyver feller on TV is handyman of sorts," Are Dee said. "Who knows what Mr. B might have seen or done working for the government? Some of those jobs change people in ways you don't want to think about. People can't un-do what they was required to do. It changes 'em. It don't appear that he's causing anybody any harm and he sure as heck isn't any danged Communist!"

"Do you think he was an assassin?" Lisa Ann asked.

"I have no idea, but my recommendation is that neither of you go pokin' into stuff that you may not want to know about. Franklin, ask yourself when the Starbrite has ever looked this good? Not for years! I'd leave him to do his job unless you've got something else troubling you,"

Franklin thought for a moment, then just shook his head back and forth, Mr. B style.

"Still, you can't help but wonder," Lisa Ann said aloud.

The Starbrite had a 'no pets' policy. It wasn't that Franklin didn't love animals, he just figured that if a room at the motel was all a person could afford, they probably shouldn't own a pet. He wound-up making an exception when a yellow male tabby cat showed up one day and chose the Starbrite as its home. Given how friendly the cat was, most everybody figured that it had been abandoned.

(For the record, it makes me furious just knowing that there are sh*t-for-brains idiots in this world who somehow think it OK to just drop off a pet in the middle of nowhere once they get tired of it. If I had my way about it, whenever we found one of those heartless pieces of crap, we'd take them to the middle of Siberia or Outer Mongolia and drop them off, just to see how well they'd fend for themselves. Feel free to add that bit of ranting to my digression list. You can even count it as two, if you want.)

While nobody ever took credit for it, the cat got named Star and would make his rounds from Number 1 to Number 12 every day, checking on renters and usually getting fed by one or more of them. Franklin liked the cat, so let things slide. It was Mr. B who took Star to the vet for a check-up, shots and to get him fixed, though he never admitted ownership. In return, Mr. B became Star's favorite human, often sitting with him outside on warm evenings or being invited into Number 12 on cold winter nights. Mr. B would buy hot dogs just for Star, cutting them up into small pieces and feeding them to the cat. In exchange, Star would bring Mr. B the occasional mouse or chipmunk that he'd caught, most times dead but sometimes still wiggling. Mr. B and Star had a great deal in common; they were both pretty quiet, neither of them seemed to have much tolerance for fools and for the most part just wanted to be left alone, except for each other.

As time went on, Star became Mr. B's constant companion, pretty much ignoring the other folks living at the Starbrite. He was always following him around, watching him work on his car or doing repairs at the motel. Unlike any other cat Franklin had ever seen, Star would jump into Mr. B's Pinto and ride in the passenger seat while he ran his errands. No matter where they went, he kept an eye on the car for Mr. B and never tried to jump out or run away.

Figuring that animals are often excellent judges of a person's character, Franklin took Star's fondness of Mr. B as a positive sign and eventually convinced Lisa Ann of the same thing.

What made Mr. B such a valuable asset to the Starbrite was that no matter how nasty the task, he always knew what to do. This became especially evident when the toilets and showers in Numbers 1 through 8 backed up with raw sewage.

When the Starbrite was built in 1958, Eustace and Willa Mae were required to install two separate septic systems, one for the first eight rooms and a second for the remaining rooms and their house. As the motel aged, the systems required increasing amounts of attention and when they broke down, things got really bad, really fast.

On one of the hottest, most miserable days in August, Lashaya Bryan started banging on Mr. B's door, hollering about the problem. Franklin was fortunate enough to be at work at the time. After walking down to Number 5 and checking on the other rooms, Mr. B confirmed that there was a serious issue with the system.

Since Franklin had recently paid to have both septic tanks pumped out, Mr. B reasoned that there had to be a clog somewhere.

Pulling out his notepad, he wrote:

Have you flushed anything unusual down your toilet?

"You mean besides the normal?" Lashaya asked.

Mr. B nodded his head up and down.

Leaning in so's nobody else could hear, she quietly said, "This is a very personal matter. I've been having an awful problem with the piles. You ever had 'em?"

Mr. B nodded his head up and down.

"My doctor thought it would help if I started usin' baby wipes for......you know.....cleaning yourself. I got the kind that says 'safe for flushing' right on the container."

She got the plastic tub and showed it to him. In the fine print, which Lashaya had missed, it said 'for most sanitary sewer systems. Not recommended for use with septic systems.' Mr. B showed the disclaimer to her and she felt real bad.

Mr. B quickly wrote notes to the other folks living in Number 1 through 8, letting them know the nature of the problem and that he was working to correct it as quick as possible.

Before Franklin ever got home, Mr. B had driven down to Wake Forest and rented a commercial sewer snake to clean out the pipes. By the time Franklin arrived, Mr. B was splattered with sewage, but the drain in Lashaya's room was still clogged. Are Dee came over to help and they all worked at trying to solve the problem well into the hot, miserable evening. Even with a fan running to move the awful stink out of Number 5, it was still overwhelming. Lashaya and most of the other renters either went out for the evening or sat outside their rooms.

Since Franklin was an engineer, albeit an electrical one, he took charge of the plumbing snake when Mr. B couldn't make any headway. While Franklin was operating it with Are Dee's assistance, Mr. B kept pointing to the instruction manual trying to tell them that something was wrong. Finally, in frustration, Mr. B reached over and pushed the reverse button on the machine, resulting in a large wad of baby wipes dislodging, along with covering all three of 'em with the other contents of the sewer pipe. It was so bad that Franklin had to walk outside and puke.

Even with his two helpers temporarily sidelined, Mr. B trooped on, removing the toilet from its flange and moving the plumbing snake back and forth for nearly an hour, with Franklin and Are Dee helping for as much as either of them could stand. Unable to dislodge the clog from inside, they took the snake outside in hopes of running it from the septic tank back into Number 5.

This tricky move required Mr. B to lean over into the tank to feed the snake into the pipe. Are Dee had called Robert Dee and Richard Lee over to help. One of 'em grabbed each of Mr. B's legs to make sure that he didn't fall into the pit of poop. Trying his very best not to gag, he slowly ran the device through the pipe, pulling out wad after wad of the offending baby wipes, along with used condoms and even a dog collar and leash. That last item was the subject of speculation for years after.

At around 9:30, there finally was a large whoosh, and fluid began moving from all the other rooms back out to the septic tank, but not before soaking Mr. B, Robert Dee and Richard Lee in stuff you don't want to even think about.

Feeling pity for 'em all, Brenda came over with a bucket of laundry detergent and a car wash brush, scrubbing and hosing down each one of 'em, since she could smell the stink all the way over to her house.

After putting Lashaya's bathroom back together and scrubbing everything down with bleach, they split up and began cleaning the other rooms, going through five gallons of chlorine bleach before they was finished. It took until near midnight to get the job done and get everything back to normal. Afterward, Franklin threw out the clothes he was wearing and took three showers that night before he finally felt clean.

The next day, Franklin typed up a notice for all Starbrite renters informing them of what not to flush down the toilets and thanking Mr. B for his quick thinking and action to get the problem fixed. Seriously, how many other motel handymen would have allowed themselves to be dropped head-first into a septic tank?

All the folks living in Numbers 1 through 8 were very thankful for Mr. B that night and told him so. This gave Franklin the inspiration to create a special award for the Starbrite's dedicated handyman. Purchasing a new plunger, he spray painted it gold and awarded it to Mr. B along with a gallon of bleach, a deck of playing cards and a fifth of whiskey. Franklin even had all the tenants sign the plunger. Calling it the "Straight Flush Award," Mr. B proudly displayed it in his room until the day he left the Starbrite Motel.

Mr. B, showing that he was a good sport, bought Lashaya a tube of hemorrhoid cream and a six-pack of 'septic system safe' toilet paper. It was one of the few times that she was actually nice to the folks involved, at least for a day or so.

It wouldn't be much of an exaggeration to say that Mr. B kept the Starbrite together with chewing gum and bailing wire, very seldom getting Franklin involved unless a really serious problem developed. In addition to knowing about plumbing, electrical and air conditioners, he somehow managed to keep the ancient ice maker running, even during the hottest weather. He seemed to have a personal relationship with the machine, knowing exactly what would break next and having the repair parts already ordered and waiting.

Part of what made Mr. B so special was the pride he took in his job. With each repair, with each crisis averted, he'd sit back afterward and smile with great satisfaction. Thinking back to what Are Dee had said about some folks just wanting to put their past behind 'em, Franklin often wondered what Mr. B had actually done in the Navy and for the CIA, but thought better of it and let things go.

One thing was for sure, it was a lucky day for Franklin and the Starbrite renters when Mr. Bazelski showed up to rent Number 12. The funny thing was that Mr. B felt exactly the same way about all of them, with the possible exception of Lashaya.

Chapter 7 – Donnie Kensler

Winters in our part of North Carolina are generally mild, with daytime highs in the low 50's and nighttime lows in the 30's. The first part of February 1985 was a notable exception.

An Alberta Clipper came down from Canada blasting the Great North State with frigid air and liked to froze us all to death. With the thermometer dropping to near zero at night, all sorts of cold temperature records, not to mention water pipes, were gettin' busted left and right. Worst of all, the weather stayed like that for nearly a week.

Marcus was making the regular rounds in his patrol car at sunset. Having reached the northern edge of Youngstown, he made a U-turn on U.S. 1, coming back south and into the village. That's when he noticed a kid walking along the shoulder of the road, wearing a light jacket and sneakers, no hat or gloves. He was carrying a small duffle bag. Pulling over, he asked him if he'd like a ride into town. The kid accepted. Getting in on the passenger side of the patrol car, Marcus immediately saw that the boy's left eye was black and blue and swollen nearly shut.

"I'm Marcus Cooper," he said, extending a hand to the boy. When he shook his hand, Marcus could see that his fingers were blue.

"Donnie Kensler," the boy said, shaking from the cold.

"You from around here?" Marcus asked.

"No, sir. I'm from north of Richmond. Just trying to get to Jacksonville, Florida."

The boy looked to be "starved-dog skinny." He was wearing a pair of jeans and as near as Marcus could tell, just a t-shirt under his jacket.

"How'd you like to have dinner at the café and warm up some?" Marcus asked.

"I would, but I'm a little tight for money at the moment."

"The Village of Youngstown has a Guest Hospitality Program, so dinner would be on us," Marcus said, making things up as he went.

"I'd like that a lot," the boy said. His teeth were chattering.

When the hamburger and fries arrived at the table, Donnie dove into them and cleaned the plate in under three minutes.

"If you'd like another one, it's covered by the hospitality program," Marcus offered.

Donnie, who was still shivering, nodded his head up and down.

"Any chance that you're running away from home?" Marcus asked.

"I ain't running away, I got kicked out."

"Is that how you got that shiner?" he asked.

Not saying anything, Donnie nodded his head up and down.

"Why don't you tell me what happened?"

"My daddy and I don't get along real well, especially after he's had a few beers. He don't bother my momma, but he's never taken much of a liking to me. Last night at 'bout 11:00 he came bustin' into my room telling me that I was a drain on his finances and now that I was 18, it was time for me to hit the road. He made things extra clear by back-handin' me. My grandma lives in Jacksonville, Florida so I grabbed what I could and started walkin'."

At that point he pulled the driver's license from his wallet and showed it to Marcus, proving that he was 18. Marcus was scribbling notes as Donnie spoke.

"I got to a McDonalds and stayed there until they were closin' up for the night. After 'most everybody left, I crawled into their dumpster and covered myself up with trash bags to keep warm until morning. Then I started hitch-hikin'. My last ride dropped me off in Kittwell and I got this far when you picked me up."

"That's near ten miles," Marcus said. "You walked all that distance in this cold?"

Donnie nodded up and down just as the second burger arrived and he dove back in.

"There's a motel across the street and I know the owner pretty well. If they've got a room, we can get you a warm place to stay at least for the night," Marcus said.

"Is that part of the program, too?" Donnie asked.

"Yup," Marcus responded.

After Marcus paid for Donnie's food, they drove across U.S. 1 and he knocked on Franklin's door. Franklin had only just gotten home from work.

"Evening Marcus!" Franklin said. "Who's your friend in the car?"

"He's a special case. His daddy beat him up pretty bad and threw him out. He made it this far from Richmond. I found him walking into town and about froze to death. Franklin, he needs a room."

Without thinking twice, Franklin handed Marcus the key to Number 8.

"How old is he?" Franklin asked.

"Just turned 18. Said he's trying to get to his grandmother's place in Jacksonville."

"North Carolina or Florida?" Franklin asked.

"Florida."

"I take it he doesn't have any money?"

"I'll cover his rent," Marcus said, reaching for his wallet.

"Not a chance, Marcus. This one's on the house."

And that's how Donnie Kensler landed at the Starbrite Motel in February of 1985.

After getting Donnie settled into the room and turning the heat up to near 80, Marcus walked over to Are Dee and Brenda's house, just as they were sitting down for supper.

"Officer Cooper, unless there's a huge crime spree goin' on in Youngstown tonight, you will sit yourself down and eat with us," Brenda ordered.

"Yes, ma'am. Thank you!"

Over supper, Marcus told Are Dee and Brenda all that he knew about Donnie and his situation.

"That poor child!" was all Brenda could say.

"Let him rest and warm up overnight," Are Dee said. "We can check out his story in the morning. If it's true, we'll figure out a way to help him. I'll talk with Franklin. I'm sure he'll let him stay at the Starbrite until things warm up some. You think he needs to see a doctor about the eye?"

"I can't be sure, but if it's still swollen bad in the morning, we should probably get him checked out."

Brenda had gone to Robert Dee and Richard Lee's old bedroom and came back with a winter coat, hat and gloves along with a pair of boots.

"I've got no idea if this stuff will fit that boy or not, but he's sure welcome to it. Richard Lee last wore those things when he was in the eighth grade."

"I'll take 'em to him after supper," Marcus said.

"Marcus," Are Dee said, "you did the right thing for that boy tonight. I'm proud of you."

"We serve and protect," Marcus said. "That was the first thing you showed me on the side of the car," he added, smiling.

The next morning Are Dee walked over to Number 8 and knocked on the door at 7:30. Donnie was already dressed and packed-up.

"I'm Are Dee Camber, the Chief of Police here in Youngstown. I understand that Officer Cooper introduced you to our Guest Hospitality Program last night. Is everything OK?"

"Yes, sir. I surely do appreciate the hospitality," Donnie said.

"How's your eye?" Are Dee asked before handing him a bag with four warm cheese biscuits that had been made by Brenda.

"Much better, thank you! I went down to the motel office and got some ice for it last night. It may not look great, but it's a bunch improved."

"I'd like you to come over to the Village Hall so that we can get some information about your family for the program records," Are Dee said.

"After that, I guess I should probably leave. Is there any law against hitch-hikin' in Youngstown?" Donnie asked.

"No law against it, but why don't you stick around until things warm up some?"

"I wouldn't want to wear out my welcome," he said.

"You won't," Are Dee responded.

Are Dee ran Donnie's license for wants and warrants. As he had expected, everything came back clean. Next, he called the Richmond County, VA Sheriff's office and asked them to check on

Donnie's mother and notify her that he was safe. During the call, he was told that the department had made several previous visits to the home over reports from the local high school about Donnie being abused at the hands of his daddy. While nothing much surprised Are Dee, the news certainly saddened him.

"Does your grandma know you're headed to her place in Jacksonville?" Are Dee asked.

"No, sir. Our phone got disconnected and I didn't have the chance to write her."

"What do you say we call her from my office?" he offered.

When Are Dee called the number Donnie gave him, it was answered by the receptionist at the Sunnyview Assisted Living Center, where they confirmed that Donnie's grandmother was a resident. Once they were connected to the grandmother's room, Are Dee handed the phone to Donnie. Listening to just half the conversation, he quickly realized that there was a problem.

When the call ended, Donnie looked at Are Dee and said, "She said that she's in a tiny apartment and that they don't allow guests to stay with the residents. She sounded like she wanted to help, but it don't seem like there's nothin' she can do."

It was crystal clear to Are Dee that the kid didn't have a clue as to what he should do next.

"When was the last time you were in school, son?" Are Dee asked.

"The day before yesterday," he answered. "I'm a Senior and on the 'B' honor roll," he added proudly.

"Why don't you make yourself comfortable here for a while? I've got some business to attend to and will be back in a bit."

Are Dee drove over to Youngstown High School and spoke directly with the principal, Charlie Eaton, then called Franklin, who was at

88

work. Next, he spoke with Howard Ellis, the manager at the Youngstown IGA, before returning to his office.

"Donnie, the Village of Youngstown Guest Hospitality Program Committee wants to extend a special offer to you. Seein' as you are 18 and legally able to make your own decisions, we'd like to offer you the continued use of a free room at the Starbrite and the chance to enroll at Youngstown High School, so's you can graduate. The Youngstown IGA happens to need a bagger, and would also like to offer you a part time job."

"This isn't some sort of charity, is it?" Donnie asked.

"It's a legitimate offer, if you want to accept it. Come spring, after graduation, you can decide whether or not you want to stick around."

It took the rest of the morning to get all the pieces set in motion for Donnie. Mr. Eaton contacted his high school in Virginia to get his records transferred and Mr. Ellis had him fill-out an employment application, though he'd already decided to give Donnie a job based on Are Dee's recommendation.

Are Dee brought Donnie home with him at lunchtime, where he met Brenda. If ever there was a stray cat or dog wandering around Youngstown, it would always find Brenda Camber who would take it in and keep it cared-for until she could locate a permanent home for the animal.

To the depths of her soul, Brenda believed that if the Lord placed someone in need into her path, she was supposed help them. Just looking across the table at that skinny kid with the black eye, she knew that there was a reason why Donnie Kensler had come into her life. It was God's will and she fully intended to answer His call.

"I'd like you to come over here for breakfast before school," she told him. "With our kids grown and out of the house, I'd sure appreciate the company."

Donnie did that for a week or so, until he got his first paycheck and could buy food for himself. Before he left for school each day, Brenda would hand him a brown-bag lunch, too. Since Donnie worked from 3:30 until 8:00 at the grocery store, Mr. Ellis made sure that he got dinner from their deli section each evening "as part of his compensation plan." Brenda had walked over to the store while Donnie was in classes and spoke with Mr. Ellis about makin' the arrangement. He understood the situation and was glad to help.

Having Donnie around also gave Brenda a chance to clean out a bunch of clothes that Robert Dee and Richard Lee had left behind, even some brand-new ones that she'd purchased in Donnie's exact size and had to wash several times so they'd look used.

If you grew up poor, as did many Youngstown residents, and know what it's like to go to bed hungry, then you naturally feel empathy for people in a similar situation. It's not that rich people don't have concern and compassion for folks less fortunate, it's just that they've never walked a mile in a poor kid's wore-out sneakers. So it was that quietly, humbly, a number of good people in Youngstown, people who lived what their religion preached, went out of their way to help Donnie Kensler and make him feel welcome. They also made sure that he never, ever felt like he was receiving charity.

After Donnie had been working for about a month, he came to Franklin and asked if he could start paying rent on his room.

"We've got a special student rate," Franklin said. "$20 a week. If that's too much, then you are welcome to stay on the Guest Hospitality Plan," he added.

Donnie was more than good with paying the student rate.

With an invitation from Brenda and Are Dee, Donnie started attending the Youngstown Free Will Evangelic Fundamentalist Church almost every Sunday, too.

What impressed the folks in Youngstown about Donnie was his strong character. Far from a freeloader, he wanted to pay his own way at every opportunity and was one of the hardest working kids they'd ever seen. His room at the Starbrite was organized and spotless. When he had a meal with Brenda and Are Dee, he immediately pitched in to clear the table and help in the kitchen. He was a dedicated student, taking his classes seriously and avoiding any tomfoolery. He worked hard at the IGA too, which really impressed Mr. Ellis. If things were slow, Donnie would offer to put up stock or flatten boxes in the back. Without exception, folks were glad to have helped the young man.

Shortly after noon on a Saturday in April, a scraggly-looking man driving a beat-up fifteen year old Chevy truck pulled into the Starbrite Motel parking lot. He looked to be in his forties, skinny, with salt and pepper hair. Franklin noticed that as he got out of his truck, he was staggering some.

Walking over to the motel office, he said, "I'm lookin' for Donnie Kensler."

"He's not here right now. Something I can do for you?" Franklin asked.

"I'm his daddy. I want to talk to him," the man said. "He does live here, don't he?"

"He does," Franklin said, "but he's not apt to be back until late evening."

"You know where I can find him?"

"Can't say as I do," Franklin said.

"I'll wait," said Donnie's daddy, as he walked back to his truck and popped the top on a Blue Ribbon beer.

Given all what Donnie had been through and judging by the looks of his father, Franklin decided to call Are Dee, who in-turn radioed Marcus, since he was on-duty that afternoon.

A few minutes later, Marcus pulled into the Starbrite parking lot, directly behind the Chevy truck and walked up to the driver's door.

"License and registration, please," he said to Donnie's daddy.

"What'd I do wrong?" he asked, reeking of alcohol.

Marcus repeated the request, "License and registration, please."

"What if I don't fu*kin' feel like givin' to you, ni**er?" he said, spitting out his window and just missing Marcus.

Skipping past the, 'I'm sure I didn't hear you correctly' part of his training, Marcus grabbed the door handle, yanked Donnie's daddy out of his seat and pushed him up against the side of the truck, where he immediately handcuffed him. Given his size, strength and anger it only took about 15 seconds to accomplish all of that. He next radioed Are Dee for back-up and he walked across the parking lot to see what was going on.

After frisking him and pulling a wallet from the man's back pocket, Are Dee handed his driver's license to Marcus. Steven P. Kensler was then given a field sobriety test, which he failed and was seated on the gravel, leaning his back against the truck. The cab had four empty beer cans on the floor and two unopened ones on the seat.

"What brings you to town, Mr. Kensler?" Are Dee asked.

"I came here to see my kid, Donnie. You know him?"

"I do," Are Dee said. "And why do you need to see him?"

"Ain't none of your fu*kin' business!" he said.

At that point, Marcus picked him up by his shirt and threw him hard against the bed of the truck.

"Excuse me, but I'm sure we didn't hear you correctly," he said to Kensler. "You want to try answering again?"

Kensler responded by puking up several beers and possibly a chili cheese dog. Marcus and Are Dee stepped aside just in time to avoid being splattered.

Spitting the last chunks of vomit out of his mouth, Kensler said, "His momma made me come. She wants me to bring him back home. I knew it was a bad idea, given what a worthless piece of sh*t he is, but I come to see him anyway."

Marcus and Are Dee walked behind the patrol car to talk.

"What do you want to do with him Are Dee?" Marcus asked quietly.

"What I want to do is take him out behind my garage and give him a few of doses of what he gave Donnie. I'm guessin' you'd like to help. What we're gonna do is get him sobered up and send him home."

"No way!? Are you serious? We've got him dead to rights on drunk driving and you want to give him a break?" Marcus said. "Why?"

"I'm not gonna argue the point right now. But think about the situation, Marcus. Given all that Donnie's been through and how far he's come, what's in his best interest? If we arrest his daddy and impound his truck, I'll guarantee you that Donnie will wind-up gettin' involved. We need to do better by that boy," Are Dee said. "Put him in the back of the car. I'll take him over to the office and we'll start pourin' coffee into him. You drive his truck over and park it behind the building."

They'd no more than pulled out of the Starbrite parking lot when Mr. B walked over with a garden hose and started spraying down and raking the mess Kensler had left in the gravel.

Instead of spending his Saturday afternoon weeding Brenda's flower beds, Are Dee sat across his desk from Steven P. Kensler and watched him drink four cups of coffee over the course of three hours, pausing only to show him to the restroom. Are Dee felt it best that Marcus go back on patrol, rather than spend any more time in the toxic presence of Donnie's daddy.

During the time they spent together, Are Dee and Kensler had said almost nothing to each other. At three, Are Dee ran Kensler back through another field sobriety test, which he passed this time.

"Your son Donnie is a friend of mine, Mr. Kensler. So instead of arresting you for drunk driving and you spending any more time with us, you're gonna get into your truck and I'll follow you up as far as the Virginia border where you will get your sorry ass out of the State of North Carolina. If you ever come back anywhere near Youngstown, I will personally arrest you for somethin' and give Officer Cooper a full hour to have a one-to-one conversation with you out in the woods. I think you should know that he was drummed out of the Marine Corps for using excessive violence and you've stirred up a whole bunch of those ugly feelings in him. Do you understand me?"

Kensler nodded his head up and down. Are Dee took him out to his truck, got into his patrol car and followed him north on U.S. 1 until he'd crossed over to the Virginia side of the border. He then returned home, where he'd discovered that Franklin had weeded Brenda's flower beds for him.

Once Are Dee got back, he radioed Marcus, asking him to come to his house.

"You OK?" he asked Marcus.

"Yup."

"I'm sorry he called you that hateful name," Are Dee said, "but I want you to know that we still did the right thing in lettin' him go."

"How's that Are Dee?"

"Was the engine running on his truck when you approached him?"

"No."

"Were the keys in the ignition?"

"Can't rightly say," Marcus responded.

"They weren't," Are Dee said. "They was in the pocket of his jeans when I frisked him. We could have nailed him for bein' drunk and disorderly, but he'd would have beat the DWI charge."

"So you did the next best thing. You convinced him not to come back to Youngstown."

"Right! Do you agree?"

"Every time I think I've learned it all, you teach me something new that I need to know," Marcus said.

"I can't never teach you humanity, Marcus. You learned all that from your momma and daddy and they sure did a fine job."

Donnie had been bagging groceries all that afternoon. While he thought he'd seen a truck that looked a lot like his daddy's, he couldn't be sure and never thought any more about it.

At the end of May Donnie became a graduate of Youngstown High School. In the five months he'd lived at the Starbrite, he put on about 15 pounds of muscle and had regained much of the self-confidence and self-worth that had been beaten out of him by his daddy. He'd written to his momma every week or two, just to let her know that he was doing fine, even if she didn't write back but once or twice in the months he'd lived in Youngstown. I guess she had her own troubles to work through.

One of the most interesting friendships Donnie made was with Mr. B, who like most of the others took a real likin' to the boy. In Donnie's spare time, not that there was much of it, he'd watch Mr. B working on his old Pinto or fixing-up something at the Starbrite.

Since Donnie seemed so interested in Mr. B's work, he took the time to show him what he was doing and how it was done, adding to the boy's set of practical skills. He was amazed at how quickly Donnie caught on and how soon he was ready to tackle jobs on his own.

It was on a warm evening in mid-June when Donnie walked across the Starbrite parking lot and knocked on Are Dee and Brenda's screen door to tell them that he'd enlisted in the Marine Corps and would be leaving for basic training the following week. The Cambers and Donnie's other friends quickly arranged a going-away party for that Saturday night. As it turned out, over a hundred folks came by to wish him good luck. It seemed that he'd touched their lives nearly as much as they'd touched his.

Donnie Kensler still sends letters to Are Dee, Brenda, Marcus and a few others from time to time, from the different parts of the world where he's been stationed. Last they knew, he was planning to be a career Marine, having been fully trained as a Motor Pool Mechanic. When Mr. B found out, he sent Donnie a note telling him how proud he was of his former apprentice!

Whether or not he ever figured out that the Youngstown Guest Hospitality Program never really existed doesn't matter nearly so much as what he learned about the good people of that community while staying in Number 8 at the Starbrite Motel.

Some things you experience can stick with you for your entire life. Kindness is one.

Chapter 8 – Eddie Franchetti

Eddie Franchetti was a lower level soldier in the Camden, NJ mob and specialized in collecting loans and protection money for his boss and uncle, Carlo. Carlo was the "Capo de Capo", overseeing the other captains in Camden on behalf of his godfather, Gerardo Santini, in Newark, who controlled most of the state. As such, Carlo was considered a trusted manager, allowing him to run his own enterprises, as long as he shared the profits with his boss.

Eddie was a numbers guy and a meticulous planner, always focused on the tiniest details of any transaction.

(So, what's any of this got to do with the Starbrite Motel? Be patient! I'll get there, it just might take me awhile.)

Unlike many of his counterparts, Eddie wore conservative suits, starched white shirts with broad striped ties and black wingtip shoes as he made his rounds. Carrying a brief case, he could easily have been confused for an accountant, an attorney or maybe even a banker. Trying to show the proper respect for the folks who did business with Uncle Carlo, Eddie always called them his 'clients.' He didn't carry a gun or any other weapon and he never hurt nobody. He didn't have to. His clients understood who they were dealing with and who eventually received the cash, so there was no need for harsh persuasion.

Every once in a while, when one of them was short of money or late on a payment, Eddie would just look at him or her like they was already laid out at a funeral parlor and say, "This is going to be a huge disappointment to my employer. We need to come to terms about your repayment plan or he'll be very upset." He always spoke to them like a real gentleman.

Folks who valued their lives or property tried their level best to avoid upsetting Uncle Carlo, so Eddie almost always returned with envelopes full of cash or agreements for catching up on any delinquent debts, including substantial interest payments. It was kind of like that revolving charge account you've got, except with much tougher penalties for paying them late and with 70% interest attached.

Uncle Carlo restricted his business activities to loan sharking and protection, leaving the nastier stuff to the other Camden capos. He generated a good income, sending a large portion of it to Gerardo on the last day of each month. One of Eddie's regular assignments was the task of loading a suitcase or two filled with cash into the trunk of his Toyota Camry and delivering them to the Palermo Social Club in Newark where they were given to one of Santini's associates.

While Eddie's job was fairly safe and relatively easy, it didn't pay nearly enough to satisfy him and the chances for advancement were limited, since Uncle Carlo's oldest son, Dom was already training to take over his papa's responsibilities. A Papa is what they call a daddy in Camden, NJ. They're strange folks up there.

Eddie aspired to be a CPA and had been taking evening college courses for nearly six years, slowly inching toward his degree. At 26, he still lived at home with his widowed momma. While he dated regularly, he wasn't ready to get serious with any girl until he'd made it in life.

Eddie had one overwhelming weakness, his greed. It consumed him day and night and he spent countless hours trying to come up with the right scheme so that he could get wealthy and still live long enough to enjoy it. Skimming collection money from Uncle Carlo was out of the question because of family loyalty and the knowledge of what would happen to him if he got caught. Becoming a permanent part of the basement floor in a new apartment building in Camden was not on Eddie's to-do list.

When his Uncle Carlo flew to Miami in February of 1985 for a three-week vacation, he asked Eddie to drive his Lincoln Towne Car down to him, flying back to Newark a couple of days later. Trying to escape the boredom of I-95, he decided to detour down U.S. 1 for a few hours. It was while cruising through southern Virginia that an idea came to him and he began work on the detailed plan that took six months to bring together.

On Wednesday, July 31st, Eddie loaded two suitcases of cash into his car and headed from Camden to Newark for his usual end-of-month delivery. What made this particular shipment unique was that it included funds gathered from several other of the Camden capos. This was a common practice, causing little concern since Carlo was trusted by his Camden counterparts and Eddie was trusted by Carlo. Driving north on the New Jersey Turnpike, he took the New Brunswick exit and headed to the deserted parking lot of a closed Woolco store. At the back of the building, he transferred the two suitcases, plus an additional one and a gym bag, from the Camry into the trunk of a four year old VW Jetta. Starting the engine of the Jetta, he walked over to his Camry and lit the fuse on two sticks of dynamite that he'd tucked just above the gas tank, along with a thousand dollars in small bills. Eddie had gotten the TNT from a demolition company owner in June, telling him it was needed for a Fourth of July party. Since he was collecting interest owed on a delinquent payment to his uncle, the client never thought twice about the request.

Eddie was just a block away when he heard the explosion. With a nearly full tank of gasoline in the Camry, he had correctly figured that there would be a heck of a bang. He pulled in to a Mobil gas station that he'd found during a scouting trip two months earlier. It had restrooms on the side of the building that were always unlocked and couldn't be seen from the front of the station. In the four minutes that he was inside the men's room and with screaming fire trucks and police cars drawing people's attention to the nearby street, he changed from the suit he was wearing into the pair of jeans, NC

State t-shirt and sneakers that were inside the gym bag. Wearing a ball cap and a pair of aviator sunglasses, he grabbed the bag and got back into the Jetta.

On his way out of town, he stopped at a Shoprite grocery store and purchased a whole four-pound Red Snapper. Back in his car, he rolled the fish inside the suit he'd been wearing, placing it into a FedEx shipping box addressed to his Uncle Carlo at his office and left it in a drop-off box. Getting back on I-95, he drove south hitting Washington D.C. Beltway traffic before crossing over toward I-85. He'd been on the road for over six hours, the sun had set and he was ready for some rest. Following his plan to the letter, he pulled into the Armada Inn at Petersburg, VA, where he'd made a reservation from a pay phone in Camden two days prior. His room was waiting for him. Staring at his three suitcases, two filled with money, he resisted the urge to start counting the cash and instead swallowed one of his momma's prescription sleeping pills, assuring him of at least eight hours of rest.

Uncle Carlo began getting calls shortly after 3:00 that afternoon, first hearing about the missed delivery from Gerardo and then receiving a hysterical phone call from his sister Angelina, who had been notified by police about the explosion of Eddie's car. Carlo called his son Dom into his office.

"What the fu*k is going on?! Have you heard anything from Eddie?" Carlo asked.

"Nothing, Pop," Dom said. "How much cash was he carrying?"

"One-point-four million," his father responded, shaking his head. "It was the bi-monthly payment. The sh*t is hitting the fan bigtime! Angelina said the cops told her that they found cash scattered around the car, but nothing to indicate that anyone was inside when it exploded. Your mother is already headed over to Angelina's house to stay with her. We need to hear directly from every guy we've got on the street to see what they know. We're going to be held accountable. Capishe?"

"I'm on it," Dom said. "You think Eddie was involved?"

"Not a chance! Your cousin is a good boy, you know that, but what he lacks is ambition. That's why I got him doin' collections. I was always hoping he'd hate the job enough to come to me and ask for a different assignment."

Dom spent the balance of the day and much of the evening speaking directly to each of the men who worked for his father. Carlo spent his time trying to calm the other Camden capos and Gerardo in Newark. He promised Santini that he'd find the cash and the culprit. Gerardo reminded him of his obligation to cover the loss, if he didn't recover the funds.

The next morning while Eddie continued his drive south, Dom brought a soggy FedEx box into his father's office and set it on his desk.

"What the fu*k is this?" Carlo asked.

"It was just delivered. It smells like fish. I got a bad feeling Pop, a real bad feeling," Dom said.

Carefully opening the box, Carlo recognized the tailored suit as one of Eddie's. The fish told the rest of the story. Carlo and Dom both immediately made the Sign of the Cross.

"That fu*kin' Nikko Rossellini is at the bottom of this, mark my words!" he said. "He's been pissed-off since the Gerardo named me Capo de Capo over him! This is just his style, old school! If that basta*d wants to start a war, he's picked the wrong guy to fu*k with! Pull the car around, I got to visit my sister and tell her about Eddie. I loved that kid!"

"We don't know for sure that he sleeps with the fish," Dom said.

"What more proof do you need, Stupido! You think they're ever going to find a body? Now go get the fu*kin' car!" Carlo responded.

No matter where you're from, even Camden, NJ, when you treat people decent and with respect they generally respond in kind, even if you're shaking 'em down for protection or loan sharking money. Because Eddie was so good at collections, he was allowed a lot of latitude in how he handled folks. The result was a whole bunch of people who were willing to do him favors. For instance, when he wanted to have a Virginia license plate (current year) for his collection, his body shop client was more than happy to pull it off a wrecked car he was repairing. Getting a Virginia driver's license with a new name took a bit more effort, but Eddie's client who worked for the New Jersey DMV was willing to get it done for the guy who had cut his interest rate from 70% down to 30%, and had helped to keep his knee caps from getting busted.

On the previous Saturday morning, Eddie had taken Amtrak from Camden to Washington D.C., hiring a cab to drive him to a used car lot in Falls Church. It was there that he negotiated the purchase of the Jetta, paying cash, showing his new Virginia driver's license with the name Edward Francis and obtaining a temporary registration and 10-day 'in-transit' Virginia license plate.

"I'm headed to California," he told the car dealer. "I'll get it permanently registered when I get to 'Frisco next week."

With everything handled, he drove north on I-95 to New Brunswick, parking the Jetta at the Amtrak station and taking a commuter train back to Camden. Eddie was home in time to have dinner with his momma and to take her to Saturday evening mass. When the big day arrived, he parked his Camry in the Woolco parking lot and walked the four blocks to retrieve the Jetta from the train station. You already know where things went from there.

Leaving Petersburg on I-85 at about 9:00 on Thursday morning, he headed south until it split with U.S. 1 just north of Henderson, NC.

102

Eddie made sure that he strictly obeyed all the traffic laws and was courteous to other drivers. During his trip to Miami, he had made a note about a middle-of-nowhere motel to stay for a few days. He wanted a place where no one would ever think to look for him.

He'd been on the road just over three hours when he stopped to top-off his gas tank in Youngstown before heading across the street to the Starbrite. After paying in cash and thanking the attendant, he pulled across U.S. 1 and into the parking lot where Mr. B was raking the gravel. It was just a little past noon on Thursday, August 1, 1985 when Eddie landed at the Starbrite Motel.

"Excuse me, you should have a room reserved for me, Edward Francis," he said politely.

Mr. B nodded up and down and walked him to the office.

"The owner said you'd be able to give me the key and would collect the rent," he said real nice.

Mr. B nodded up and down again and handed him a registration card and scribbled '$35.00 due today' on another piece of paper.

When Eddie reserved the room, Franklin told him that Mr. B was a mute.

Filling out the registration card as Ed Francis from Charlottesville, VA, he pushed it back to Mr. B along with two twenty dollar bills.

"Where's a good place to eat around here?" Eddie asked.

Mr. B pointed to the Carolina Country Café and handed him back a five dollar bill along with a key for Number 10.

"Thanks," Eddie said. "You can keep the change."

Mr. B had never received a tip before, so just kind of stared at the money before he put it in his pocket.

"It's nice that somebody gave that old guy a job," Eddie thought to himself.

"A New York accent and an NC State shirt, plus the man gives me a big tip. Nobody who lives at the Starbrite gives tips. Something's not right about him," Mr. B thought.

Franklin pulled into the Starbrite parking lot at 6:45, just as Ed was walking back from his second meal of the day at the café.

"I've got to find a different place to eat tomorrow," he thought to himself, not a big fan of country cookin'.

"Are you Mr. Francis?" Franklin asked.

"I am," said Eddie. "You must be Franklin."

"I am," Franklin said, real friendly.

"The retarded guy got me all checked in this afternoon and collected the rent," Eddie told him.

"Mr. B isn't retarded. He's actually a very smart man and handles all our maintenance. He's just mute, like I told you on the phone," Franklin said, somewhat irritated.

"Sorry, no offence meant!" Eddie offered quickly.

"None taken. What brings you to Youngstown, Mr. Francis?" he asked.

"I'm here to check out the area for future business development," he responded.

From his response, Franklin strongly suspected that something wasn't right about this guy.

Eddie had backed his car into a space directly in front of Number 10, bringing only the suitcase with clothes into the room. Waiting until 11:45 that night, when he assumed that the other tenants would be asleep, he quietly opened his door. He first replaced the temporary license plate on his car with the current-year Virginia plate. Being as quiet as a mouse, he then opened the trunk and brought the two suitcases filled with cash back inside his room.

Mr. B had heard the door open two units down, got up and stood at the window of his darkened room, observing the activity via a slightly lifted slat in his Venetian blinds. Having a full moon to light up the parking lot he saw everything Eddie was doing.

Once back inside his room, Eddie locked the door, checking it twice and softly opened both bags to begin counting the cash over the next hour.

"Holy Mother of God!" he said out loud.

He knew there'd be a lot of money, but one-point-four million dollars was more than he could have ever dreamed of.

Closing the suitcases and moving them across the room, he opened his clothing bag and pulled out a 25-caliber silver plated pistol, placing it on his nightstand. The man who never carried a weapon, now felt the need for some personal protection.

Waking up on Friday morning, he got going quickly, knowing that he had business to attend to. While he wasn't too concerned about the security at the Starbrite, he also didn't want to take any unnecessary chances.

When Eustace and Willa Mae had updated the rooms in the early-70's, they'd added dropped ceilings to make the place feel more modern. Standing on a chair, Eddie pushed back one of the white fiber panels and stuffed stacks of twenty, fifty and hundred dollar bills on three of the panels surrounding it, before sliding it back into place. By the time he was done, he'd emptied the first suitcase.

Eddie then slid the second suitcase, still filled with cash, under the bed and placed the empty bag in front of it. He placed the twenty-five caliber pistol in the nightstand drawer, next to the Gideon Bible and walked out the door of Number 10, checking the lock twice.

"Follow the plan to the letter and everything will be fine," he reassured himself.

Wearing a Navy blue golf shirt and grey slacks, Eddie drove into Raleigh and found an office supply store, just off Millbrook Road. There he purchased a good quality leather brief case, similar to the one he used when making collection visits on behalf of his Uncle Carlo.

After having lunch at a local barbeque restaurant, he returned to Number 10 at 1:30, bringing his new briefcase into the room with him. Eddie checked to make sure that nothing had been disturbed in his absence, and was relieved to find that everything was exactly as he'd left it four hours earlier.

Pulling the suitcase filled with cash from under the bed, Eddie filled his new briefcase with as much as it would hold, just over $100,000, before closing it. He replaced the larger bag under the bed then carefully slid the twenty five caliber pistol into the belt of his dress slacks and pulled out his shirt to cover it. Once he was inside his car, he transferred the gun to the glove box and re-tucked the shirt. Everything up to that point was exactly as he'd planned it.

Carefully pulling out of the Starbrite parking lot, he drove to the Quincy Farmer's Bank branch across U.S. 1, having decided that it would be a good first place to open an account.

"How can we help you today?" asked the friendly teller.

"Do you offer safe deposit boxes?" Eddie asked.

"Not at this location, but our main office in Henderson has 'em. You've got to have an account with the bank to rent one," she said.

"Can you give me directions?" he asked.

"Let me write them down for you," she said. "If you open an account up there, please tell them that Darlene at the Youngstown branch sent you."

"I certainly will," Eddie responded as Darlene handed him the directions.

After opening a savings account at the main office of the bank with a thousand dollars, Eddie then rented a six by twelve inch, two foot deep safe deposit drawer, the largest available. Sitting inside the bank's private room for safe deposit box customers, he counted out the stacks, transferring the cash from his briefcase to the drawer before closing it and calling for a teller to help him replace it in the Quincy Farmer's Bank vault.

Driving back to the Starbrite, Eddie couldn't have been much more pleased with himself.

"Everything is falling into place perfectly," he said to himself, as he reentered his room, kicked off his shoes and laid back on the bed.

The next morning, Eddie refilled his briefcase, placed his pistol in the Jetta's glovebox and drove south into Raleigh. Having done some research, he had found a bank that was open on Saturday mornings and had safe deposit boxes available. There, he repeated the process from the previous day, opening a savings account before renting the safe deposit box, which he filled with the contents of his briefcase.

Deciding to give himself a well-deserved day off, Eddie spent Sunday touring the Duke Gardens and University campus in Durham, finding an excellent restaurant where he enjoyed an early dinner, before returning to Youngstown.

Monday and Tuesday were spent driving to banks with a filled briefcase, opening accounts and securing safe deposit boxes at five additional locations. While the process was painstakingly slow, Eddie never once varied from his original plan and by the end of the day on Tuesday had placed all the cash from his second suitcase securely into bank vaults in Henderson, Wake Forest and Raleigh; seven locations in total.

According to his plan he'd take the remaining cash, currently being stored in the drop ceiling of Number 10, with him when he left Youngstown the following morning and planned to place it in banks once he got to his final destination.

After all his hard work, Eddie decided that he'd earned a decent meal and a drink, so stopped at a steakhouse just north of Raleigh and indulged in a medium-rare 10 ounce filet and two Johnny Walker scotches. It is fair to say that Eddie was extremely proud of himself.

"A failure to plan, is a plan to fail. Extraordinary planning produces extraordinary results!" he thought.

"Would you like another cocktail?" the pretty waitress asked.

"What the hell! Sure!" he responded, celebrating his success.

After paying his tab and leaving the steak house, Eddie started to feel the effects of the three drinks as he drove back to Youngstown.

"I really should have stopped with two," he said to himself.

Cruising into town at fifteen miles an hour over the speed limit, he slammed on the brakes to avoid overshooting the turn into the Starbrite. Looking in his rearview mirror, he saw the blue lights of Are Dee's cruiser as he pulled into the parking lot.

Leaning down to the driver's window level, Are Dee said, "I'll need your license and registration please."

"Sure officer," Eddie responded as he pulled his Ed Francis, State of Virginia license from his wallet. When he reached for the temporary registration in the glovebox, Are Dee saw the butt of Eddie's silver plated pistol. As he handed Are Dee his license and registration and he walked back to his cruiser, Eddie let out a long, scotch scented breath.

"Marcus, are you available for back-up?" Are Dee radioed.

"I'm on the north side of town. What's your 10-20 (location) Chief?" Marcus replied.

"Starbrite parking lot," he responded.

When Eddie saw the second police cruiser pull in with its blue lights rotating, he began running various options through his head. If Ed Francis gets a ticket, he'll just pay it on the spot and be polite. If Ed Francis gets arrested for drunk driving, let's hope he doesn't have any prior offenses. He can post bail and get out of town tomorrow.

Before Eddie could get to the third "if" Are Dee came up to the driver's window, his hand resting on the butt of his gun. Marcus was standing next to the passenger window, his hand also resting on the butt of his gun.

"I want you to get out of the car very slowly, Mr. Francis, and lean against it, placing your hands on top of your head," Are Dee said in a slow, deliberate manner.

"Officer, I realize I may have been speeding, but this seems a little extreme," Eddie said.

"Please do exactly as I told you," Are Dee said, in an all-business manner.

"Of course," Eddie replied.

Marcus came around from the passenger side of the car and frisked Eddie, feeling several items in his pants pockets.

"Please empty your pockets, front, sides and back, on the hood of the car," Marcus instructed.

Eddie did as he was told. Are Dee had gone back to his cruiser and returned with a large manila envelope.

"We're gonna take an inventory. Marcus will write down all the stuff and give you a copy. Do you understand?" he said before they started.

Eddie nodded his head as Marcus read off the items.

"Money clip with $381 dollars, room key to Number 10 at the Starbrite motel, seven bank deposit slips, seven small keys....looks to me like they may be for safe deposit boxes, wallet with five one hundred dollar bills. Chief, I felt around the inside of the billfold, like you taught me. Tucked behind the lining I found a MasterCard in the name of Edward Franchetti and a New Jersey driver's license also in the name of Edward Franchetti."

Are Dee looked over at Eddie, frowning.

"I smelled alcohol on your breath when I stopped you. Marcus is going to administer a field sobriety test and breathalyzer while I run both of these driver's licenses for wants and warrants. Before I do, is there anything you'd like to tell me?"

Eddie moved his head back and forth.

Coming back a few minutes later, Are Dee looked at Marcus.

"Chief, he blew a one-point-one," he said.

"Put the bracelets on him, Marcus," Are Dee said.

"Mr. Francis, when I ran your Virginia driver's license for wants and warrants, it seems that you don't exist in their system and the number on your license belongs to an 88 year old woman in Roanoke."

"There has to be some sort of clerical error," Eddie said, thinking back to the New Jersey DMV clerk who obtained the license for him.

"The other problem is that plate on your car is stolen. It belongs on a '78 Firebird that was wrecked in New Jersey back in April. The good news is that your New Jersey license has no outstanding tickets. The bad news is that Edward Franchetti, the name on your other license, is wanted for questioning in the matter of a vehicle explosion up there, by the New Brunswick police department. The good news is that we can tell your momma that you're alive and well. She filed a missing person's report on you with the Camden, New Jersey Police Department," Are Dee added.

"Is there anything else officer?" Eddie asked.

"Yup, there is," Are Dee said. "Since I saw what I think is a handgun when you opened your glove box, we have probable cause to search your vehicle. I'm going to place you in the back of my patrol car while we conduct our search."

"Am I under arrest, officer?" Eddie asked.

"Where would you like me to start? We're charging you with drunk driving, using a false identity and driving with stolen license plates. You're in a heap of trouble, boy!"

He finally said it! After all those years, after hundreds of arrests, after over a hundred pages and eight chapters, Are Dee finally said it!!!

"You're in a heap of trouble, boy!"

(That's it! I can quit all this writing stuff and go back to working at an auto parts store! If I were a drinking man, I'd probably have one of those Johnny Walker scotches that Eddie likes. But I digress....again.)

Are Dee came back to his cruiser a few minutes later with another manila envelope, this one bulging at the sides and containing the now unloaded silver plated pistol.

"Mr. Franchetti, do you have a handgun permit? For weapon with the serial number filed off?" Are Dee asked, already knowing the answer.

"Read him his rights, Marcus," he said.

"Before Marcus transports you over to the county jail in Henderson, we're goin' over to my office and we're gonna call your momma. She needs to know that her son is alive and well."

"At least for now," Eddie thought. "At least for now."

After making the arrest in the Starbrite parking lot Are Dee had taken Eddie over to the police department office inside the Youngstown Village Hall. Having no vehicle impound lot, Marcus just parked Eddie's Jetta in front of Number 10 at the motel and drove his patrol car across the street, joining them.

Eddie had been placed in a chair directly across the desk from Are Dee.

"Take the handcuffs off him," Are Dee told Marcus. "He ain't goin' nowhere 'til after we make this call."

"Mr. Franchetti, once we take you over to the county jail for questioning, you'll be granted one phone call to the party of your choice. What we're gonna do now is call your momma, who I'm guessin' is worried sick about your welfare."

Eddie nodded his head up and down.

Are Dee dialed the number in Camden, NJ and Angelina Franchetti picked up on the third ring.

"Ma'am, this is Are Dee Camber, Chief of Police in Youngstown, North Carolina...."

"Oh dear God, don't tell me anything bad has happened to Eddie."

"Well, yes and no. He's fine and sittin' across the desk from me, however, we've arrested him on a number of charges. He'll be transferred to the Quincy County Jail over in Henderson later this evening. Yes ma'am, Quincy County in North Carolina. Yes ma'am, of course you can speak with him. That's why we called."

Are Dee handed the phone to Eddie.

"Hi Ma," he said.

"Eddie, thank God you're OK. I've been saying novenas to Saint Jude for two days, praying that I'd hear your voice again."

"I'm fine, how are you?" he said.

"You're fine! Is that all you've got to say?! I've been going out of my mind with worry, thinking you were laying in a ditch somewhere or at the bottom of Raritan Bay! Your Uncle Carlo is so torn up he can barely talk! He's been calling here day and night, hoping I'd hear from you. Where have you been?"

"I really can't talk about it right now, Ma," he said. "I'm not exactly in a private location."

Are Dee looked over the desk and smiled at Eddie.

"I understand. I'm just so thankful that you're OK. Look, no matter what kind of trouble you're in, Carlo told me that he'd come get you and bring you home. He said he'd give a million bucks just to put his arms around you."

"No need to call Uncle Carlo, Ma. This is just a little misunderstanding. Nothing I can't handle on my own."

"Don't be foolish, Eddie. My brother has connections and he was so concerned, you just can't imagine."

"Really, I can handle this."

"Nonsense, as worried as we've all been, I'm going to ask him do go down there to South Carolina and get you sprung."

"North Carolina, Ma. I'm being held in North Carolina."

"Whatever. I am just so relieved to know that you're safe! Thank God!!"

On Thursday morning, Eddie was charged with the crimes Are Dee had arrested him for on the previous night. He was arraigned in front of a Magistrate in Henderson and bail was set at $7500.

It came as no surprise to him that his Uncle Carlo showed up first thing on Friday morning and posted his bond. Eddie had spent a good piece of his time at the Quincy County Jail trying to come up with a new plan, this time hoping just to stay alive.

As he was being released, he was given back his wallet, money clip, safe deposit box keys and a number of other items that were taken from him at the time he was pulled over in Youngstown. He was also given a list of items currently being held by the Youngstown Police as possible evidence or impounded, including the items he'd brought into his motel room, as well as his car and his pistol.

Changing from his orange jailhouse jumpsuit back into the clothes he was wearing on Wednesday evening, he was escorted to where Uncle Carlo was waiting.

It scared Eddie half to death when Carlo said absolutely nothing to him as they walked out to his Lincoln Towne Car. As he had expected, Dom was sitting in the driver's seat. Carlo opened the back door and got in next to Eddie.

"Eddie, we have a situation," Carlo started. "If it was anybody but you, we'd have an immediate solution to the problem. Badda-bing, badda-boom! The thing is, Angelina begged and pleaded with me to find a different way to handle this matter. The only reason you might survive this betrayal of your own flesh and blood is because I don't want to break my sister's heart, though I haven't ruled out breaking your fu*kin' neck! Gerardo gave me the OK to resolve this matter at my discretion, so here's how things are gonna play out. You're gonna return the money, all of it, to me and Dom today. Dom is gonna break both your legs when we get back to Camden, but he promised your mother that he'd to do it real gently. As soon as you get out of the hospital, you're gonna take your mother and move to Florida. You'll be banned from further family business for life, which in your case will be very short if there's any further complications. Capische?"

"Uncle Carlo, I am so sorry," Eddie started.

"I don't wanna fu*kin' hear it! The only thing I want to know is where you put the money."

Eddie gave Dom the instructions on how to get to each of the seven banks where he'd opened accounts and safe deposit boxes. Stopping only to buy a duffle bag, they went to each location, where Eddie retrieved the contents of each box and closed his accounts. After each stop, with Dom carefully watching, Eddie emptied the cash into the trunk of the Lincoln.

"We'll count it when we get back," Uncle Carlo warned. "Nephew or not, if it isn't all there, I'm gonna make an example out of you in a very unpleasant way."

Eddie shook his head up and down, understanding the consequences.

With a trunk full of uncounted cash, Dom drove north on U.S. 1, eventually getting on I-85 and cutting over to I-95 for the long trip back to Camden.

It was after 10:00 p.m. when they were just outside of Delaware City, Delaware. Dom told his father that they needed gas and pulled into a truck stop just off the expressway.

Eddie asked his uncle if it was OK to use the restroom.

"Sure, but I'm going with you," Carlo said. "I need to hit the can, too. Don't think about doing anything stupid, Eddie, or it'll be the last dumb thing you do."

With his uncle still in a Men's Room stall, Eddie asked if Carlo wanted a coffee for the road. Figuring that with Dom standing in the truck stop lobby, there wasn't much risk in letting his nephew buy the drinks, he said, "Black with two sugars."

While still inside the Men's Room, Eddie saw the sign for the trucker's showers and locker room and ducked inside. He quickly found a window and crawled out into the dark parking lot of the truck stop.

Returning to the truck stop lobby, Carlo looked at Dom and said, "Where's Eddie?"

"With you, Pop," Dom said.

"Does he fu*kin' look like he's with me?? You check outside, I'll see if he's still in the building," Carlo said. "If you find him out there, don't wait until we get home. Break his legs now."

Walking between the big rigs, Eddie spotted a large moving & storage company trailer with an Oregon address painted on the side. Walking up to the cab, he knocked on the window and asked the driver, "Any chance you're headed west?"

"Yeah, to Portland. What's it to you?" the driver said.

"Would three-hundred in cash get me a ride there?" Eddie asked.

"Hop in," the driver said.

Chapter 9 – Stan Marbury

Divorces can be pretty ugly and Stan Marbury was living proof of how bad they can get.

He and his wife Yvonne had been married for eleven years and had two kids, a boy who was nine and a little girl who was six. Stan was the manager of the DollarMasters variety store in Franklinville and had been transferred there in 1983. While he didn't make much money, he and his wife were able to swing the purchase of a double-wide on an acre lot, just north of town.

Stan's store was on the 'marginal' list of his company's locations and his job was to turn it into a money-maker for the chain as quickly as possible. According to his boss, he either had to increase sales, reduce operating costs or do both. That became even tougher when the Piggly-Wiggly next door to Stan's store closed-up, reducing the number of folks coming to the shopping center.

One of the quickest ways to lower operating costs was for Stan to work more hours. Since he was salaried, it didn't cost the company any more money if he worked sixty, seventy or even eighty hours a week doing the things they'd otherwise have to pay hourly employees to handle.

Working all those hours didn't sit too well with Yvonne, since she was taking care of the kids and working three days a week for an insurance agency. Feeling awful lonely, she began sharing her sorrows with her boss, Ricky Faircloth, who was sympathetic to what she was going through. They started having lunch together, which seemed harmless enough, even though they was both married. It didn't take too long before they was taking their lunch breaks at the double-wide. In other words, they were having an adulterous affair.

Deciding that they'd be happier together than with the people they was married to, Yvonne and Ricky began figuring out a plan to make things happen. Yvonne cleaned out her and Stan's checking and saving accounts and had the locks changed on the double-wide on the same day she had divorce papers served on him at work.

Since she had a serious jump-start on Stan, who was already working himself half to death and being as he was exhausted and beat down, he foolishly agreed to all of her divorce demands and eventually had to declare bankruptcy. Between child support and alimony payments, Stan was left with about $50 a week to live on. In other words, he was flat busted. That's how he landed at the Starbrite Motel in May of 1985.

'In other words,' was Stan's favorite expression and he used it in almost every sentence he spoke, or so it seemed.

"I need a room to rent. In other words I'd like to move in to the Starbrite. I work a lot of hours. In other words I'm the store manager. The car has a miss. In other words it's not running right."

This had grated on Yvonne's nerves for all time they were married, but it was a habit that Stan simply couldn't break. The employees at his store heard him say it constantly, but shrugged it off as just another benefit of having a minimum wage job at DollarMasters.

"I need you to dust the shelves on aisle seven. In other words they need cleaning. You need to work on register 3 today. In other words you're going to be a cashier."

Because Stan worked so many hours, Franklin had a special arrangement for receiving his weekly rent payments. Since Stan was living in Number 11, he'd knock on Mr. B's door either late on Friday night or early on Saturday morning and exchange $35 for a rent receipt. Mr. B would give Franklin the payment the next time they were together. In other words, it was an alternate method for paying.

When things went sour between Yvonne and Ricky, she decided to move back home to Valdosta, Georgia with the two kids and live with her parents. Stan wanted to wage a custody fight, but lacked the money to hire an attorney. In other words, he lost the chance to see his kids on any kind of regular basis.

To make things worse, Stan had been placed on probation by his District Manager. Even with his best efforts, he still wasn't able to make his store profitable. The truth was, his company had burned out the four previous managers trying to turn a sow's ear into a silk purse. In other words, Stan had been given an impossible task and was failing at it.

After paying his weekly rent, Stan had just $15 a week for food, gas, car insurance and any other expenses. As a result, he was eating a whole lot of Raman noodles and grabbing up any expired food from the variety store, rather than throwing it in the trash. To further trim operating expenses, he was also working virtually every hour that the store was open.

On the surface, Stan Marbury might seem like just another poor fool who was being eaten alive by fate, but that was not the case. He was a bright feller with a strong (ridiculous) work ethic. Most of all Stan was resourceful. Since he knew that he couldn't possibly work any more hours, he found a better way to increase store traffic, drive up sales and make more money for himself. In other words, he got involved in selling drugs.

With the shopping center where his store was located slowly going downhill, Stan noticed that a couple of young local rednecks had started spending a lot of time at the far corner of the parking lot, near a thick stand of Carolina pines. Several times each hour, people drove up to 'em just long enough to say hello. Since business at his store was so slow, he often worked alone. In between customers, Stan would watch what was happening and he eventually came to the conclusion that drugs were being sold.

After two weeks of observation, Stan left one of his hourly employees in charge of the store and walked across the parking lot where he introduced himself to a very reluctant Bubba Thompson and Xavier Carlyle.

"I've been watchin' you boys from my store," Stan said. "I want you to know, I make no moral judgements about what people do, so long as it don't affect me. In other words, I don't really care that you're selling drugs."

Neither Bubba nor Xavier would make eye contact with Stan.

"But sooner or later the police are gonna see what you're doing and haul you off to jail."

"Wouldn't be the first time," Bubba said almost proudly.

"I got an idea that might help you stay in business, assuming you was willing to cut me in for a small piece of the profits. In other words, I'm proposing that we become partners."

"Why would we trust somebody we just met?" Xavier asked.

"Because you don't have much choice. I've been takin' pictures from my store and have three rolls of film safely stored as my insurance policy against you boys doin' anything stupid. Here's your problem; you stick out like a watermelon in a field of cotton. Hangin' out in the corner of the parking lot, you may as well have a neon sign on your truck saying 'Drugs for Sale!' In other words, you need to be a whole lot less obvious."

Stan then handed them two boxes of Crackly Pops, his store's house brand of candy coated popcorn.

"What's this sh*t?" Xavier asked.

"That's your ticket to selling more of whatever it is you sell and keeping out of trouble with the law."

"We only sell pot," Bubba offered.

"Will you shut the fu*k up?!" Xavier barked.

"Let's say that you buy Crackly Pops from me, a case at a time for $100 and I let you set up a table in front of my store where you resell 'em at a dollar a box, with the proceeds going to support an orphanage in Haiti."

"That don't sound very profitable to me," Bubba said.

"Hear what the man has to say," said Xavier.

"For folks just passing by, you sell 'em the Crackly Pops and give the money to charity, nice and legitimate. For folks wanting Super Turbo Crackly Pops, you sell 'em a box with a nickel, dime or quarter bag inside. In other words, just like it says on the box, a prize in every package!"

"How'll we know which is which?" Xavier asked.

Stan reached in his pocket and pulled out three cards with peel and stick dots.

"You color code the boxes. Nothing on the ones for the public. Red, green or blue dots for the special boxes. You do everything right out in the open with a much lower risk and you raise some money for that orphanage."

"What's in it for you?" Bubba asked.

"A case of Crackly Pops sells for $24, or a dollar a box. I'll buy 'em at that price and sell 'em to you for $100. My profit will cover your rent for being in front of the store and for showing you the idea. As long as you sell the special boxes to customers you know and trust, the risk is pretty low. In other words, you should be fine."

What Stan didn't tell Bubba and Xavier was that he'd be in the clear if they ever got caught, since all he was selling was Crackly Pops.

"All you gotta do is pay a $100 for the first case. I'll even draw up the signs for you. In other words, you could start as early as tomorrow," Stan offered.

"What the fu*k! Let's give it a try," said Bubba.

"Do you trust this guy?" Xavier asked.

"Maybe, maybe not, but he might just be one of them marketing geniuses you hear about all the time. You know, like Ronald McDonald."

In addition to making $76 dollars on each case of Crackly Pops for himself, Stan also believed that people coming around to buy pot might spend some money at his store.

The next morning the boys arrived at 8:30, a half hour before the store opened. Stan had purchased the case of Crackly Pops the night before and had them in the back of his car along with the peel and stick dots and signs. As he had instructed, they brought a folding table to place in front of the store. After he collected his money, Bubba and Xavier went back to their truck and began opening a few boxes, placing bags of pot inside and re-sealing them with tape before adding the appropriate dot. Following Stan's advice, they had two cardboard boxes. One for the legitimate Crackly Pops and one for the special ones.

Stan put up a sign in the store's break room saying that there would be a charity fundraiser taking place in front of the store and encouraging his employees to help support the Haitian orphanage.

If Stan had underestimated anything, it would have been the demand for pot in Franklinville. Bubba and Xavier's regular customers continued coming around to their new location, taking home their dope in Crackly Pops boxes. Some of 'em even bought an extra box to help fund the orphanage. Feeling more comfortable with purchasing their marijuana out in the open, they increased what they bought with some of 'em even selling the extra to their friends and family, expanding the distribution network. Stan's entrepreneurial plan was working! (That was another one of those Astoria (Queens) words.)

As business took off for the boys, they started buying as many as three or four cases of Crackly Pops from Stan in a good week. He was clearing over $300, tax free, almost every week. He didn't want to know what the boys were making, but the truth was they were hauling in more cash than they'd ever seen, so much so that they had to add extra marijuana plants to the ones they was growing in the garden patch owned by Bubba's grannie.

Keeping to Stan's plan, they went to the post office every Saturday and got a money order for what they collected for the Sisters of Perpetual Abstinence Orphanage and sent it off to Haiti, knowing that they were doing something good for all those poor children. Since they were makin' so much money, they began adding some of their own cash to the donations. This especially paid off when the local police started to notice their activities, suspecting that the boys might be keeping the donations for themselves. When they questioned Xavier about it, he showed 'em the weekly USPS money order receipts. Satisfied with their investigation, one of the cops even ponied-up for two boxes of Crackly Pops, the civilian variety.

Stan raised the store's inventory of Crackly Pops to meet demand and also noticed a sharp increase in the sales of snack food items. He reasoned that people smoking dope would have a bad case of the munchies and he was well prepared to meet their needs. Those same customers also bought other stuff while they were shopping for small alligator clips in the electrical section, butane lighters and cigarette papers. It was just under two months before the store was back in the black.

Rather than risk having his store stand out too much within the DollarMasters chain, Stan kept adding time to the hourly employee's schedules, keeping the store profitable but not so much so that he might be promoted to another location. In other words, he was sandbagging.

In appreciation for Bubba and Xavier's weekly contributions, the Sisters of Perpetual Abstinence Orphanage sent them real nice thank you letters on a regular basis and included photos of the children they were helping. They was so proud that they displayed 'em on their folding table in front of Stan's store.

"That little Jose is sure lookin' happier," Xavier said, holding up before and after photos.

"I'd bet that's because he's gettin' enough to eat these days," said Bubba.

Just after Thanksgiving, the boys went into the DollarMasters and bought up $300 of toys, packed 'em up and shipped 'em off to Haiti.

To keep an eye on things, Stan insisted that Bubba and Xavier could only sell Crackly Pops when he was working at the store. Since Stan was now back to a reasonable schedule, the boys generally were open for business from 10:00 to 6:00, but they and their special customers were just fine with that.

Even with his greatly improved financial situation, Stan continued to stay at the Starbrite, saving as much as he could so that he could eventually deal with his ex-wife, Yvonne. In other words, he was fixin' to take her to court.

It had been over a year since Eddie Franchetti had been arrested. After Are Dee and Marcus thoroughly searched his room and confiscated his belongings as evidence, they did the same with his VW Jetta. They had found nothing in the car that added to the case, and since there was no impound lot in Youngstown nor space at the Village Hall, Are Dee handed Franklin the keys and asked him to store it behind the Starbrite.

A couple of times each month, Mr. B would start the car and drive it around the parking lot to keep the battery charged and even washed once or twice.

Stan drove a nine-year-old, beat-to-hell Chevette that was falling apart at the seams and only ran on three of its four cylinders. He badly needed a new car, but didn't want to spend any more money than he had to for a replacement. Having missed the Eddie Franchetti parking lot arrest and drama because he was working at the DollarMasters store that night, he had no idea why the Jetta was parked at the Starbrite, so he asked Franklin about it.

"That's a nice looking car you keep behind the motel. Who does it belong to?" Stan asked.

"It's owned by a former renter who I guess is in jail now," Franklin responded. "The Youngstown Police asked me to store it for 'em."

"If you find out it's for sale, I might be interested," Stan replied. "In other words, I'm shopping for another car."

Thinking about the car and its owner, Franklin called Are Dee.

"Eddie Franchetti was released a couple of days after his arrest," he said. "His uncle came down from New Jersey and posted his bail. When Franchetti didn't show up for his court date, the uncle forfeited seventy-five hundred dollars. There's been an arrest warrant out for him but nobody's seen or heard from him, here or up north. Why do you ask?"

"Well, I was wondering what to do with his car? It's been sitting here for over a year."

"That's a good question, Franklin. I'll look into it and get back to you."

The following Saturday, Are Dee wandered over to Franklin's house, knocking on the door before letting himself in and grabbing a cold soda-pop out of the refrigerator.

125

(As a small digression, carbonated soft-drinks are generally called 'sodas' in the South and East. In the North, Midwest and West, they are called 'pop.' If you're ever in doubt, you can always refer to 'em as 'soda pop,' to play it safe. Just another small detail courtesy of your author. You're welcome!)

"Make yourself at home," Franklin said, smiling.

"Already did," Are Dee responded. "You know, you're a whole lot more pleasant when Lisa Ann is here. Just sayin'. I got some news about that Jetta you've been storing. First off, it doesn't appear to belong to anybody."

"How can that be?" Franklin asked.

"Franchetti purchased it illegally using a false ID. The State of Virginia can't issue a title to somebody that doesn't exist. I tried to call Franchetti's mother, but her phone's been disconnected and he's nowhere to be found. Since you've stored the car for over a year, you've got a legitimate lien on it. I called the NC Motor Vehicle Division and they said that you can file for an abandoned vehicle title. They'll do a search on the VIN (vehicle identification number) and if there's nothing that trumps your lien, they can issue a title to you."

"It sounds complicated. I don't know that I've got the time to mess with it," Franklin said.

"I figured you'd say that. Since I was already so deep into it all, I filed the paperwork for you. Forged your signature on the title application, too, in case you want to prosecute," he said, smiling broadly.

"I owe you one! Thanks!"

Three weeks later, a title arrived in the mail for the Jetta, made out in Franklin's name. He left a note on Stan's door asking him to please see him when it was convenient.

With Stan's reduced work schedule, he'd gone back to paying his rent directly to Franklin and stopped over that afternoon.

"You asked me about the Jetta we've been storing. Turns out I'm now the owner and I'm open to selling it."

"I'd like to look it over," Stan said. "In other words, can I take it for a test drive?"

"It's got expired plates and no insurance. Let me call Are Dee so that he or Marcus don't arrest you," Franklin said as he handed Stan the keys.

After returning from his drive and looking over the Jetta from stem to stern, Stan asked Franklin what he wanted for the car.

"I checked the Blue Book wholesale value with a dealer in Raleigh. It's worth $1800. I'd sell it to you 'as-is' for $1600."

"How about $1500 cash?" Stan asked.

Franklin held out his hand to Stan and said, "Done!"

By the spring of 1986, with his store earning a small but steady profit, Stan applied for and received a transfer to manage a new DollarMasters location in Valdosta, GA. His partnership with Bubba and Xavier had allowed Stan to sock-away nearly $10,000 that he planned to use toward hiring a good attorney. In other words, he was now prepared to do battle with Yvonne for better access to his kids.

On his last day at the Franklinville store, he said his good-byes to all the employees just before walking out to the sidewalk to speak with Bubba and Xavier.

"We're gonna miss you Stan," Xavier said. "You sure taught us a bunch about marketing."

"And helped make us a lot of money, too," Bubba added.

"We want to wish you the best of luck in getting your kids back," Xavier said, starting to choke up.

"Before you go, we've got something special for you," Bubba said, handing Stan a box of Crackly Pops with red, green and blue peel and stick dots placed on it.

"Thanks, boys," Stan said, all teary-eyed. "I want you to promise me that you'll be careful and stay out of trouble."

"We will," they both said.

With that, they exchanged awkward guy hugs and Stan drove back to the Starbrite to pack his things and head for Valdosta. In the privacy of Number 11, he opened the box the boys had given him and found ten $100 bills.

"How about that," he said.

Yvonne had been doing a considerable amount of soul-searching in the months since she'd moved back to her parents' house. After telling her momma the full story about how she'd sinned with Ricky and how she'd treated Stan, she was strongly encouraged to pray for guidance in getting her life back on track. When her kids told her that their daddy was moving to Valdosta, she made the decision to see Stan and walked into the new DollarMasters store a few days after he'd arrived.

"Hey," she said.

"Hey yourself," he said back.

"Can you talk for a couple of minutes?' she asked.

"I 'spose so, let me take you back to my office," he said as he led her to the back of the store.

"I've missed you, Stan. The kids have, too. I've made some awful mistakes. I broke one of the Ten Commandments, a big 'un, and I'm guessing I hurt you pretty bad. I really made a mess of things and I am so, so sorry. I mean that with all my heart," she paused to wipe the dripping mascara off her cheek. "Do you think there's any possibility that you could ever forgive me? I would give my life for a second chance."

Stan stood there, pondering the situation for a few seconds as Yvonne's heart was pounding right through her size 38DD Wonderbra.

All of the anger that Stan had felt through the divorce and Yvonne's move to Valdosta suddenly took a backseat to what was in the best interests of his kids. Stan took a couple of deep breaths, thinking carefully about what he should say. People make mistakes, he reasoned with himself. He'd made his share. Yvonne was only asking for a chance to make things right.

"I can't make any promises, but if you'd like to have dinner sometime, we can start trying to figure things out. In other words, I'm at least willing to talk about it."

"Thank you, Stan. I know I don't deserve it, but thank you. A second chance is all I'm asking for," Yvonne said, her mascara now dripping down to her jawline. "The kids asked me how soon they could see their daddy."

"Given the custody situation, that's pretty much up to you," he responded.

"From now on, how about anytime you want to see them. No more restrictions, I swear on the Holy Bible."

"That would be good. I'm off on Saturday, how about then?"

"Sure, and you'd be welcome to stay for supper after, if you'd like."

As Stan walked Yvonne out of the store, he handed her a box of Crackly Pops. "On the house," he said, though she never did understand why he did that.

With a new manager at the Franklinville DollarMasters, selling dope in front of the store just wasn't the same for Bubba and Xavier, even though they were savin' $76 dollars on every case of Crackly Pops. Things really changed for them when they got a handwritten letter from the Sisters of Perpetual Abstinence Orphanage telling them about a new building project for the children and that they were seeking volunteers to come down to Haiti and work for on the construction for a few weeks. The Sisters had included several recent photos of the children, including little Jose.

"Xavier, maybe we should think about retiring from the marijuana business while we're money ahead and not in any legal trouble?" Bubba asked.

"We could take a vacation down in Haiti for a couple of weeks and decide while we're there," Xavier offered.

"Do you think we can drive it or should we fly?"

Opting to fly to Haiti, they landed in Port Au Prince and took a bus to the orphanage. For as poor as some folks were around Youngstown and Franklinville, Bubba and Xavier were absolutely stunned by the level of poverty they rode past. Fortunately, the Sisters of Perpetual Abstinence Orphanage appeared to be in reasonable shape and well run, though hardly up U.S. standards.

They were warmly greeted by the Mother Superior who showed them to the room they would share. Before supper, they were invited to meet the children. It was when they were introduced to little Jose, that they were hooked.

Originally planning to stay for two weeks to help with the construction of new housing for the kids, they kept extending their trip, working six days a week to improve the living conditions.

It was while they were there that Bubba became interested in plants other than marijuana. One of the Sisters took notice and helped him to learn the names of the local flora and fauna and showed him new growing techniques. Bubba was given responsibility for the landscaping around the new facility and worked tirelessly to come up with a design and get all the plants placed.

Early on, Xavier became deeply moved by the graphic crucifix of Jesus hanging in the orphanage chapel. He found himself praying there every morning with the children, even though he wasn't Catholic. The Mother Superior had told him that he had a wonderful gift for relating to children and wondered if he was active in a church back home. She was surprised when he told her that he'd never been baptized.

At the end of three months and with the construction project completed, both men reluctantly knew that it was time to go back home. (Their experience at the Sisters of Perpetual Abstinence Orphanage had changed them both in ways you can't imagine, but that I'll tell you about later in the story. You won't even have to ask.)

Chapter 10 – Robert Dee and Richard Lee Camber

Robert Dee Camber had the first three years of his life to be an only child, pampered and adored by his momma and daddy. He could vaguely remember them happily telling him that he would soon have a little brother or sister and that he was excited to be having a new playmate. Then Richard Lee came along, fussing and crying all the time. His momma was always telling Robert Dee to be careful and gentle with the baby, even when Richard would grab a handful of his older brother's hair and yank so hard that it made him cry. As his baby brother got older, they actually began to play together and before long they became friends.

To no small extent, they were like a couple of bear cubs, wrestling and scraping from the time they woke up in the morning until they went to bed at night. But, it was always just play fighting, never anything mean or ugly.

When Robert was seven and Richard was four, their cousin Franklin came to live next door with Eustace and Willa Mae. Robert was old enough to understand the concept of death and what had happened to Franklin's parents. Without Are Dee or Brenda saying a word, he started looking out for his little cousin, much the same way he did for his brother. He'd keep watch over Richard and Franklin when they went into the woods, to make sure they didn't get bit by a snake or eaten by the monsters that lived in the thick stand of spindly pines that grew behind their house.

When the two younger boys entered kindergarten, it was Robert who got in trouble for punching a second grader who cruelly teased Franklin about his parents being dead. Franklin was upset and crying, so Robert sat down next to him reminded him that Uncle Eustace and Aunt Willa Mae were his parents now and that he and Richard would become his blood brothers next time one of them got a cut. Richard sat next to his brother, nodding in agreement. The bond between the three boys was as solid as concrete, especially since Eustace and Are Dee was also so close.

As they was growing up, Robert and Richard was always trying to outdo each other regardless of the risk to life and limb. Climbing up a tree so's they could parachute down using one of Brenda's umbrellas or trying to ride a bicycle backwards, sitting on the handlebars were just a couple of the stunts that resulted in Doc Benson having to stitch up one or both of 'em. Franklin was far more cautious and generally waited to see if his cousins had survived before attempting things for himself.

While their momma considered her sons to be hellions, their daddy would shrug things off and say, "Boys will be boys."

This only seemed to set Brenda off all the more.

Richard and Franklin were in the same class up through the ninth grade. Franklin was the smarter of the two, and would patiently help Richard with his homework, taking his time to make sure his cousin understood the lesson. In high school, Franklin was assigned to college prep classes, while Richard opted for general education and vocational courses. With Robert graduating and enlisting in the Army, Richard and Franklin stayed close, though they were moving in different directions socially. Like his older brother, Richard liked dating the wildest girls at Youngstown High School, often drinking moonshine and carrying on with 'em out at the millpond. Franklin preferred quieter girls and was content holding hands or getting just a kiss at the end of an evening.

"If the girl's agreeable, don't be afraid to go for the homerun," Richard advised Franklin, before handing him a condom. "Keep this in your wallet, so's you'll always be prepared." Franklin did exactly that, not removing it until it was needed during his sophomore year of college.

After both boys graduated from Youngstown High School in May of 1977, Franklin went on to NC State that fall while Richard applied for work and was hired at the Bennington Textile Mill in Wake Forest. Robert, who had served his hitch in the Army was already working at Bennington the day his younger brother arrived.

Robert and Richard had shared a bedroom ever since Brenda and Are Dee brought their sister, Patrice, home from the hospital. As grown men, who'd long outgrown the bunkbeds in their parent's house, they decided to pool their resources and rent a two bedroom single-wide at the Paradise Trailer Court, just off U.S. 1, a couple of miles north of the textile mill.

Brenda was open and honest about her concerns, as soon as she'd heard what they'd done.

"You do know I love ya's both, right?" she said as they nodded in agreement. "So don't think I'm tryin' to be ugly when I say that neither of you can cook so much as a can of beans nor figure out which end of the vacuum cleaner you plug into the wall. You boys do a lot of work around here and I proud of you both, but were it not for Patrice and me, you and your daddy would starve to death in a filthy house."

The boys couldn't argue with anything their momma had said. From the time they was big enough to help their daddy, they'd worked outside, mowing and trimming the lawn, weeding their mommas flower and vegetable gardens, washing the car and they even helped Franklin take care of the property at the Starbrite. Brenda blamed herself for their lack of any domestic skills, even though they was both like a couple of raging bulls in a china shop and had done far more damage than good anytime she'd tried to show 'em how to cook or clean.

"As a housewarming gift, I'm gonna buy you all the basics you'll need to survive on your own and Patrice has volunteered to try teachin' you two what I couldn't," Brenda said. "I want you both to promise me that you'll pay attention to her." The boys nodded in agreement with their momma.

On the first Saturday afternoon that Patrice came to the trailer, she nearly gagged when opening the refrigerator and finding uncovered, raw hamburger that had gone bad in a serious way. Since neither of her older brothers were receptive to takin' lessons from their baby sister, Patrice proposed another plan.

"I'll come over once a week and clean up this pit," she said. "While I'm here, I'll even cook up a casserole or something else for you to eat during the week, but I expect to be well compensated," Patrice said.

"How's twenty dollars a week sound?" Robert asked.

"Thirty sounds a whole bunch better, since I've got to clean your bathroom, too," she said.

"Can you start now?" Richard asked.

Though Brenda never asked the boys or Patrice, she pretty-well knew that their little sister was covering for them again. Patrice did her job well, having to occasionally wake-up one of 'em at two or three in the afternoon to clean a bedroom or having to scrape petrified pizza off the coffee table. In spite of a temptation to do otherwise, she never said anything to the boys about seeing the evidence of serious carrying on's in the trash and the occasional pair of panties under a bed.

The arrangement worked great until Patrice left for UNC Wilmington in the fall of 1983. Before heading to college, she found a replacement housekeeper for the boys. The girl was a 17 year old junior at Youngstown High School, Faith Culver, and was just as pretty as she could be.

"Before you two Romeos get any ideas, I want to remind you that she's serious jail-bait and her daddy won't hesitate for a heartbeat to have either of you locked up," Patrice said to her brothers. "Do I make myself clear?"

"Is that all what you think of your two big brothers?" Robert Dee asked, his feelings hurt.

"I love you both," Patrice said, going over to kiss each of 'em on the cheek, "that's why I'm making sure you stay out of trouble. And I want you to show that poor girl some respect. Don't be tossing your rubber wrappers where she can see 'em."

By the mid-80's the U.S. textile industry had started getting beat to death by competition from Asia, India and even Egypt. Patriotic citizens who had "Be American, Buy American" bumper stickers on their trucks started buying $22 golf shirts for $12.99 at the You-Know-Who Supercenter and not looking at where they was being made. It didn't matter that the shirts only lasted about half as long as the American made ones, so long as they was cheap.

(I could go off on a long and fact-filled digression about the impact of foreign products being dumped in the U.S. and how lobbyists with sacks full of cash came to own the best politicians that money could buy and how those same elected officials turned a blind eye to the destruction of the American middle class, but I probably won't. It would just raise my blood pressure and further convince my family that I've become a crazy old coot, not that they need much encouragement.)

With reduced demand for American-made textiles, mills across the south began reducing production or shutting down entirely. By early 1986, the Bennington Mill in Wake Forest had trimmed its workforce by twenty percent after two years of hiring freezes and attrition, but it still wasn't enough. As the bottom was dropping out, the layoffs began and things went from bad to worse for hardworking folks with limited education and skills.

On the last Friday in February, both of the Camber boys along with a group of other workers were given their termination notice as part of a RIF (Reduction In Force), which was the Human Resources term for permanently eliminating jobs with no hope of those folks ever being brought back. As part of the process and to make sure nobody could bring an age discrimination lawsuit, for every older worker who was laid-off, a younger one was also shown the door. A total of fifty-eight good people, who had done their jobs to the best of their abilities and were loyal to their company were walked out to their cars by rented security guards, just like they was criminals. How it was handled was disgraceful!

Having spent their paychecks nearly as fast as they'd earned them, Robert Dee and Richard Lee were facing the unpleasant reality that they'd probably have to give up their trailer within the next few weeks unless they found new jobs. Their rent would next come due on the fifteenth of March.

Franklin and Lisa Ann heard all about the layoffs during Sunday supper with Are Dee and Brenda. Robert Dee and Richard Lee were both there, too.

"You boys can move home and have your old room back," Brenda offered, far more excited about the possibility than were her husband or sons. "It would beat payin' rent on that trailer."

"We'll get thirteen weeks of unemployment benefits. We may get lucky and find new jobs before that runs out," Richard Lee said.

"Or not," said Robert Dee.

"You boys might want to think about startin' a business," Are Dee said. "That way, you'd be in control of your own destiny."

"The only business we ever ran was R&R Lawn Mowing Service," Richard Lee said, laughing.

"But we did make some good money," his brother added.

When Robert Dee was 13, he began offering to mow lawns for people in Youngstown. He loved being outside and did terrific work, often getting additional customers from word-of-mouth recommendations. Things went so well that he brought Richard Lee

137

in as partner the second summer. Robert would mow, Richard would trim and clean-up. Over the course of the next three summers, the boys ran a successful business and managed to stay out of trouble, at least for the most part.

"What if you went back into the lawn maintenance business? You could tow a trailer behind your pick-up for the equipment and drive into North Raleigh. There's lots of rich folks who want all that stuff done for 'em," Are Dee suggested.

"How'd we finance all that?" Richard Lee asked.

"Your daddy and me will loan you the money to get started," Brenda said, without checking with Are Dee and avoiding his eye contact.

"If you want to cut back on livin' expenses while you get things started, I've always got a couple of empty rooms at the Starbrite," Franklin said. "You could each have your own space and stay rent-free until you get the business goin'."

"Franklin, that's very generous of you," Are Dee said, "but you've got a motel to run and shouldn't be offerin' to give away your income like that."

"Daddy's right," Robert Dee said. "We appreciate your offer, but couldn't accept it."

"You can give me any reason you want," Franklin said, "but y'all are my family and if the day ever comes when I can't help my only kin, then I'd just as soon shut down the Starbrite. My offer stands and there's nothing any of y'all can say to change my mind. If the situation was turned around, any of you'd do the same for me, and don't say you wouldn't."

"Franklin, I love you like a cousin!" Richard Lee said smiling.

And that's how the Camber brothers, Robert Dee and Richard Lee, landed at the Starbrite Motel in March of 1986.

Knowing that his cousins could be serious partiers, Franklin moved Richard Lee into Number 3 and Robert Dee into Number 9, to keep 'em separated some.

Working with their momma to get all the proper paperwork filed, finding a good used trailer and buying commercial-grade mowing and trimming equipment, Camber Brothers Lawn & Landscaping was ready to go by the first of April.

Lisa Ann helped Robert Dee and Richard Lee design fliers that they distributed on a neighborhood by neighborhood basis, starting with the more expensive subdivisions in Wake Forest and working into North Raleigh. They also had a second phone line installed at their parent's house, so's that Brenda could answer business calls for them.

Franklin helped them with a route plan, to minimize travel and maximize the efficiency of their company. With all the growth in the area and so many new subdivisions popping up, the brothers figured they wouldn't have any trouble in filling their schedule. They were wrong.

Are Dee had warned his sons that they should expect some lean months before things got going. Thinking that the world was waiting for Camber Brothers Lawn and Landscaping, the boys spent all of April and nearly half of May wondering if the new phone line was working. With their unemployment benefits just covering their operating expenses, they began wondering what they'd gotten themselves into, especially since they now owed their parents $7500.

Doing what their momma suggested, they prayed for guidance each night. As they was leaving church two Sundays later, Pastor Thorpe asked them to come by his office the next day.

"Boys, I don't know if you are aware of it or not, but Mr. Hadley, who has been our custodian for many years, is leaving us at the end of this month," the Pastor said. "We've found an older gentleman to replace him, but handling the mowing of the church property and cemetery is more than he wants to take on. Your daddy told me about your new business venture. I was wondering if you could fit our work into to your schedule."

Smiling back at the preacher, Robert Dee said, "I think we can fit you in."

After some polite negotiating back and forth, Camber Brothers Lawn and Landscaping was hired that morning by the Youngstown Free Will Evangelic Fundamentalist Church as their first large client!

With one full day a week taken up with work at the church, they slowly began getting additional jobs, mostly in North Raleigh. Following their daddy's advice, the boys kept their company lean and mean, with the two of them working as many hours as it took to get through the summer of 1986, eventually hiring four boys from Youngstown High School on a part-time basis to help 'em out. With his blessing, they borrowed Are Dee's pick-up so that they could divide into two teams for the busiest part of the season.

To their credit, Robert Dee and Richard Lee were slowly starting to make money and pouring most of it right back into the business. The first thing they did was to start repaying the loan that their parents had given 'em. To keep their personal expenses to a minimum, they continued living at the Starbrite and walking across the parking lot to eat many of their meals at home, at their momma's insistence. By July, they started paying rent at the Starbrite, at Franklin's reduced 'family rate' of $30 dollars a week.

Being so busy, neither of the boys had the time or energy for any of their previous tomcatting activities. Richard Lee even abandoned his lifetime goal of making love to 100 women, and reset the number down to 75.

Franklin and Lisa Ann had been a couple for just over two years when they rented a cabin near Linville, in the North Carolina Mountains and spent an extended four-day weekend together in early November that same year. With beautiful fall colors and the rustic one-bedroom cabin with its antique brass bed, it had turned out to be exactly the kind of romantic get-away they'd both hoped for.

The temperature had dropped into the low 30's on their second night, so Franklin built a roarin' fire in the fireplace, where they snuggled-up after the scrambled-egg supper that he'd cooked for 'em.

"Did I tell you that Marie turned in her notice at Piedmont and is taking a job with Global Airways? She going to be working out of their Atlanta hub and moving there," Lisa Ann said.

"No," said Franklin. "When's all that gonna happen?"

"Next month, just before our lease expires," Lisa Ann responded.

"Well, the only logical thing for you to do would be to move out of your apartment and in with me," he said.

"The only logical thing to do?! Franklin, you sure know how to make a girl feel special!" Lisa Ann said.

"Can I get a do-over, if I ask real nice? Please?" he begged.

"I'd say you need one. Are all electrical engineers such romantic devils?" she asked laughing.

"Lisa Ann, I love you with my whole heart. There is nothing in the world that I'd like more than for you to move in with me. We already share one heart, let's share one house," he said.

"Much better!" she said. "Who knows, you keep talking to me that way and you might even get lucky tonight."

"I get luckier every minute I'm with you," he said.

"Oh Franklin! How could I not accept your offer? Shall we seal the deal with an electrical engineer's handshake or by making passionate love in front of the fireplace all night?" she said, teasing him with all her might.

"I'll bring in some more logs, why don't you fetch the blankets and pillows."

"I take it you've opted to skip the handshake," Lisa Ann said.

And that's how Lisa Ann Prescott landed at the Starbrite Motel, albeit in the owner's home, in December of 1986.

Since Lisa Ann was already spending at least a couple of nights at Franklin's house every week and since she and Marie had been renting a furnished apartment, moving took nothing more than filling three suitcases and packing a handful of boxes with the few things she'd gotten in the three years they'd shared the place.

On move-out day, Marie gave her a hug and wished her and Franklin the best.

"I'll expect an invitation to the wedding," Marie said.

"What are you talking about?" Lisa Ann replied. "We're not planning to get married, at least not right away. We haven't even seriously discussed it."

"As your friend and now former roommate, I'll bet you a crisp $20 bill that you'll be Mrs. Delworth within the next twelve months," Marie said.

"Maybe Ms. Prescott-Delworth," Lisa Ann laughed.

"He's a good guy, Lisa. If you could have him cloned, I'd be more than happy to take a copy. I really thought you'd started dating Gomer Pyle when I first met Franklin, but I was sure mistaken. He's somebody special."

"I could always introduce you to one of his cousins," Lisa Ann suggested.

"I thought we were friends?" Marie laughed. "You may recall, I've already met Robert Dee and Richard Lee."

"Oh, yeah."

After completing the fall leaf blowing, raking and removal jobs in November, Robert Dee and Richard Lee spent December servicing all their lawn care equipment and thinking forward to spring and the possibility of expanding the business, especially since it was starting to do so well. If they were to add a third truck, trailer and people they'd have to find the right person to run the additional crew.

After Bubba Thompson had returned from Haiti in September, he immediately enrolled at Raleigh Community College taking classes in horticulture. While he wasn't a great student, the subject matter held his interest, though by the end of winter term, he'd realized that book learning wasn't for him.

Reading through the Help Wanted section of the April 8th, 1987 edition of the Quincy County Weekly Tribune, he saw an ad that interested him and called Camber Brothers Lawn and Landscaping to see if he could have an interview for the job.

When they met the next day in Number 9 at the Starbrite, Robert Dee and Richard Lee liked that Bubba was a plain-spoken country boy, like themselves. What impressed them the most was his extensive knowledge of plants.

"Have you ever done any landscaping work?" Richard Lee asked.

"Not for pay, but I did a bunch of volunteer work while I was helping at an orphanage in Haiti last year. The Mother Superior even wrote me a letter of recommendation," he said before pulling out the envelope.

Bubba had thought to bring photos of the work he'd done in Haiti along with samples of his design work drawings from college.

At the end of the interview, Robert Dee and Richard Lee told Bubba that they'd get back to him, one way or the other, within the next two days.

"I don't want to hire him to run a crew," Robert Dee said later to Richard Lee.

"Why not? I think he'd be perfect," responded his brother.

"What if we hired him as our Landscape Designer and expanded that part of the business? Like daddy's always sayin', we need to be more visionary in our thinkin'. How many times have customers asked us about replacing shrubs or plants when we was doin' other work? We'd make more on landscapin' than on mowin'.'"

"What if we compromised, and had him runnin' a crew three days a week and doin' the other stuff for two or three days more? Bubba could gain experience and we'd still cover the extra maintenance work," Richard Lee suggested.

With the correct path found, the Camber brothers hired Bubba to start the next week. They trained him in running a lawn maintenance crew first and he caught on real quick. They also bought him supplies for designing landscaping layouts. That's what turned out to be Bubba's passion! He spent his own money to order books about plants and shrubs and practiced doing designs every chance he got.

By the middle of their second summer in business, Camber Brothers Lawn and Landscaping was raking in cash in addition to grass clippings, and needed a full-time manager for the third crew. Bubba was busy helping their existing and new customers create garden oases in their back yards, which not only paid his salary but generated enough additional profits for the boys that they were considering hiring a crew just for the landscaping part of their business. Things were finally working out better than expected!

It was on a Sunday afternoon in late July when Robert Dee was buying a six-pack of soda-pop at the IGA that he ran into his former housekeeper, Faith Culver, who was now 21. He hadn't seen her since he and Richard Lee had moved from their trailer over a year prior. Taking to heart the warning Patrice had given her older brothers, both of them always treated Faith respectfully and never even considered asking her for a date, no matter how pretty she might have been.

"That was then, this is now," Robert Dee said to himself, just before startin' up a conversation with her in the parking lot.

Faith was every bit as sweet as she was beautiful and Robert Dee wanted to ask her out, real bad.

"I was wonderin' if you'd like to go out for dinner sometime?" he asked, worried that she'd turn him down, given the 10 year difference in their age.

"I've got to be honest Robert, with the reputation you and Richard Lee have, I think my parents would have a problem with me going out with you, much as I'd like to. I'm still living at home with my momma and daddy. They're as strict as they were when I was in high school!" she said.

"I might have been some wild as a kid, but I've matured a bunch and would like to show them and you that I can be a respectful gentleman. What if I was to come to your house and let 'em get to know me?" Robert Dee asked, meaning every word of it.

"That'd be fine," Faith replied. "I'll ask my momma to set an extra place for supper tonight."

Not knowing that Faith had a serious crush on him when she was their housekeeper, Robert was positively amazed by the invitation. He went back to Number 9 and cleaned-up, asked Brenda for the pecan pie she'd made for her and Are Dee's Sunday supper and showed up with it at Faith's house exactly at 6:00.

(There's a bunch more to the story, but that'll be covered in my next book, *Camber Brothers Lawn & Landscaping*, available just as soon as I find a literary agent who doesn't send form rejection letters to aspiring authors and can negotiate with a publisher who specializes in "humorous Southern romance.")

(On second thought, maybe I should cover the rest of the Robert Dee and Faith's part of the story in this one.)

Chapter 11 – Lenny Crosley

Lenny Crosley was born and raised in Youngstown and had been in Robert Dee's class from kindergarten through high school.

Without being ugly, it's fair to say that Lenny was never the sharpest knife in the drawer, though there's little doubt in my mind that he'd actually checked to find the sharpest one, since Lenny had a real obsession with knives; the bigger the better. He especially loved wearing the sheath containing his prized machete, which stretched from his belt to down near his knees.

Lenny was a small guy, standing just five feet, four inches tall and weighing only 135 pounds, with slick black hair worn in a Mullet style. While he was generally a pleasant enough feller, he suffered some from a "little man complex," which resulted in him getting into losing fights from time to time. All it took was some smart-aleck making fun of Lenny's height and he'd come all unglued and be ready to do battle with somebody twice his size. Those brawls never seemed to end well for Lenny, but fortunately, he was never foolish enough to pull out one of his prized knives in the heat of the moment, no matter how much he might have been tempted.

Given his size and penchant for strutting around with his machete at his side, some of the less sensitive locals had tagged him with the nickname "Machete Man," and had no hesitation at shouting the name out to him if they saw Lenny walking down the street.

While Are Dee and Marcus had counseled him about wearing the machete in public, he wasn't breaking any laws and all they could do was suggest that it was a bad idea, not that Lenny was listening to them much.

Lenny's daddy had passed years before and his momma had recently remarried. His new step-daddy didn't think that a thirty year old man should still be living at home and encouraged Lenny to find a place of his own, especially given his level of discomfort with the boy's fondness for what he considered to be "sharp bladed instruments of death."

Having never held a job for longer than a couple of years, at best, Lenny somehow convinced his second cousin, the owner of the Youngstown gas station, to hire him for the evening shift, from 6:00 to midnight, Monday through Saturday.

With his first paycheck in hand and his step-daddy's boot at his back, Lenny approached his old friend Franklin about renting a room at the Starbrite and that's how he landed in Number 7 in September of 1986.

While Franklin and the Camber brothers didn't think much about Lenny sitting in front of his room and sharpening his knives with a honing stone, it made Marcus, Mr. B and some of the other renters nervous.

"Are you sure he's alright in the head?" Mr. B wrote in a note to Franklin. Franklin assured him that, unless provoked, Lenny was pretty harmless.

Lenny's second cousin had strictly forbidden him from wearing his machete during working hours, though he did allow him to bring it to the gas station and keep it hidden under the counter. Wanting to be prepared for any potential emergency situation, Lenny had started practicing Samurai moves with the machete, while in the privacy of his room at the Starbrite.

To his credit, Lenny confessed to Franklin that he'd done some damage to the room and reimbursed him for the shredded curtains and the two electrical cords that Mr. B had to replace.

Late on a Saturday night in mid-November, all of Lenny's training and preparation paid off when a pick-up truck with two teenage punks pulled up in front of the gas station, just before closing. Lenny was standing next to the cash register when they walked in, looking around to see if anyone else was in the building. When one of them flipped open a switch blade and demanded that Lenny hand over the money in the cash register, the adrenaline and years of pent-up anger kicked in like a turbocharger and he whipped out his machete, slicing the small knife in half and taking-off the tip of the robber's index finger as he buried the massive blade into the countertop.

The two would-be robbers ran for their lives and their truck, leaving the fingertip and a trail of blood behind. When Marcus arrived on the scene, he immediately thought that someone had been shot or beaten to death, from all the carnage.

Even with the Highway Patrol assisting in the attempted robbery investigation, they were never able to match an impression from the severed tip to any fingerprints on file.

In a small community like Youngstown, the story of Lenny foiling the robbery spread like wildfire and he was quickly elevated to "legend" status, with young boys coming to the gas station, asking him to show them his razor-sharp weapon for destroying criminal activities. Rednecks who might otherwise have considered hassling Lenny about his size, now gave him a newfound level of respect.

A few days later, standing in front of the bathroom mirror in his room at the Starbrite, Lenny wondered to himself if his momma could sew him a super-hero suit with a double-M on the chest for "Machete Man." He was shaken from his fantasy by a knock on his door. It was Are Dee, who he invited inside.

"Lenny," he started, "while we're all real proud of what you did the other night, I want to talk to you about the risk you took. If one of those boys had a gun on 'em, I think the outcome would have been considerably different. I can understand how all the positive attention you've been gettin' can make a feller feel invincible, but you're not....none of us are. There is no amount of money in that cash register that's worth you gettin' shot dead."

Lenny reluctantly nodded his head in agreement, figuring that Are Dee might be right. "Still, I stopped 'em! It may have been dangerous, but it was worth the risk to me," Lenny said, proudly.

"You got lucky this time, son. Real lucky. If it happens again, please, for the sake of your momma, just give them the money and live to fight another day. Whilst we're on the subject of surviving, I want to again recommend that you quit walking around town with that danged machete. You're just invitin' trouble," Are Dee said.

Are Dee had no more than walked out the door when Lenny began thinking about ways he could improve his skills and protect himself, even against someone carrying a gun. With business at the gas station being slow that evening, Lenny killed some time by looking through the Quincy County Weekly Tribune, where he saw an ad for a new business in Wake Forest that gave him a brilliant (by his standards) idea.

The following afternoon, before his shift started at the gas station, Lenny drove south on U.S. 1 and found "The Master Kowalski School of Martial Arts," located in a former auto body shop building. Walking in, Lenny was impressed by the rows of padded mats on the floor and the bank of six foot mirrors lining one wall. There was also the unmistakable smell of automotive paint thinner still in the air.

Lenny was greeted almost immediately by a heavyset middle-aged man wearing a white karate suit, a gi, held together with a black belt. He bowed as he introduced himself. "I'm Sensei Kowalski, Master Instructor of the ancient martial arts," he said. "How may I help you?"

Getting right to the point, Lenny asked, "How much would it cost for you to teach me some Samurai machete knife moves so's I could disarm somebody carryin' a gun?"

Back in 1986, long before texting, "WTF!" hadn't yet been invented, but if it had, you can bet that Sensei Kowalski would have used it in response to Lenny's request.

While the original intent of The Master Kowalski School of Martial Arts was to teach self-defense, discipline and how to earn a black belt in eight months or less, business had started off pretty slow and the Sensei needed to sign-up any potential new student who walked through the door.

"First, you'll need to go through all the steps required to earn a black belt in the martial arts. Once you have achieved that level of skill, then we could work on more specific defensive moves. While the training I teach doesn't involve weapons, I suppose we could make an exception and do some individualized lessons."

"I've got $125," Lenny said. "What'll that get me?"

Thinking that the $125 would cover another newspaper ad, Sensei responded, "Six one-hour lessons." Though he wanted to add, "And a down payment on life insurance," he held it back.

Through December and into January, Lenny drove to the Dojo (school) for his weekly one-hour session in the basic-basics of disarming another person. Feeling that his student was in no way prepared to add weapons training to his instruction, Sensei said, "Lenny, while you've gained much knowledge, you still need more to be proficient at the skills you desire."

"What will another hundred bucks get me?" Lenny asked.

"Five more lessons," Sensei responded.

"Done," Lenny said.

By the end of February, Lenny had run out of money for additional training and Sensei Kowalski had about run out of patience in dealing with him, and so they parted ways with a bow to one-another. As Lenny was leaving the Dojo, the words "dead man walking" kept going through Sensei's mind.

Remarkably, one of the benefits of Lenny's martial arts training had been a huge improvement in controlling his anger, when provoked.

If nothing else, Sensei had taught him to remain focused and calm during an attack, regardless of any verbal taunts, and to respond decisively when required. With his newly gained confidence, Lenny only occasionally wore his machete and was far more comfortable in his dealings with other people.

On a Friday night in late March of 1987, just before closing, Lenny saw a familiar looking pick-up truck pull up in front of the Youngstown gas station. Two young men, both wearing stocking masks over their faces, entered. One of them was carrying a gun; the second one, Lenny noticed, was missing the tip of his right index finger.

Figuring that they hadn't stopped by for a social visit, Lenny responded correctly when they demanded the money from the cash register. He calmly set the cash drawer on the counter, while the man missing the fingertip stuffed the money into his pockets as the other man, holding the gun, headed for the truck.

"Put your hand on the counter," Fingertip-man ordered to Lenny as he pulled out a large hunting knife. "We've got some business to settle, runt."

Realizing what was about to happen, Lenny obeyed the order while breathing slowly and carefully reaching under the counter to pull up a sawed-off shotgun with his free hand.

Aiming at the chest of the man in front of him, Lenny calmly said, "You should never bring a knife to a gun fight."

Looking inside the gas station and seeing the situation, his partner scrambled for the pick-up truck and peeled out of the parking lot, leaving him behind.

Are Dee arrived several minutes after receiving the 9-1-1 call, to find Lenny still calmly pointing the shotgun at the robber.

After the second attempted robbery, video cameras were installed inside the gas station. But Lenny, this time agreeing with Are Dee, felt that being lucky twice in one lifetime was more than enough.

A few weeks later, he applied for a job refueling airplanes at the Raleigh-Durham airport and was hired. With a larger salary and a newly-found desire to escape being a Youngstown legend, he rented an apartment near his new job and left the Starbrite for good.

While driving through Wake Forest, on his way to his new apartment, Lenny stopped at The Master Kowalski School of Martial Arts and gave Sensei his beloved machete, after telling him about the attempted robbery and how much his training at the Dojo had helped him.

"I don't think I'll ever need it again," Lenny said "and wanted you to have it."

"I'll be darned!" Master Kowalski said.

In honor of Lenny's progress and the gift, Sensei put the machete on display in the lobby of the Dojo.

Mr. B was cleaning up Number 7 to get it ready to re-rent, when Franklin walked in to check-out the condition Lenny had left it in and noticed several machete marks that were in the woodwork.

"Do you want me to replace the trim?" Mr. B wrote.

"I think it adds character to the room," Franklin said. "Leave it be."

Chapter 12 – Phyllis & Norman Prescott

By March of 1985 Lisa Ann and her momma hadn't spoken a word to each other in over three years and there were no signs that the ice was even close to thawing, even though her daddy, Norman, regularly poked at both of them to bury the hatchet.

"I'm flying down to Raleigh next week," Norman said to Phyllis. "Why don't you come with me and visit Lisa? Don't you think it's time the two of you got back together?"

"Certainly, as soon as she calls and apologizes. You do know that flights go in both directions. She could come up here anytime and straighten things out."

"She's her mother's daughter, Phyllis, and every bit as stubborn as you. Maybe even more so. Seriously, wouldn't you like to see Lisa? You know, a few days out of the Canadian winter might just do you a world of good."

Phyllis nodded her head, in hopes that Norman would drop the subject.

"Did I tell you that she has a regular boyfriend?"

"Have you met him?" Phyllis asked.

"Not yet, but she tells me that he's from a small town north of Raleigh."

"So she's dating Jethro Bodine?"

"She said that he's an Electrical Engineer at Esterhouse, where she works. A really smart guy."

"Who no doubt has hopes of moving up in the evolutionary chain?"

"Come on, Phyllis! You haven't even met him. Besides that, what do you care? You apparently don't love our daughter enough to take the higher ground and get your relationship back on track."

Well played, Norman! He'd just tossed a guilt card right in the middle of her poached salmon!

"I'll think about calling her," Phyllis said, "but no promises."

As was their regular routine, after dinner Norman retreated to his den to watch TV or read productivity reports from work. Phyllis usually spent her evening reading in their living room. Wanting to talk with Norman about a dinner party they were to attend on the upcoming weekend, Phyllis went into the den and found him sound asleep in his recliner, with the TV tuned to *The Dukes of Hazard*.

"Seriously," she thought, "couldn't he watch _anything_ more intelligent than this drivel?"

Before she turned off the TV and woke up Norman, she sat down and found herself watching a few minutes of the episode.

"Oh, for the love of God," she said, disgusted with herself for wasting her time, as she clicked off the remote.

That night Phyllis had a horrible dream. She dreamt that Lisa Ann had become Daisy Duke and had a bulging, pregnant stomach sticking out between her tiny top and short shorts. Phyllis was there, too, helping her take care of several barefoot grandkids, all of whom were in need of baths.

"Maw-maw," one of them called to her, "Jethro Junior has done sh*t his diaper again."

Lisa Ann turned to her and said, "I sure appreciate you helping out 'til I get this young'un birthed."

At that moment, Jethro Senior drove up in a Dodge Charger with a Confederate flag painted on the roof. Norman was in the passenger seat. The horn was playing "Dixie."

Phyllis work up with a jolt, looking over at Norman who was soundly sleeping. The digital alarm clock that read 2:35 a.m.. She never got a wink of sleep for the rest of the night.

Sipping her third cup of black coffee the next morning, while Norman ate his bran flakes, Phyllis said, "I've given it a lot of thought. I'm going to call Lisa this evening."

Phyllis spent most of her day contemplating what she should say to her daughter and how she should say it. She even rehearsed the conversation in her head a few times.

As soon as Norman had retreated to his den after dinner, she dialed the number for Lisa Ann's apartment in Morrisville.

"Hello," Lisa Ann said at the other end.

There was a long pause.

"Hello, anybody there?"

"It's me," Phyllis said.

"Mother? Is everything alright? Did something happen to Dad?"

"Everything is fine, except between you and me," she said. "Do you have a few minutes?"

"I suppose so," Lisa Ann responded.

During the fifteen minute conversation Phyllis did her best to mend the fences between her and Lisa Ann, without ever apologizing for anything and without putting any blame on herself. Lisa Ann mostly listened to her mother drone on about the high hopes she'd always had for her and the willingness of her momma to overlook things from the past, if Lisa Ann was open to doing the same. Near the end of the conversation Phyllis said that she was planning to fly to Raleigh the following week with Norman and wanted Lisa Ann to have dinner with them.

"I'll be there," she said to her momma, though she had more reservations than the Cheesecake Factory on Mother's Day.

Cuddled up to Franklin on Friday night, Lisa Ann said, "I don't know why I accepted the invitation, other than being curious about what Mother may have up her sleeve. I'm always glad to see my dad. I want to introduce to you to him, I just don't think this is the right opportunity."

"You need to settle your hash with your momma before you go bringing a stranger into the picture," he said. "There'll be plenty of things you'll want to talk over and that need to be said between you and her."

"You're no stranger, Franklin. You're my boyfriend, my lover, my best friend," she said as she gave him a kiss.

"You're really something, Lisa Ann Prescott!"

"Something good or something bad?" she asked, smiling.

"Something wonderful and somebody I love," Franklin said.

"I love you, too," she responded.

"Even though I'm just a Youngstown hayseed?"

"Because you're Youngstown hayseed and because I just love seeing the look on your face when I do this….."

(We can move on to the next part. I'm reasonably sure you get the picture.)

Lisa Ann's daddy cashed in a whole bunch of his Marriott points and upgraded to a suite for his visit the next week. He figured that it would be better to have Room Service bring in their supper than to risk what might happen if things went sour between Phyllis and Lisa Ann in some fancy restaurant. In other words, he was more than a little scared and who could blame him.

By the time 7:00 pm rolled around, Norman had returned from his business meetings and Phyllis had been primping in the bathroom for a solid hour.

"She's our daughter, not the Queen of England," Norman said, having an urgent need to use the bathroom that Phyllis had been hogging. "She's seen you without your make-up."

Lisa Ann knocked on the door a few minutes later, giving her daddy a big hug as he let her in. Phyllis made a grand entrance from the bedroom, hugging her daughter and kissing her on the cheek.

"You look wonderful dear," her momma said to her.

"So do you Mother," Lisa Ann replied before an awkward silence hit the room.

"Can I pour either of you a glass of wine?" Norman asked. "I've got a very nice merlot."

"Yes," they both said.

Keeping mostly to small talk during dinner, both Phyllis and Lisa Ann were on their best behavior, neither of them wanting to deal with the elephant that was in the middle of the room. Finally, Phyllis took a shot at it.

"Have you considered returning to college and getting a bachelor's degree?" she asked.

"I really don't need one at this point. I've got a good job working directly for three of the company's vice presidents and I help the owner's administrative assistant with some of that work, too."

"But Lisa, you've got so much more potential than just being an administrative assistant."

"I like what I'm doing. Working at Esterhouse makes me happy. I like feeling happy. It's a relatively new emotion for me."

"Meaning exactly what?" her momma asked.

"Meaning that I've spent so much of my life being miserable that being happy feels really nice for a change. I may not be working on a cure for cancer, but I really like what I'm doing and like the people around me."

"I always thought you were a very happy child," Phyllis said.

"Of course you'd think that, Mother. I was the child you wanted me to be. It didn't matter if I was so unhappy that I wanted to run away from home. As long as you kept pushing me to be your model girl, surely I must have been happy. Right?"

"Children don't know what's in their best interests. It's their parent's job to steer them in the right directions."

"I don't disagree, but there's a huge difference between steering and bulldozing," Lisa Ann said. "If you're really interested in seeing what happiness looks like, you should meet Franklin and his family. They are some of the happiest, best adjusted people I've ever seen."

"He's the boyfriend your father told me about. So he has a big ol' happy country family?"

"Franklin's parents died when he was little. He was raised by an aunt and uncle. When they passed away Franklin's cousin and his wife sort of reeled him into their family."

"That sounds like a very sad life," Norman said.

"Just the opposite. They are small town people, who care about their family more than anything, extended or otherwise. They don't have much materially, but they have their faith.....they live their religion, and they care deeply about the happiness of their kids and each other."

"Are they related to the Walton's? Good night John-boy and all that garbage," Phyllis said.

The look that Norman shot at Phyllis told her in no uncertain terms that she'd gone way too far.

"I'm sorry Lisa, that wasn't a very nice thing for me to say," Phyllis offered.

"If you want to know the truth, they probably are a bit like the Walton's and there's nothing bad about that."

There was another one of those long silences that generally screams that folks are uncomfortable.

"Mother, did you ever, even once, ask me if I was happy? Does it matter to you in the least that I'm happy now?"

"Of course it does, what kind of parent do you think I am?"

"If I answered that honestly, I doubt we'd ever speak to each other again," Lisa Ann said. "Look, I've got to go to work in the morning, so I think it's time for me to hit the road."

"Wait Lisa, please, there's something that needs to be said before you go, and I'm the one who needs to say it. Another glass of wine, Norman."

He refilled her glass just in time for Phyllis to take a long swig.

"I'm sorry that I hurt you. I'm sorry that I wasn't the mother I should have been or the mother you wanted or needed. I'm sorry that I made your life so miserable. It was with the best of intentions, but that doesn't change how it impacted you. I only want what's best for you Lisa."

"Of course you do," Lisa Ann said as insincerely as possible, before allowing the significance of her mother's words to sink in. She paused long enough to realize that she'd just heard an apology from a woman who had never considered the possibility she could be wrong about anything.

"Thank you, Mother. What you said means more to me than you'll ever know."

"I do want to make things right between us. Really. I'll try my best to show you that I mean it and if at some point you'd let me meet Franklin and his family, I promise not to embarrass you in any way," Phyllis said.

As she headed to the door, Lisa gave her momma a hug, a real one, and she gave one to her daddy, too.

After she left, Norman turned to Phyllis and said, "That was a good start. Thank you."

As Lisa Ann walked out to her car, she decided not to return to her apartment and drove out to Youngstown instead. When she pulled up into the Starbrite parking lot she saw that Franklin's lights were still on.

Franklin opened the door of his house as she was getting out of her car.

"You're up kind of late for a school night," she said.

"I figured you might be coming this way. Wanna talk?"

"Not so much. What I'd really like to for you to just hold me."

"I'd be honored, Miz Lisa Ann."

Lisa Ann continued to keep a safe distance from her mother, but they did begin speaking by phone once a month. One of the things that helped thaw the relationship the most was that Lisa Ann had started calling her momma and daddy on the evening of major holidays throughout the year and sharing details of how she'd spent the day with Franklin and his family. Like a little girl telling her friends about Disney World, Lisa Ann was awestruck by what Thanksgiving, Christmas and Easter meant to the Cambers and their guests. The true meaning of each holiday and the joy of sharing them brought her a level of happiness that she tried her best to communicate to Phyllis and Norman. The truth was, they were getting jealous of the people who had captured the heart of their daughter. And that was what led the Prescott's to ask Lisa Ann if they could rent a room at the Starbrite for Easter weekend 1987.

Norman had met Franklin nearly a year earlier while in Raleigh on a business trip and was genuinely impressed by him and he'd told Phyllis as much. Since he was the man their daughter was now living with, she wanted to meet him and the other people who had become so important to Lisa Ann. They both wanted to see firsthand what made Franklin's extended family and Youngstown so special.

"Please tell me that the Starbrite will be full that week or let me remind them that you only rent by the week," Lisa Ann said to Franklin.

"First off, you know it's never full. I consider it a good week when ten out of twelve rooms are rented. Tell your parents that we'll have a room for them as our guests."

"They can afford the thirty-five dollars, Franklin."

"That's not the point Lisa Ann, they're family and I don't charge family."

"They're not your family," Lisa Ann said.

"Well, maybe not yet," Franklin said in a not-so-subtle manner.

"What am I going to do with you?" Lisa Ann asked.

"I was hopin' the same thing you did with me last night."

When the time for their visit came, the only room Franklin had available for Phyllis and Norman was Number 7, two doors down from Lashaya Bryan. Wanting to make a good impression, he asked Mr. B to repaint the room in robin's egg blue and the bathroom in gloss white. Mr. B checked all the electrical circuits to make sure there were no dead outlets, replaced all the lightbulbs, shined up the plumbing fixtures and installed a new toilet seat. Wanting to avoid Lashaya, Franklin waited until she was at Wednesday night Bible Study before he swapped out the old black and white TV in Number 7 for his own 25 inch color Sony, with a remote control. Without telling Lisa Ann, he convinced Brenda to drive in to Raleigh and buy new sheets, bedspread, pillows and curtains for the room. As far as the Starbrite went, the Prescott's would be staying in the Presidential Suite.

Landing in Raleigh on Good Friday, the weather was warm and the sky was cloudless, which was especially good for the Prescott's, coming from Ottawa, where snow was still on the ground. Lisa Ann picked up her parents at the airport and drove them out to Youngstown and got them settled in their room. Franklin came down the minute he saw Lisa Ann pull-in and he was introduced to Phyllis, who sized him up like a hog buyer at a 4H auction. Making good on her many promises to Lisa Ann, Phyllis went out of her way to be as warm as she knew how, starting with giving him a hug.

"It is such a pleasure to finally meet you Franklin. I've heard so many wonderful things from Lisa. Thank you for such gracious hospitality."

"It's a pleasure to meet you, too, Mrs. Prescott," he said, "and to see you again, Mr. Prescott."

"This is a lovely room. Lisa tells me that the motel has been in your family for years."

"My aunt and uncle built the place and ran it until they passed. They left it to me, but I'm afraid it won't be here much longer. They're planning to widen U.S. 1 and the Starbrite is right in the way."

"What will you do?"

"Don't know for sure yet. Maybe buy a place in Raleigh to be closer to work or a few acres out here and build a house. The Lord works in mysterious ways, I'm sure he'll show me the right path."

Phyllis had a snarky response on the tip of her tongue, but kept her word to Lisa Ann and said, "I'm sure he will. Lisa told us that she's been attending church with you for several months."

"We may even get her baptized one of these days, if she chooses. She sings the hymns with the voice of an angel."

"I'll bet she does," Phyllis said, remembering the voice lessons that she forced Lisa Ann to take.

"Lisa told me that you were just awarded your first patent, for some sort of micro switch. Very impressive. Congratulations!" Norman offered.

"It's really not a big deal, just an idea I had for a senior project when I was finishin' up at NC State. Seems like it took forever to get it approved," Franklin responded.

"Don't be so modest," Norman said. "I've known telecom engineers who been at it for decades and never gotten a patent approved."

Franklin wanted to shift the subject away from himself as quickly as possible.

"We'll give you some time to settle in and come back about six-thirty. Brenda and Are Dee are looking forward to having you over for supper tonight." Franklin said.

"That would be wonderful," Phyllis responded. "I think we'd both like to freshen-up a bit."

Alone in their room, she and Norman looked around and found it to be much more pleasant than they'd anticipated. Old, but nicely decorated, it reminded them both of the places where they'd stayed early in their marriage.

"Do you remember when this was the best we could afford?" she asked Norman.

"I want to remind you that Lisa was conceived in a room just like this on our trip to the Finger Lakes," he said with a big smile.

It was a memory that Phyllis hadn't thought of in years, but smiled thinking back to the passion she and Norman had once shared and the overwhelming love they felt for each other in those days. What ever happened to those feelings, she wondered sadly?

Phyllis changed into a pair of slacks and a light sweater. Norman put on a pair of Dockers and a casual button-down shirt. It wasn't long before Lisa and Franklin came for them and they walked over to Are Dee and Brenda's house together.

"This is really a lovely little town," Phyllis said.

Are Dee and Brenda lived is a single story, three bedroom brick house that was built in the mid 50's. In the 60's Are Dee had added a full length porch to the front and a decade later he and Brenda had completely remodeled the home. It wasn't anything fancy, neither was it a tarpaper shack. More than anything, it was a warm, inviting place where the Cambers made everyone who came in feel welcome.

Knowing how important it was to Franklin that she and Are Dee make a positive impression on the Prescott's, Brenda had scrubbed the house from top to bottom. Since Robert Dee and Richard Lee would be working late that evening, she suggested that they stop to eat on their way back to the Starbrite. Finally, she ordered Are Dee to change out of his uniform before supper.

"Why would I do that?" he asked. "What if Marcus needs back-up? Even when I'm off duty, I'm still on-duty, you know that!"

"Your only duty tonight is to make sure that Lisa Ann's parents understand that Franklin comes from good, upstandin' people, not a bunch of country bumpkins."

"But we are country bumpkins," he protested.

"Hush up and do as I asked, for once in your life. This is important Are Dee! I mean it. We're all the kin that boy has in the world and we're doin' this for him. Now go put on your blue dress shirt."

Are Dee knew she was right, even for as much misery as Brenda was currently putting him through.

When he went into the bedroom to change clothes, he saw his favorite blue shirt hanging in the closet with plastic over it.

"Danged if she didn't take it to the dry cleaners!" he said to himself.

Are Dee had just come out of the bedroom when he saw Franklin, Lisa Ann and the Prescott's walking across the front porch. Sticking his head into the kitchen, he said to Brenda, "Show time!"

In return, she gave him 'the look,' indicating her lack of amusement.

After showing everyone in, greetings were exchanged. With everyone now on a first name basis, Phyllis offered to help Brenda with the meal preparation and Norman sat down with Are Dee in the living room. They were four people who had absolutely nothing in common with one-another other than Franklin and Lisa Ann, but recognizing the importance of the evening, they all made their best efforts to make each other feel comfortable.

Norman and Phyllis had brought two bottles of wine, a Cabernet and a Chardonnay, not knowing what Brenda was making for supper. I don't know as anybody at the table knew the correct wine for chicken fried steak with milk gravy, so both bottles were opened.

166

"You must forgive me for making such a pig of myself," Norman said after supper, "but that meal was wonderful! I don't know when I've ever tasted home cooking like that! And the banana pudding was so good I was tempted to lick the plate."

"I have to agree," Phyllis said. "If that's country cooking, then Brenda must be a master chef."

The funny thing is that both complements were absolutely sincere.

"If you had any doubts about how I got this big, now you know the reason," Are Dee said.

"Y'all hush! You're makin' me blush," said Brenda.

Franklin and Lisa Ann offered to clear the table and load the dishwasher while her parents and the Cambers retired to the front porch to enjoy the mild Carolina spring evening.

"Norman, have you ever tasted moonshine?" Are Dee asked.

"Never," he said. "I suppose a man in your profession confiscates some from time to time."

"Yeah, that or I just go straight to the best 'shiner I know and buy a quart," he said with a big smile.

Pulling out two glasses and a Mason jar, Are Dee carefully poured some of the clear liquid into each container.

"It's a touch stout," Are Dee said, "so you might want to start with just a sip."

"Since they're gonna drink that stuff, how about another glass of wine for you, Phyllis?" Brenda offered.

With everyone's glasses filled, Are Dee proposed a toast. "To family," he said.

"To family," they all repeated as the glasses clinked.

Norman took a small sip of the moonshine and started turning bright red.

"What that lacks in smoothness, it more than makes up for in strength," he said, coughing slightly.

"I know y'all got plans to spend tomorrow with the kids," Brenda said, "but I do want to invite you to Easter sunrise services on Sunday. They're gonna be down by the millpond and something really special this year."

"We'd be honored," Phyllis said and she meant it.

The next morning while still in bed, Norman looked over at Phyllis and said, "I can't remember when I've had such a good night's sleep."

"With all the moonshine you drank last night, it's a wonder you can remember anything at all," she said smiling.

For the first time in years, she leaned into Norman and snuggled up next to him.

Their Saturday spent with Franklin and Lisa Ann went far better than anyone might have expected. They spent much of the time driving around Youngstown looking at vacant land, as well as checking out several neighborhoods in Wake Forest and Raleigh. It was while they were touring a model home in a new subdivision just off Durant Road that Phyllis noticed a small bedroom just off the master.

"That would make a great nursery," she said, before even thinking about it.

It was the warm look exchanged between Franklin and Lisa Ann that told her just how serious they were about one another.

"Smooth, Phyllis, very smooth," Norman said, as he tickled her ribs and laughed, once they were alone outside.

Norman bought everyone dinner at Churchill's in North Raleigh before they drove back to Youngstown.

Deciding to walk the six blocks to the millpond the next morning, the Prescott's, Cambers, Franklin and Lisa Ann gathered next to the water, along with a group of worshipers from the Free Will Evangelic Fundamentalist Church. Lisa Ann was amazed to see her parents holding hands as they walked over.

"Norman, what got into you last night?" Phyllis whispered, smiling. "You were like a teenager!"

"I couldn't help myself," he whispered back, "It was like being back at the Finger Lakes Lodge again."

Pastor Thorpe began the service. "Brothers and sisters, we are here today to celebrate the resurrection of our Lord and Savior, Jesus Christ, on this beautiful Easter morning. I selected this spot for our sunrise service because it's a place where I've come to over the years to feel closer to God. I have always been humbled by its beauty and its serenity."

"I want to share with you the news that this will be my last Easter to serve our church. With the relocation of our congregation and construction of our new building, I will be retiring at the end of the year and turning over my responsibilities to someone younger and healthier who can help our congregation to grow and spread the word of the Lord."

"Since this will be my last sunrise service as your pastor, I wanted to bring y'all here and help you to cast away your sins on this Easter morning, ask the Lord for forgiveness and start anew, rebirthed, on this special day."

"On the tables to your right are stacks of stones and pieces of chalk. I want each of you to pick up a stone and write a sin upon it that's burdening your heart. Then, I want you to throw that stone into the pond. Ask the Lord for forgiveness and salvation! Cast away your sins on this Easter morning, knowing that Jesus died on the cross for you, so that you could be forgiven and could live forever in the house of our Lord."

After the beautiful, moving sunrise service, they started to walk to Brenda and Are Dee's for country ham biscuits. Franklin asked Norman to stay back for a minute while the others headed home.

"Mr. Prescott, I want you to know how much I love your daughter."

"I know that, Franklin," Norman said. "You'd have to be blind not to see what the two of you feel for each other."

"The thing is, I'm a pretty old fashioned guy. I believe in traditions. So before I ask Lisa Ann to marry me, I want to get your blessing."

Norman turned to face Franklin, placing his left hand on his shoulder and shaking his right hand.

"You have it, Franklin," he said. "I know you'll be a good husband and father. When are you going to ask her?"

"Soon, real soon," he said.

The Prescott's had a 2:00 p.m. flight back to Ottawa, so said their good-bye's to the Cambers after breakfast. Franklin and Lisa Ann drove them out to the airport and walked them as far as the security check-point.

"This has been a wonderful trip," Phyllis said. "Franklin, you are very fortunate to have people like Brenda and Are Dee in your life. I want you to promise that you'll take good care of our daughter and that the two of you will come up to Ottawa for a visit this summer."

"Yes, ma'am," Franklin said.

"Lisa, I've never seen you so happy! It's all any mother could want for her child," Phyllis said, with tears in her eyes. "I love you, sweetheart."

"I love you too, Mom," Lisa Ann said. "You too, Daddy."

After a round of hugs, the Prescott's went through security and on to their gate.

"So what do you think, Phyllis?" Norman asked.

"I think we just spent a weekend with our future son-in-law and his family and I couldn't be more pleased," she said.

"You know, it's just a short drive from Ottawa down to the Finger Lakes. What would you think about booking a long weekend there this summer?"

"How about a full week?" she asked.

Chapter 13 – Inita Mann and Fonda Dix

With construction having already started on the U.S. 1 widening project to the north and south of Youngstown in the late spring of 1987, Franklin was enjoying a string of 'no vacancy' weeks at the Starbrite. Road workers were trickling into the area from out of town and needed cheap, temporary housing. It was only because some of them had returned to their homes for an extended Memorial Day weekend break that he found himself with two empty rooms.

Spring had been unusually brief that year and a late May heatwave had driven the temperature to just above the 90 degree mark with humidity at 80%. People were jumpin' into swimming pools just to dry off some. As Stan Marbury would say, "In other words, it was a normal summer day in North Carolina."

With the window air conditioner running at full blast, Lisa Ann and Franklin were sitting in front of it trying their best to keep cool, when they heard a couple of car doors close in the parking lot.

Now, there is no question that Franklin Delworth was an intelligent and good hearted man. I've already established those virtues in the previous chapters. But growing up at the Starbrite and living in a small, sheltered community like Youngstown, he could sometimes be innocent in the ways of the world.

He looked out and saw two women walking toward the motel office. Lisa Ann had also seen 'em.

"They're hookers, Franklin," she said.

"How can you tell that from this far away?"

"I grew up in Queens. I know a hooker when I see one. Trust me on this, they're hookers."

"They look like a couple of nice ladies to me," he said.

Before Lisa Ann could offer any additional comments, they came into the office.

A probably true fact of history is that hookers got that name during the Civil War (also see Northern War of Aggression) when a group of prostitutes began following the camp of Union General "Fighting Joe" Hooker. Whether or not Fighting Joe partook of the ladies may never be known, but he most likely condoned their presence amongst his officers and enlisted men. If you ever heard the term "camp followers," it pretty much means the same as hookers and for all the same reasons. (It's been awhile since I digressed, so I felt entitled to this little one.)

"How can I help you ladies?" Franklin asked.

"Do you have rooms for the next three nights?" asked the redheaded one.

"I've got two empty rooms, but as the sign says, we only rent by the week. Thirty-five dollars, paid in advance."

The redhead looked over at the brunette. "Whatcha think, Inita?"

"Let's go for it," she said.

"Can you give us two that are next to each other?" the redhead asked.

"As it happens, Number 1 and Number 2 are available."

"Far end, away from things," the brunette observed.

"We'll take 'em," the redhead said.

As Franklin handed them registration cards, he looked over into the living room to see Lisa Ann rolling her eyes.

The brunette filled out the card as Inita Mann from Fayetteville and the redhead was Fonda Dix from Virginia Beach. If Franklin had been even remotely as savvy as his late aunt and uncle, he might have asked to see their driver's licenses or wondered why their car had a Pennsylvania plate. Instead, he smiled at the women and took the $70 cash.

"Fonda," Franklin said, "that's a very unique first name."

"It was my mother's maiden name. We're distant cousins to Henry, Jane and Peter," was her reply.

"What brings you ladies to town?" he asked.

"We're therapists," Inita said, without adding any additional details.

Lisa Ann chose that moment to walk over to the office counter and stand next to Franklin. It was a clear territorial indicator to the ladies.

Franklin walked them down to Number 1 and Number 2, handed them the keys and said, 'Hope you enjoy your stay at the Starbrite."

"Thank you. I'm sure we will," responded Fonda.

When he got back to his house, Lisa Ann was sitting in a living room chair with her arms and legs crossed.

"I need a man and fond of dicks?!! Could it be possible that those aren't their real names? Are the local authorities aware that you've decided to open your own house of ill repute, Mr. Delworth?" she said.

"Say what?"

"Franklin, did you bother to look at those two?"

"So they were dressed a little trashy. That proves nothing! You ever seen the girls that Robert Dee and Richard Lee date?"

"I sure have. You ever wondered why Brenda doesn't invite them to Sunday supper?"

"Besides that, don't you have to have a degree to be a therapist?" Franklin asked.

174

"Therapists, my ass! The only degree those two earned was from Bee-Jay You! Franklin there will be no trade-outs for the rent, under any circumstances. Are we clear on that?"

"Are you nuts?"

"Are we clear?"

"Lisa Ann, you know that I haven't looked at another girl since I met you. What could they possible offer that would make me even consider something like that?"

Lisa Ann got up from her chair, crawled into Franklin's lap and whispered into his ear.

"No way! Are you serious? That's disgusting! Are you makin' that up?"

"So we're clear?"

"Absolutely."

"Good," she said as she started working at the buttons of his shirt, no doubt concerned that Franklin might have been getting hot.

On Sunday morning, when most of the rest of the folks in Youngstown were headed for church, Inita and Fonda decided to start looking for a building for their new business venture. After driving most of the way north to Henderson then doubling back south, past Wake Forest, they found three possibilities, all closed business locations. There was a gas station building with three service bays, a lawn and garden repair shop building and a mobile home sales office with large parking lot.

It was the closed mobile home sales office, three miles north of Youngstown that held the greatest interest.

"I like the parking lot, we could put up a privacy fence and park cars behind the building," Fonda said.

"I was hoping we could find at least two-thousand square feet. The office looked smaller to me. We really need to see the inside," Inita added. "It did say for sale or lease."

"We can call the real estate agent tomorrow. We need to go in pretty conservative, remember, we're in the' heart of the Bible belt."

Hoping that the agent might be available on Memorial Day, Fonda used the pay phone in the Starbrite parking lot to call. It turned out that he owned one of them new cell phones, so he answered from his car on the way home from Atlantic Beach.

"Sure," he said, "I can meet you there at four this afternoon. It's a great property! Plenty of potential and it's on the east side of U.S. 1, so it won't be affected by the road widening. Are you interested in buying or leasing?"

"Leasing," Fonda said. "We're looking for a 36 month net-net agreement with an option for months 37 through 60 with no increase unless precipitated by inflation, and then tied to the actual rate as established by the Consumer Price Index."

A net-net lease would mean that the girls would pay for all the improvements needed for their business as well as ongoing repairs and utilities. The only thing the owner would have to cover is property insurance and taxes. The agent was already favorably impressed.

Meeting them at the property, he found the two ladies conservatively dressed in business-appropriate pant suites. Both were wearing glasses and had on only a small amount of make-up. They both were carrying portfolio pads and were making lots of notes and drawings. They certainly appeared to be proper businesswomen.

After showing them the property, an 1800 square foot building with four offices, a bathroom and reception area, he asked, "What do you think?"

"I don't know," said Inita. "It's going to take a lot of renovation to meet our needs, it's further out of town than we'd like and it's smaller than what we'd hoped for. How is it zoned?"

"That's the thing. Because it's over a quarter mile from any residential property or other businesses, it is zoned for General Usage, which around here means you can use it for about anything you'd like. We're pretty easy when it comes to zoning issues. What are you planning?"

"We are both therapists, so wanted to create a joint office and establish new patients in the area," Fonda responded.

"What type of therapy do you do?" he asked.

"We specialize in personal relaxation treatments for people undergoing a great deal of stress or anxiety in their lives. It's massage based," she answered, professionally and without hesitation.

Since the property had sat empty for a considerable amount of time and the owner was facing foreclosure proceedings if he didn't get it filled soon, the agent was more than willing to take their explanation at face value and try to cut a deal.

"I can draft a lease tomorrow and you could have occupancy immediately. It'll cost you $950 a month, with a two-thousand dollar security deposit," he said, swinging for the stands.

It was Inita who laughed first.

"If your goal was to insult our intelligence, then you're succeeding. Let's cut the crap and get down to what it's really worth. According to the sign in the window, the last business that was here closed two years ago, so demand for the property is minimal at best. The parking lot needs work and we'll have to invest four or five thousand just to get the building back to a point where we can use it. $450 per month and a $1000 security deposit. Take it or leave it."

The agent immediately realized that this wasn't the first rodeo for Ms. Mann and Ms. Dix.

"Six-fifty and I think I can get the owner to agree," the agent said.

Inita looked over at Fonda, who nodded her head.

"Make it five-fifty with no security deposit. That's our final offer," Inita said.

"I'm not sure the owner will agree to that," said the agent.

"Why don't you use your cell phone and call him," Inita suggested.

Excusing himself to make the call, the agent returned less than five minutes later.

"We've got a deal," he said. "I'll draw up the lease in the morning. You can either come to my office or we can meet here and I'll give you the keys as soon as it's signed."

As they were about to leave, the real estate agent turned to Fonda. "If you don't mind me asking, Ms. Dix, are you any relation to the lady they named the state mental hospital for in Raleigh; Dorothea Dix?"

"She was a distant cousin, I'm told," was Fonda's answer.

"Imagine that!" said the agent.

That one simple question was the inspiration for the "The Dix Massage Therapy Center," as it said on the sign, though their appointment cards did have a disclaimer saying that they weren't affiliated with the Dorothea Dix Hospital in Raleigh.

With a classy looking illuminated sign near the highway, four therapy rooms and a privacy fence shielding the parking lot, Inita and Fonda opened up for business on the 20th of June. The ladies contacted Franklin to see if he might have a couple of rooms available for two of their incoming Associate Therapists, but the Starbrite was full-up.

It was at a Saturday evening supper with Are Dee and Brenda that the subject came up.

"No vacancies! I'll bet it's been awhile since you've seen that at the Starbrite?" Are Dee said.

"In a way, it's kinda too bad," Franklin responded. "The very thing that's gonna cause the Starbrite to be torn down is what's filling it up these days."

"How's that, Franklin?" Brenda asked.

"I'm full-up because of highway workers," Franklin answered.

"That and a couple of hookers," Lisa Ann added, casually slippin' it in.

"Lisa Ann, you don't know that," Franklin responded.

"Franklin," Are Dee said, "if we're talkin' about the women in Number 1 and 2, they're hookers alright."

"How can you be so sure?" he asked.

"When you've been in law enforcement as long as I have, you can tell from a block away. I wasn't going to say anything unless they started usin' the Starbrite as a business location, but they're hookers. You do know that they opened The Dix Massage Therapy Center, north of town? It's a massage parlor. We can't prove anything yet, but I can guarantee there's illicit activities goin' on there."

"You serious?" Franklin said.

"Last week, we stopped a local preacher, who will remain nameless, for a busted taillight. Marcus was out that way and saw him pullin' out of the place," Are Dee said. "When Marcus asked if his massage

179

had a happy ending, the preacher said 'let he who is without sin cast the first stone.' They're hookers alright."

"Are Dee do you think this is appropriate supper table talk with two ladies present?"

"It's OK, Brenda," Lisa Ann said. "I told Franklin they were hookers the minute I saw them."

As their client list grew, Inita and Fonda had to bring in more Associate Therapists and eventually placed a double-wide on the property they were leasing so's they could house all their girls. While the Quincy County Sheriff, the State Highway Patrol and Chief Camber all knew they were running a house of pleasure, they had yet to come up with any solid evidence, a complaining customer or anything else that could be used to shut 'em down.

In October, after Inita and Fonda had been renting their rooms from Franklin for five months, they approached him with a business proposition. Perhaps 'business opportunity' might be a better choice of words.

"We'd like to rent all twelve rooms at the Starbrite on an on-going basis," Fonda said.

"We'll up what you're getting from $35 dollars a week to fifty," Inita added.

"And how exactly would you be usin' those rooms?" Franklin asked.

"With the growth of the Dix Massage Therapy Center, we've got a number of clients who require overnight treatment. We also have several more Associate Therapists who need housing," Fonda said.

Having been teased for all those months by Are Dee and Lisa Ann, Franklin didn't hesitate in his response.

"Ladies, while I appreciate your generous offer, we've got some people who've been livin' here for years and don't have any place else to go. I couldn't evict them, it just wouldn't be right. The Starbrite is gonna be sold to the DOT soon and torn down as part of the U.S. 1 project, once it gets to Youngstown. Those folks sure don't need to be displaced twice."

"Would it make any difference if we offered sixty a week?" Inita asked.

"I'm afraid not. My mind's set regarding this matter."

"If you change your mind, you know where to find us," she added. "Here's a coupon for 50% off on a treatment, if you're ever interested. Given how much we value this relationship, either Fonda or I would perform your therapy personally."

"I'll certainly keep that in mind. Thanks," he said.

It wasn't long after that three large motorhomes were parked behind the privacy fence at the Dix Massage Therapy Center to handle patients with special needs. That was probably the straw that busted the camel's back.

After a long string of citizen complaints over the type of business the ladies were running, the Sheriff's department finally raided the place on New Year's Eve, charging five Associate Therapists with prostitution. Inita and Fonda were also charged with running a brothel. The Sheriff, who had lost his re-election bid in November, decided to publish the names of the patients receiving treatment at the time of the raid. I 'spect most of those boys had some serious explaining to do back at home.

With the Dix Massage Therapy Center padlocked and their Associate Therapists busted, there was really no reason for Inita and Fonda to stick around, once they'd posted bail. Heading for greener pastures, at least pending their trials, the ladies decided to turn-in their room keys and leave town.

"I guess you finally figured out what we do for a living," Inita said to Franklin.

After Marcus ran the Pennsylvania plate on their car that previous fall, Franklin knew that Inita was really Kelli Ryman from Philadelphia. Fonda was her younger sister, Edie. Both had been arrested for soliciting and prostitution several times, in Pennsylvania and in eastern North Carolina, near the armed forces bases.

"I've known for quite a while," was all he said.

"You never let on. You always treated us respectfully. How come?"

"My Aunt Willa Mae taught me to judge not, lest ye be judged," Franklin said.

"Thank you, Mr. Delworth," she said.

"You're very welcome, Miz Ryman," he said. "I hope you and your sister have a safe journey."

"As long as it's out of Quincy County?" she asked.

"Wherever you go," he said.

He watched as their car turned left out of the Starbrite parking lot, heading north on U.S. 1.

Chapter 14 – Sealing the Deals

In mid-February of 1987, Franklin, Are Dee and three-dozen other Youngstown property owners received a certified letter from the Department of Transportation informing them of what they already knew, their property was in the path of the U.S. 1 widening project. The letter said that they'd be contacted by a DOT representative and given an official offer for their land in May.

Franklin, Lisa Ann, Are Dee and Brenda had a serious conversation about the whole subject the weekend after they'd received their notifications.

"I think we should get two appraisals on our property and have those in our back pocket when the DOT makes their offer," Franklin said.

"I agree, but you've also got to consider what the potential value of the land will be after the new road gets built. Remember Franklin, be a visionary!" Are Dee said. "You've got eight acres that each have 208 feet of road frontage and are 210 feet deep. If you was to sell the DOT a sixty-foot right of way to your property and let 'em pay you for the Starbrite and your house, you'd still have eight lots that were a hundred-fifty foot deep with all that prime road frontage. Keep in mind that there's thirty-two acres of farmland behind you. With that and your land, some smart developer could put a big shopping center back there. But you'd hold the key, since they'd need your land to make it work."

"Who's gonna build something like that in Youngstown?" Franklin asked.

"Maybe nobody today, but in another ten years that land could be worth a whole bunch of money. Think of it like putting cash in the bank and just collecting interested for a few years," Are Dee added.

"Where's that gonna leave us?" Brenda asked.

"Our property is a hundred-fifty foot wide by a hundred foot deep. Once the DOT gets their sixty foot of right-of-way, they might just well have all of it," Are Dee said. "We're just gonna have to decide where we want to live after that. You were the one who got me thinkin' about retirin' again and movin' up to Lake Gaston."

"You wouldn't have to twist my arm," Brenda said.

It turned out that the DOT representative sent to handle the Youngstown project was a bald, short, pudgy sixty-five year old government bureaucrat named Mort Samuels, a Real Estate Field Negotiator who was on his very last assignment before retirement. The Youngstown negotiations were given to Mort as a final 'up yours' from his supervisor, a South Bronx transplant named Dick Felton. From the time Dick came into the department, he'd thought that Mort was just coastin' until retirement, which was actually pretty-much true. With no negative reviews in his employment file and only months before he'd be gone anyway, Felton gave him every crummy assignment that came along. Youngstown would be his last before starting his government pension.

The DOT allowed their field representatives a $40 per diem expense allowance to cover housing and food. Mort loved good food and drink, so would always stay in the cheapest accommodations he could find and make up the difference by treating himself to a nice meal every night. That's how Mort Samuels landed in Number 8 at the Starbrite Motel for the month of May 1987.

Unfortunately for Mort, the only restaurant in Youngstown was the Carolina Country Café, which barely met his lowest standards for breakfast or lunch, but certainly not for dinner. Rather than drive into Raleigh each night, he made the decision to buy a couple of fifths of his favorite bourbon, a handful of good cigars and three blocks of gourmet cheese along with some crackers. Having traveled for the DOT for years, he had amassed a large quantity of undated restaurant receipts, which he used to cover the costs of the 'out of scope' items. Instead of going out for an evening meal, he'd unwind from the day by sitting in his room listening to an FM classical music station on his portable radio and having a couple of cocktails while slowly enjoying a cigar and snacking on the cheese and crackers.

Slowly consuming two or three drinks over the course of three or four hours in the evening left him mellow, but certainly not drunk, so he would continue working on paperwork well into the night.

Mort's objective was to negotiate the land required for the U.S. 1 widening project. The DOT needed at least a sixty foot right-of-way in order to add a median strip, along with two twelve foot lanes and shoulders, which would create the new southbound portion of the highway. The current U.S. 1 would serve as the two northbound lanes and be completely repaved at the end of the project.

For Mort, negotiating the property deals in rural areas was fairly easy, since so much of it was farmland. Trimming the right-of-way off a large farm and paying the landowner was a cut and dry process in the majority of situations.

If a house or barn was in the direct path of the road or going to be too close to the new highway, than the deals got tougher and more expensive to make. In some cases, the structures could be lifted and moved further back on the property. This was a good option, especially for some of the beautiful old farm houses that had been owned by the same families for multiple generations.

To Mort's credit and that of the DOT, they were respectful of the numerous tiny family cemeteries that fell in the path of the highway and managed to skirt around them, protecting the final resting places with fences and markers.

The most complex negotiations began as Mort started meeting with property owners inside the Village of Youngstown itself. Knowing the emotional issues attached to the Free Will Evangelic Fundamentalist Church and its overall impact on the community, it was first on his list. He'd actually come into town in January to get it handled and a reasonable offer was made for the property. The cemetery was nearly 150 feet away from the path of the new road, so it wasn't going to be affected.

A final deal was struck with the Church Management Committee and approved by voice vote from the entire congregation. Land was purchased on West Holden Street, about a half-mile from the current location and ground was broken for the new church building. The money paid by the DOT easily covered the price of the new property and provided a 30% down payment on the new structure, but still left the congregation with a nearly $600,000 mortgage. Some in the congregation felt that the Pastor and Management Committee had lost their minds and were building a cathedral, rather than a country church, but with the steady growth in the area and the increasing number of folks coming to services and Sunday school, the majority of members approved of the project. Best of all, the timing was such that the current church building could be used until the new one was completed.

Prior receiving an offer from the DOT, Franklin paid for two appraisals on his property, one from a company in Raleigh and a second one from a firm in Henderson.

As he and Lisa were looking over the results, she said, "Is it OK if I call my dad and see what he thinks? He's relocated a bunch of employees over the years and may know somebody who has experience in things like this."

"That's a great idea, if you don't think he'd mind," Franklin said.

"He'll be happy to help. You know, he really does like you Franklin, even if you are sleeping with his daughter," she said smiling.

"Do you think it bothers him that we're living together?" Franklin asked.

"You do mean living in S-I-N!" she responded, again smiling. "Baby, there's nothing wrong in his eyes or anybody else's about how we live. We are a loving couple."

"How about you? Are you OK with how things are?" Franklin asked.

"I love you very much," she said, without really answering his question.

Mort Samuels, wearing his hard-nose game face, met with Franklin on the Wednesday of his first week at the Starbrite and presented an offer that was significantly less that the average of the two appraisals.

Lisa Ann called her daddy in Ottawa and told him all about it. He asked Lisa Ann to photocopy everything and send it to his associate at the Raleigh Nortel offices.

"He'll look it over on his own time and let us know what he thinks. He owes me a favor," Norman said.

A week later, Norman called their house, wanting to speak with Franklin.

"They're trying to low-ball you Franklin. Your appraisals prove that. My guy says that you should be able to push for them for another 15%, but recommends you ask for twenty."

Mr. B knew just about everything that ever went on at the Starbrite and had already come to realize that Mort Samuel's had a fondness for bourbon and cigars. The empty bottles tossed into the dumpster and the cigar butts had shown up on Mr. B's radar within the first week of his stay. After contacting a former associate in Washington, he also knew that the Youngstown project would be Mort's last one prior to retirement.

Mr. B gave Franklin a note suggesting that he meet with Mort on the last Thursday he was to be staying at the Starbrite and as late in the evening as possible. Though Franklin didn't quite understand why, but trusted Mr. B and scheduled the second negotiation for 8:00 that night. When Mort returned to his room at 6:00 for his usual unwinding time, he saw a bottle of ultra-premium bourbon and two Cuban cigars sitting at the door to his room.

"Thank you for being a valued guest of the Starbrite Motel! Wishing you safe travels," the card on the bottle said.

Without Franklin's knowledge or approval, Mr. B had taken it upon himself to drive to Raleigh and purchase the bourbon. The illegal cigars were sent to him by a friend in the State Department.

Armed for a hardcore negotiation, Franklin was pleased to see that Mort was in a happy, accommodating mood when they met in the motel office at eight that evening. Rather than threatening to play the eminent domain card, he spoke to Franklin like a long lost buddy. In the end, Mort upped the DOT offer by the full 20% Franklin had requested and tossed in a $2500 relocation allowance. Their agreement was reached and signed by 9:00 and Mort headed back to his room to enjoy more of the wonderful gifts he'd found earlier that evening. Even though accepting them was a direct violation of DOT written policy, Mort didn't much care since he'd be retiring as soon as he got back.

"Screw the policy!" he said to himself while opening the bottle, takin' in the aroma of the velvet smooth liquor before pouring a double and lighting up one of them fine stogies.

As a result of Mort's negotiations, the DOT agreed to pay Franklin $421,000 for the sixty-foot right of way, the Starbrite Motel and his two bedroom house. He could keep running the Starbrite until they were ready to bulldoze the property. The DOT would give him a month's notice prior to the time he'd have to vacate.

Even though Are Dee and Brenda had pushed back hard on the DOT's offer, in the end they were paid $164,000, or 5% less than the appraised value for their house and property. Like Franklin, they could stay in-place until the land was actually needed. Are Dee and

Brenda had met with Mort at 3:00 p.m. on the same day as Franklin, when he wasn't in nearly as friendly a mood.

(While what both of 'em received may not seem like a lot of money to you, keep in mind that we're dealing with 1987 dollars which today would be worth....well....a whole bunch more. Math was never my strong suit. Some may be thinking the same could be said about my writing, too.)

Mort Samuels returned to his office the following week to complete the last of his paperwork, clean-out his desk and enjoy a slice of 'Happy Retirement' cake with his co-workers. He also turned-in 28 days of expense receipts that each ran between $38.50 and $39.75, per diem. The accounting folks were always amazed about how he never went over the allotted amount.

As a retirement gift, his co-workers all pitched in and bought him a box of his favorite cigars. Mort and his wife were packed and headed to their new condo at Ft. Myers Beach before the first of June.

Dick Felton was actually very impressed with how well Mort had done with his final assignment and that only a handful of the negotiations would result in the DOT invoking the eminent domain law. He also felt that Mort had done a great job when comparing tax and appraised values to what was paid for all the properties, with one notable exception. Go figure.

With the deal finalized for the sale of the Starbrite Motel and payment to be received in July, Franklin and Lisa Ann began to seriously look for a new place to live. Since they had plenty of time to make their decision, Franklin's engineer mind kicked in and all their choices were analyzed thoroughly. More than a bit too thoroughly for Lisa Ann who felt that ultimately it should be Franklin's decision since the house would be his, paid for with the money coming from the Starbrite.

Franklin couldn't understand why she wasn't more engaged in the house-hunting process, given their relationship. It was on a Sunday afternoon when Lisa Ann had driven into Raleigh to do some shopping that he walked over to get some advice from Brenda, who knew immediately what was causing the problem.

"How long have you and Lisa Ann been together?" she asked Franklin, already knowing the answer.

"Two and a half years," Franklin said. "What's that got to do with this?"

Brenda looked at him like he had a third eye in the middle of his forehead.

"And how long have you two been living together?" Brenda asked.

"About a year-and-a half," Franklin responded.

"What kind of commitment have you made to Lisa Ann?" Brenda asked him.

"What do you mean? She knows I'm committed to her," Franklin responded.

"I swear, you'd think I was talkin' to Robert Dee or Richard Lee," Brenda said. "Let me ask you the way Lisa Ann's daddy might, what are your intentions regarding that sweet young lady, Franklin?"

"I want to marry her."   ,

"Dear Lord, give me the patience to deal with this man!" Brenda said, looking toward the ceiling. "That's wonderful, but don't you think that maybe you should ask her if she'd like to marry you?"

"Sure, when the time is right," Franklin said.

"And when will the time be right, after bein' together for two and a half years and wantin' her to buy a new house with you? Franklin, it's time for you to buy Lisa Ann a ring and ask her if she wants to be your wife. How can she be excited about building a future with you, when you can't manage to make a lifelong commitment to her? Do you need me to spell it out more clearly for you?"

"No ma'am," he said. "I understand what you're gettin' at."

"Good," Brenda said, "I was afraid I'd have to start drawing you a diagram."

"I already asked her daddy for his blessing when her parents were here in April," Franklin confessed.

"And what did he say?"

"He gave me the green light," Franklin responded.

Shaking her head in amazement, Brenda said, "Franklin, please promise me that you won't say 'green light' when you discuss this with Lisa Ann. That was two months ago and you still haven't asked her?"

"I haven't found the right opportunity," he said.

"Find it, Franklin and find it soon," Brenda said.

"Yes, ma'am."

Once Lisa Ann had returned home, Franklin asked her, "How many vacation days do you have left?"

"I don't know, probably seven or eight. Why?" she asked.

"I think we should go somewhere special," Franklin responded.

"We've already told my parents that we'd fly to Ottawa in August, where else do you want to go?"

"Someplace just for us, someplace romantic," he said.

"I thought we were looking for a new house," Lisa Ann responded.

"That can wait."

"Ok, where do you want to go?" she asked, just a bit confused by Franklin's sudden change in direction.

"Where's the most romantic place you can think of?" he asked.

Lisa Ann paused for a minute and then smiled. "I loved the cabin at Linville. It was wonderful."

"You're right! It was a special place," Franklin said, also smiling. "Let me call 'em and see what dates are available. Are you OK with that?"

"Sure. What's up, Franklin?" Lisa Ann asked, just a bit skeptical.

"Does something have to be up for a guy to want a romantic weekend with the girl he loves?"

"I guess not," she said, "but this is kind of out of the blue, especially for you."

Franklin called to cabin's owners and found that it was available for the second weekend in July. He and Lisa Ann both scheduled Friday and Monday as vacation days, repeating their long weekend from the previous November.

Getting some more advice from Brenda, Franklin skipped the chain jewelry stores and visited a family-owned business in downtown Raleigh, picking out a classically styled engagement ring with a square, Princess-cut diamond.

Showing it to Brenda a few days later, she said, "You did real good, Franklin. Real good!"

Lisa Ann thought that Franklin was behaving a bit odd, but wrote it off to all that was going on with the sale of the Starbrite and having to find a new place to live after spending most of his life in the two bedroom house that he'd soon have to leave. The decision do go to the mountains for a long weekend didn't make much sense to her, but she still thought it would be a nice get-away.

Unfortunately, Mother Nature was intent on messing up Franklin's plans. The first tropical storm of the season hit on Friday, coming up from the Gulf of Mexico right through the Appalachian Mountains of North Carolina. The storm extended the travel time to Linville to nearly six hours. Driving on slick mountain roads in the pouring rain, with the windshield wipers flapping had made Lisa Ann slightly carsick, too. Once they got to the cabin itself, they were both drenched bringing their coolers and luggage inside. Unlike their fall visit, it was hot and muggy even at the higher altitude and the cabin didn't have air conditioning. To make matters worse, the power went out just before nine that night.

Deciding that their best option would be to sleep in the cabin's screen porch and get some cooler air, they moved the mattress and bedding out there. The steady rain tapping on the metal roof, the flashes of lightening and sound of distant thunder along with the flickering candlelight transformed an otherwise disastrous day into the romantic night that Franklin had originally hoped for.

"This is wonderful," Lisa Ann said. "If we ever get rich, will you buy this cabin for me?"

"Just for you?" Franklin asked.

"Yup, and if you play your cards right, I might let you come here, too," she said smiling.

"I'd be honored, Miz Lisa Ann."

"So tell me the truth, why the get-away weekend in the middle of everything else that's going on?" she asked.

"I've got something on my mind. Something that I need to talk to you about," he said.

Concerned, Lisa Ann said, "I thought we could talk about anything at home. It must be serious for us to need to come all the way up here."

"About as serious as things can get," Franklin said.

"Are you OK? You're not sick or anything?" she asked.

"I'm fine, at least for someone in my position," Franklin said.

"What position is that?"

Reaching under his pillow and pulling out the small box containing her engagement ring, Franklin looked at Lisa Ann in the candlelight and said, "The position of asking you if you'd marry me. Will you be my wife?"

Lisa Ann instantly started crying, but managed to nod her head up and down anyway. Finally she said, "Yes."

It rained all through the night and well into Saturday morning. When they woke up sometime after eight, Lisa Ann looked down at the ring she was wearing on her left hand, confirming that she hadn't dreamt Franklin's proposal.

"Can we stay here forever?" she asked Franklin.

"Just until Monday morning," he said.

"If you buy us this cabin, we could make love out here anytime we wanted," she said.

"If we moved up here, how would we make a living?"

"Do you always have to think like an engineer?"

"Not always," Franklin said, reaching over to kiss his fiancée and hold her in his arms.

When they got back to Youngstown late on Monday afternoon, the first person they planned to tell about their engagement was Brenda, who was beside herself with happiness. Are Dee also happened to be home at the time.

"What a blessing! We'll need to throw a big party to celebrate! Any idea when you'll have the wedding?" she asked.

Looking at each other, Franklin and Lisa Ann realized that they hadn't quite thought that far ahead and started laughing.

"Given how long Lisa Ann's put up with you already, I recommend getting' the knot tied pretty quick before she changes her mind," Are Dee said to Franklin.

"No chance of that. He's stuck with me," Lisa Ann said just before she kissed Franklin.

Calling her parents in Ottawa that evening, Phyllis said, "I'm hardly surprised, but absolutely delighted and so happy for you, Lisa!"

"You know that Franklin asked me for our blessing when we were there in April," Norman told Lisa Ann. "I wondered what was taking him so long to pop the question."

"He was just waiting for the right romantic moment to sweep me off my feet," Lisa Ann said smiling, "and he succeeded!"

Franklin and Lisa Ann eventually decided to have the wedding after they got the question of where they'd live resolved.

There was no question that Mort Samuels negotiations in Youngstown had caused a bunch of folks to start lookin' for new places to live.

Are Dee and Brenda bought a nice piece of land on the North Carolina side of Lake Gaston and hired a contractor to start building 'em a cozy three bedroom home and boathouse. With his knee bothering him every time it got damp outside and Marcus doing such a fine job, Are Dee planned to retire in the spring, but had yet to tell the Village Council. He wanted to make sure that everything was properly lined-up so's Marcus would be named as his replacement. While he had no doubts about Officer Cooper's abilities, he was still only 27 years old, which would make him the youngest Police Chief in the state. Are Dee also planned to recommend hiring two additional officers and getting them fully trained before he left the department.

Franklin had notified all the Starbrite tenants that he planned to keep the motel open until the DOT gave their final thirty day notice to vacate. He figured that they'd have until at least April or May before he'd have to close the Starbrite for good.

Robert Dee and Richard Lee had decided to ride things out at the motel until the end, since they could still stay there for just $30 per week. Taking a wait and see attitude, they figured they could always rent another trailer together, if need be.

In August, an acre plot of land on the southwest side of Youngstown, just off Rogers Street, came on the market. Spending a Sunday afternoon walking every inch of the property and discussing what kind of house they'd build and where they'd place it on the land, Franklin said, "We'd be stuck with makin' the commute into Raleigh every day. With Brenda and Are Dee moving up to Lake Gaston, things will be a bunch different, too."

"You don't think they'll want to come down to see their grandkids every couple of days?" Lisa Ann said.

"Whose kids are we talkin' about?" he asked.

"Whose do you think?! When the time comes, I want to raise our family in Youngstown," Lisa Ann said. "Are you good with that?"

"Better than good. Have I told you how much I love you today?" Franklin asked.

"Just today?" she asked, "I was hoping that you loved me every day."

When Franklin purchased the property, he deeded it in both of their names, wanting to make sure that Lisa Ann understood that they were partners in everything going forward. Hiring a local builder, they finalized the blueprints and broke ground in October for a two-story, 2500 square foot home with an oversized garage. With three bedrooms and a small room off the master that could be used as an office or a nursery, they were ready to start the next phase of their lives.

The builder promised that the home would be ready before the end of April.

Chapter 15 – Faith Culver

After extending an invitation to Robert Dee for Sunday supper, Faith Culver returned home to tell her momma and daddy about their upcoming guest for later that evening.

Vince and Norma Culver were salt-of-the earth folks, but two of the most conservative people to ever live in Youngstown. After they'd moved to town in 1970 for Vince's job as a foreman for the Wake Forest-Youngstown Electrical Co-Op, they attended the Free Will Evangelic Fundamentalist Church for several months before finding it too liberal for their tastes. So, twice a week they drove down to Wake Forest on Wednesday nights and Sunday mornings to worship at the Central Carolina Orthodox Christian Tabernacle, the most straight-laced, no drinkin', no smokin' nor foolin' around, take-the-Bible-literally church 'most anywhere.

Vince was one of those guys you could easily pick out in a crowd of a hundred men. Still wearing the flattop hairstyle he'd sported since the mid-50's and standing at just over six feet tall, he was hard to miss.

Most folks would tell you that Norma was where Faith got her beautiful looks. Now in her late forties, she had the face of a much younger woman and could have easily passed for Faith's older sister. With the same dark hair and eyes as her daughter, she was a beautiful lady.

Faith was the eldest of their two children, with her brother Eric just two years behind her. When her parents found out about her takin' a job as Robert Dee and Richard Lee's housekeeper, they insisted that the boys give her a key to the trailer so's she could do the cleaning when they was at work, or more specifically, not in the same place at the same time as their daughter.

After graduating from Youngstown High School in 1985, she enrolled in nearby Lewiston College and made the thirty-mile commute daily, since her folks weren't comfortable with her living on a co-ed campus. Faith had been allowed to date starting during her junior year of high school. A beautiful, petite girl, with deep brown eyes and long, dark hair she had more than her share of boys who wanted to take her out, but only of a few of 'em ever made it through her parent's screening process.

Since she had been old enough to understand about the birds and the bees, her parents had made it absolutely clear that 'good girls saved themselves for their husbands' and that any premarital fooling around was a sin that would result in eternal damnation. While she didn't completely agree, she did respect her folks and made a commitment to be pure and chaste until her wedding night, regardless of the temptation.

As part of her momma and daddy's screening of her dates, each boy had to come to their house and properly meet Faith's family, giving her parents the opportunity to reject any feller that was deemed unacceptable for their daughter. Robert Dee Camber already had at least two major strikes against him before he ever got to the Culver's door.

In a small community like Youngstown, where everybody knows everybody else's business, the Camber boys had both earned a reputation for having wild times with wild women on Saturday nights and showing up for church on Sundays, most often severely hung-over. Richard Lee was the worst of the two and Robert Dee didn't fall far behind his younger brother. But, since starting Camber Brothers Lawn and Landscaping a year earlier, both of 'em had settled down a whole bunch.

The second strike came in the form of Are Dee. While still a deputy on the Quincy County Sheriff's Department, he'd had the audacity to ticket Vince Culver for driving fifteen miles per hour over the posted speed limit. Vince was headed south on U.S. 1, running late for a Wednesday night Bible Study class that he was supposed to be leading. Feeling that he was doing the Lord's work, not unlike a priest rushing to give somebody the Last Rites, Vince pleaded not guilty and the case came up before the Youngstown Magistrate about six weeks later.

Hearing both sides of the story, the Magistrate's gavel came down with the words "guilty as charged," and gave Vince his choice of paying a $25 fine or serving ten days in the county jail. Weighing the option of becoming a religious martyr versus using up a week's worth of vacation time to serve his sentence, he reluctantly paid the fine. Vowing to never forgive Are Dee Camber, he overlooked that part of his nightly prayers about "forgive us our trespasses, as we forgive those who have trespassed against us."

When Robert Dee showed up at the Culver's front door at six that Sunday evening with one of his momma's fine pecan pies in hand, he was already swimming seriously upstream. Vince was grudgingly polite but cold as ice toward Robert Dee. Norma was only slightly warmer and more pleasant.

After finishing supper and offering to help with the dishes, Vince had hoped Robert Dee would leave and the issue would be closed. Instead, Faith invited him to sit down in the living room with her parents.

Looking over at Robert, Vince said, "I've heard that your lawn mowing business is going pretty good."

"We're about eighteen months in and the lawn maintenance part has grown to the point that we've got three crews. The landscaping design piece has expanded beyond what we'd ever expected. We've really been blessed."

"A simple 'yes' or 'no' would have been all you needed to say," Vince said. "Are you boys still staying at your cousin's 'sin bin' motel?" Vince asked.

"I don't know what you mean about sinnin' there, but yes, we're both living at the Starbrite to keep our expenses down," Robert Dee said.

"I hear tell that he's been rentin' to two whores," Vince said.

"Vincent, please!" Norma said to her husband.

"Mr. Culver, my cousin Franklin is as good a man as I know and is a devout Christian. I'm not familiar with the women you're speakin' about, but I can assure you that there's no activities of that nature goin' on at his motel," Robert Dee responded.

"If your cousin is such a devout Christian, then why's he and his girlfriend livin' together outside of wedlock?" Vince asked.

"Vincent Culver, that's more than enough," Norma said to her husband, "besides, Faith has something for all of us to hear."

"I thought I might read from the Bible this evening," Faith started. "I want to start with Matthew 18, verses 21 and 22. *Then Peter came to Jesus and asked, 'Lord, how many times shall I forgive my brother when he sins against me? Up to seven times?' Jesus answered, I tell you, not seven times, but seventy-seven times."* In Luke 6:37, it says, *"Do not judge, and you will not be judged. Do not condemn, and you will not be condemned. Forgive and you will be forgiven."* And in John 8:7 it says *"When they kept on questioning him, he straightened up and said to them, If any one of you is without sin, let him be the first to throw a stone,"* Faith ended.

"That was lovely, dear," Norma said to Faith.

"Momma and Daddy, Robert Dee would like to take me out on a date. Are you both OK with that?" she asked, handing her Bible to her daddy and looking straight at him.

"I guess so," he reluctantly responded, looking down at the book he was holding in his hands, "As long as no alcohol is involved and you get home at a decent hour."

"Thank you, Daddy," she said.

"Would next Saturday night suit you, Faith?" Robert Dee asked politely.

"That would be perfect," she responded.

For their first date, Robert Dee brought Faith to a quiet Italian restaurant in Raleigh. Sitting across the table from each other, he found himself unable to break contact with the beautiful set of deep brown eyes that were looking back at him. He listened intently to every word she spoke. He was truly taken by her intelligence and good humor, but it was her warm smile and gentle laugh that he found to be the most attractive. Faith was different from any other girl he'd ever spent time with, and she was quickly drawing him in like a hummingbird to a flower.

Getting her back home by 9:30 that night, he ended their evening by walking her to her parent's front door where she gave him a sweet kiss on the cheek.

"Can we do this again?" he asked.

Faith gave him another kiss on the cheek and said, "I was hoping you'd ask that."

After their third date, Faith asked Robert Dee to go to church with her family the next day and he agreed. In exchange, her momma asked him to have Sunday supper with them, where Vince treated him entirely different than the first time he'd been over. In spite of their original misgivings, the Culver's were pleased with how respectful Robert Dee was to their daughter and the entire family.

The following weekend, Faith attended the Youngstown Free Will Evangelic Fundamentalist Church with the Camber family. At Sunday supper, Brenda and Are Dee were amazed and delighted by their son's new girlfriend. Faith especially hit it off with Lisa Ann, who was close to her in age.

After they'd left, Brenda looked at Are Dee and said, "Who was the man who brought that precious girl to our table? I know he looked like Robert Dee, but he surely didn't act like our son."

Are Dee agreed. "Did you see how he was lookin' at her all evening? My guess is that the boy's finally growed up and wants to be with a good woman like his momma."

Later that evening, when Robert Dee took Faith home from supper with his parents, he asked if it was OK to kiss her. When he did, the electric spark between the two of them jumped like an arc welder. It was when he kissed her for the second time that her daddy turned-on the porch light, but it still didn't dampen the moment.

Before she went inside, she whispered, "I love you Robert." And he whispered the same back to her.

Treading more cautiously than he ever had with any other girl, Robert Dee continued taking Faith out for dates on Saturday nights all through September and October, usually accepting his now regular invitation from her parents to attend church with their family on Sunday morning.

Richard Lee couldn't, for the life of him, understand how Robert Dee could be so interested in a girl who he'd never slept with, but knew that this was a tender subject with his older brother, so just let it be.

In early November, after leaving a movie, they started some serious kissing in Robert Dee's truck. He knew they were heading into uncharted territory so he was going extra slow and cautiously.

Faith looked at him, smiled that wonderful smile of hers and said, "You think maybe we should go to your room?"

Hearing those same words from any other girl he'd ever dated, Robert Dee would have burned half the tread off his tires to get to the Starbrite. But Faith was different from any of them others, sweeter, more innocent and most certainly the one who had completely stolen his heart.

Knowing everything about Faith and the Culver family that he knew, and considering how Satan himself was testing them both that night, he looked at her and said, "I love and respect you so much, Faith. As much as I want to, I can't take you there until we're married. Would you marry me?"

She said, "I will, Robert, I will."

After considering all their options and their pressing desire to get married as soon as possible, the pair decided to elope two days later.

The two of them went to church with Faith's parents on Sunday and Robert Dee had Sunday supper at her parent's house. After getting back on Sunday night, Robert Dee told his brother that he wouldn't be at work until Thursday and that Richard Lee would have to cover for him. When he pressed his older brother for the reason why,

Robert Dee said that for once in their lives he just couldn't tell him what was going on.

On Monday, Faith skipped her classes at Lewiston College and met Robert Dee at the mall, where they purchased wedding rings. After having lunch, they drove to the Wake County Courthouse in Raleigh, got their marriage license and were hitched on the spot by a Justice of the Peace. From there, they checked in at the downtown Holiday Inn and consummated their marriage before calling Faith's momma to break the news.

When Vince Culver heard about their elopement, he hit the roof and initially wanted to call out the FBI to arrest Robert Dee and charge him with _anything!_ It was Norma who calmed him down and brought some reason to the man.

"Faith told me that she'd kept her promise to us," she said. "She waited until she found a good Christian man and now they're married. She's 21 and there ain't nothing we can do except welcome him into the family. Besides that, I really like Robert Dee and think he'll make a wonderful son-in-law."

Thinking over his options and realizing that he had none, Vince threw in the towel saying, "You're right. I can live with it all as long as Faith don't join that heathen church where the Cambers go."

Vince was way too proud to ever fess-up that he could have been wrong in judging somebody. The truth was that he actually liked Robert Dee and thought that deep down, he was a good man.

And that's how Faith Camber came to live at the Starbrite Motel in late October 1987.

Once Brenda found out about Robert Dee and Faith, and even though she was upset that two of her kids were now married and that she hadn't gotten to attend either of their weddings, she decided to be the peacemaker for the family and invited everyone to their house for supper on Wednesday night.

Brenda and Are Dee were both more than pleased that one of their boys had married such a nice girl and was finally settling down. They could not have welcomed Faith into the Camber family more warmly. The same went for Richard Lee, Franklin and Lisa Ann.

Are Dee looked at his oldest son and said, "I am proud of you Robert Dee! You found yourself a girl who you can build a future with. Now, there's no pressure from me, but your momma does want a grandbaby or two so's that she can properly spoil 'em."

While that first gathering was a little strained, Are Dee helped soothe the situation by greeting Vince with a big smile and apologizing for writing him a ticket back 1981. Vince admitted that he should have gotten over it long ago, as the two men shook hands.

Brenda and Norma hit it off pretty good too, having known each other in passing with both of 'em living in Youngstown.

While Vince still didn't approve of Franklin and Lisa Ann's living arrangement, he figured that it wasn't much of his business after all, since they was actually pretty nice folks, once he got to know 'em.

Whether the Cambers and Culvers wanted to admit it or not, both families were cut from the same bolt of Southern cloth, sharing similar values and traditions. More than anything, both sets of parents wanted their children to have a strong marriage and a happy life together.

As a special treat, Brenda had arranged for an international long distance phone call to Uruguay, so's that Robert Dee could tell his little sister about marrying Faith. With her momma begging her, Patrice agreed that she and her husband, Alejandro, would come home for Christmas so that the Cambers could finally meet their son-in-law and everybody could be together for the holiday.

It was after spending their first night in Number 9 at the Starbrite that Robert Dee realized a single room in the old motel would never do for his new bride. That weekend they began looking for a home where they could really start their life together.

A week before Christmas, they made a down-payment on a house in a new subdivision in Wake Forest. Faith's parents gave them $1000 wedding gift to use toward the home and offered to continue paying for her classes at Lewiston College, where she'd graduate in the spring. Hearing about the Culver's generosity, Are Dee felt an overwhelming desire to one-up Vince, so he and Brenda gave the kids $2000 toward the house.

Enjoying an egg nog together at a combined family gathering, Vince asked Are Dee, "Now that we're all family, tell me the truth, was you always planning to give 'em that big gift?"

Had Vince not been smiling when he asked the question, Are Dee might have answered different.

"Probably not," he said with a big laugh, "but they sure picked a fine house to raise a family and I kinda figured we was both makin' a contribution towards our future grandkids. I can't think of a better investment, can you? You think we outta call a truce?"

"Before or after we both go broke?" Vince said, also laughing.

Chapter 16 – Jack Esterhouse

Jackson Esterhouse was the son of a Detroit auto executive and grew up in Grosse Pointe, Michigan. He earned an MBA from Harvard in 1956 and sought out a growing industry where he could invest some of his family's money. With the surge of post-war consumer product manufacturing, he figured that electrical switching devices for factories was a good place to start. Just days after graduation and with the help of his daddy, he purchased Raleigh Electrical Products, a marginally successful operation that held several underutilized patents. Under Jack's leadership, Esterhouse Electrical Manufacturing expanded rapidly both through organic growth and acquisition.

Jack believed that Esterhouse Manufacturing should be the marketplace innovator and to that end created a Research and Development Department that was the envy of the industry. He encouraged his engineers to file new patents on the Esterhouse products they were creating and made sure they were well rewarded when one was issued. Because the engineers worked on Jack's timeclock, Esterhouse Electrical was always a co-owner of the patents.

Jack also believed strongly in recruiting the best and brightest people he could find and his Personnel Department was constantly on the lookout for college graduates with good potential. That's how Franklin Delworth landed at Esterhouse shortly after earning a degree in Electrical Engineering from NC State in the spring of 1982. What made Franklin especially standout to the Esterhouse recruiter was that he already had a patent pending for a micro-switch that he'd developed during his senior year of college.

After spending a year learning all he could about Esterhouse manufacturing processes and working on an assembly line, Franklin was promoted to the R&D Department and was the youngest engineer in that group. It was during a meeting in the Executive Boardroom in 1984 where he met Lisa Ann Prescott for the first time.

Over the years, Jack Esterhouse had earned the nickname "Take it Back Jack" among his employees, since virtually everything he promised them came with fine-print disclaimers that easily allowed him to back out of raises, benefit improvements or just about anything else. As a result, Jack had some serious credibility issues with the people he depended on most to help grow Esterhouse Electrical Manufacturing.

With rising production costs and increased competition from Asia, Jack was looking for ways to keep Esterhouse growing. That's what prompted his first meeting with Dong Long Woo, a Chinese industrialist, in late 1985. After over six months of negotiating, the decision was made to start shifting a portion of Esterhouse product production to China, beginning in early 1987. The move caused considerable concern among Esterhouse workers at the Raleigh plant. So much so that Jack held three employee meetings, one for each production shift, talking with his assembly line workers and assuring them that their jobs were secure.

"We are committed to building the best electrical switching apparatus in the world right here in Raleigh, North Carolina," he said. "Our China expansion will only involve legacy products, where competition is toughest. All new products will continue to be built here, all research and development will continue at this facility and we anticipate little to no reduction in staffing."

It was the last part of Take It Back Jack's last sentence that didn't set so well with 'Team Esterhouse' and caused panic meters to go off all over the plant. After seeing several of his best engineers jump ship for other companies, he invited the entire R&D department to have lunch with him in the Executive Boardroom, so that he could plug some of the leaks.

"I want to congratulate Franklin Delworth on his first patent while here at Esterhouse. In keeping with our company policy, Franklin will receive a $1,000 bonus and a point-two-percent royalty on each new switch of his that we sell. Let's give him a big hand."

During the meeting, Jack also recognized the outstanding work of four other engineers with bonuses and heaps of praise.

None of the people in the room were fools and the smell of Take It Back Jack B.S. was running strong in the air, especially during the question and answer portion of the meeting.

"Mr. Esterhouse, you've gone to great lengths to assure us that our jobs are secure and I know I speak for the others in this room when I say how much that's appreciated," said a company veteran.

There was tepid applause after he said it.

"But, we hear a lot of rumblings from the folks working on the assembly line about their jobs shifting to China. With the number of observers coming here from Woo Industries, you can understand how they feel. Can you clarify your position on the Manufacturing Division?"

"That's a good question and a very reasonable concern. It's also part of why I brought you all in here today," Jack said. "The globalization of our industry has required some rethinking on the part of virtually company leader in our category. New partnerships, that wouldn't have been considered even two or three years ago, are being formed to keep companies like ours in a strong, competitive position."

"At four o'clock Eastern time this afternoon, Mr. Woo and I will announce the merger of our two companies into Woo-Esterhouse Manufacturing. The merger is subject to Federal Trade Commission approval and is planned for the first quarter of next year."

There was dead silence in the room.

"As I've said from the beginning of our relationship with Woo Industries Limited, we plan only to move the production of legacy products abroad. By forming this strategic partnership, we will open up the growing Chinese market to our products, lower manufacturing costs and steer our ship into the best trade winds in our history," he said, just as proud as a peacock.

What Jack didn't say about the merger and strategic partnership was that Woo Industries was actually buying a 70% stake in his company, resulting in nearly twenty-million dollars going straight into his bank account. Since Woo-Esterhouse would technically be a new company, all of the items made in the U.S. could be classified as legacy products and therefore subject to being moved to Chinese plants. Yet another Take It Back Jack half-truth had been spoken!

"We can't make this happen without a strong commitment from every member of the R&D team. As an incentive and to better cement our relationship with all of you, each R&D team member will be gifted 500 shares of stock in the new company, which will be fully vested at the end of five years. If we meet our goals for new growth, those shares could be worth as much as a fifty-thousand dollars for each of you."

One of the other itsy-bitsy details that Jack didn't share with his team was the fine print attached to the deal that included each engineer signing a two year non-compete agreement and that leaving the company for any reason, getting fired, laid-off or quitting, would result in a 100% forfeiture of their stock, prior to vesting. It wasn't long before the folks in R&D department were referring to the incentive as Take It Back Jack's Golden Handcuffs.

True to his reputation, Jack Esterhouse kept his word for a while. There were no production layoffs during the balance of 1986 and the first half of 1987. There were no new hires, either. Looking at Personnel records going back to the start of his company, he knew that about 11% of his production workforce would leave on their own in any given year. He'd already reduced his assembly line workers by almost 9% by the time the merger took effect. If he played things out as planned, he'd achieve the desired 40% reduction in the Raleigh workforce by 1990, without ever laying-off a soul or paying out a nickel in separation benefits.

Jack's personal life closely mirrored his business life. At age 53, he was currently on this third marriage, his personal fortune saved by the 12-page prenuptial agreement each of his wives signed prior to walking down the aisle. It was rumored that Take It Back Jack even had disclaimers placed in his actual wedding vows.

Part of the merger included an innovative "worker exchange program." Select Esterhouse employees from Raleigh were recruited to visit the Woo plant in Beijing to better understand their methods and culture. The reciprocal arrangement worked great, with most employees visiting only for a week or two. Some of the engineering and senior management staff visited for up to a month.

Lisa Ann had been working for a group of Esterhouse vice presidents for over three years. She regularly filled-in for Jack's administrative assistant when she was sick or on vacation, so she was certainly no stranger to Mr. Esterhouse.

In early March of 1988 she was called into his office. Joining them was the V.P. of Personnel and Linda McCrery, Jack's executive secretary. Given the people who were present, Lisa immediately thought she was about to be fired.

"Sit down and relax, Lisa. You look scared half to death," Jack said in a fatherly manner. "We've got good news for you."

In spite of Franklin's misgivings, Lisa had always liked Mr. Esterhouse, so immediately felt at ease by what he'd said.

"We've got a truly unique opportunity for you. That's why we're all here. As you know, we've had great success with the worker exchange program. It's helped bridge many of the cultural gaps between our company and Woo Industries. As part of that program, I'm planning to spend about half my time in Beijing over the next two years and Dong Woo will be doing the same here. I'll need an administrative assistant while I'm in China. With Linda's children in elementary school, she isn't able to accept the assignment, but she very strongly recommended you for the job."

Bill Kingsford, the VP of Personnel took over. "We looked over your employment file and saw that you have an Associate's degree. Since Jack will be spending the second and fourth quarters of this year and the first and third quarters of 1989 in China, we felt there might be an opportunity for you to study over there when you weren't working. At Jack's request, Mr. Woo personally contacted the University of Beijing and they have agreed to accept you as student during your non-working time. At the end of the assignment, you'd come home with a Bachelor's degree and a terrific opportunity to advance your career at Woo-Esterhouse. If you accept the position, we'll not only continue your current salary and cover all your housing expenses, but we'll also pay for your educational costs."

It was Linda McCrery who spoke next, "Lisa, I know that you and Franklin are engaged and there is nothing that any of us want to do to disrupt your personal life, but if you could delay your plans for two years, we can provide you with a once-in-a lifetime opportunity."

"Wow," Lisa Ann said, "that's a lot to take-in. I certainly want to talk to Franklin about it before I can give you an answer. Is there any chance that he could go, too?"

Bill Kingsford looked over at Jack for direction.

"Lisa, we're going to be downsizing the R&D department later this year. The announcement won't be made until May or June. I want you to know that anyone impacted by the change will be given a very generous outplacement package," Jack said.

"Is Franklin going to be laid-off?" she asked.

213

"No," Jack said, "he's an extremely valuable asset to our team and his job is secure."

What Take It Back Jack didn't say was that most of the layoffs would impact the highest-paid, senior level engineers, making for a substantial reduction in payroll costs and shifting the increased workload to younger people who would be less apt to push-back.

Lisa let out a sigh of relief.

"But with the reduced staffing, it's critical that he stay here in Raleigh," he added.

Jack got up from behind his desk and moved to the empty chair next Lisa Ann, "This is a big decision for you and we can all appreciate the position we've put you in. That said, we're going to need an answer, one way or the other, by Friday."

"That soon?" she asked.

"I'm afraid so," Jack answered. "I want you to take the rest of the day off. Linda has already offered to cover for you. Go home, clear your head and think things through. Opportunities like this don't happen very often."

"Thank you, Mr. Esterhouse," Lisa Ann said, "I'll give you an answer by Friday morning."

Without giving Franklin any details, Lisa Ann called his extension to tell him that she was leaving early and that she'd see him later that evening. As she drove home to Youngstown, she kept looking down at her engagement ring and wondering how Franklin would react to the offer.

Instead of going inside the house, she walked over and knocked on Brenda's door.

"My gracious! What's wrong?" Brenda said, seeing her at the door. "You look pale as a ghost."

Over a glass of wine, Lisa Ann shared the whole story with Brenda, who reached across the table to hold on to her hand and give the kind of maternal comfort that Phyllis had never been able to offer.

"They've sure put you between a rock and a hard place," Brenda said. "My guess is that Franklin will be mad as all get-out about that part. You asked for my opinion. If I say that you should go to China and Franklin was to ever find out, he'd never forgive me. Besides, I don't know if that's the right decision. If I say that you should stay, you may lose your job and you'll certainly lose a chance that other folks would kill for. So what you need to do is search your heart for the right answer. Do what's in your heart, Lisa Ann. Even if it's the wrong decision, it will be the right one for you."

Giving Brenda a big hug as she left, Lisa Ann looked down at her watch and saw that it was 5:30. Since Franklin would be home in less than an hour, she called the new Youngstown Pizzeria and ordered a delivery.

When Franklin came in, he knew immediately that something was wrong. Lisa Ann walked over, gave him a quick kiss and then just rested her head on his shoulder, holding his body tightly to hers.

"Do you want to tell me what's goin' on?" he asked.

"Can I just hold you for a while longer first?"

Over a beer and the pizza, she shared all the details of her conversation earlier that day with Jack Esterhouse and the others.

"This all sounds like another classic Take It Back Jack deal. While you may get part of what's promised, I can guarantee you won't get everything they outlined. If you do, you'll be the first," Franklin said. "Do you know what you're gonna do?"

"The only thing I know for sure is that I don't want us to be apart for two days, let alone two years," she said.

"Lisa Ann, whatever you decide, we can work through it," he said. "It won't be easy, but as much as we love each other...." His voice trailed off.

"What do you think I should do, Franklin?"

"Do you want the Selfish Me to answer or the Understanding Me? The Selfish Me would tell you that our plans are already set. The new house will be ready in a few of weeks, then we've got to start thinking about the wedding."

"And what would the Understanding Franklin say?" she asked.

"He'd say that he loves you with all his heart and that if this is truly a once-in-a lifetime opportunity and it's what you want, then you should go for it. He'll be at our new house waiting for you."

"Franklin, I don't know what I should do! Help me decide!"

"No, Lisa Ann. You've got to decide what's best for you and we'll deal with whatever else happens. I love you and don't want you to go, but I won't try to stop you if your heart says you should do it."

Chapter 17 – Some of the Others

With the folks I've written about in several of these chapters, you probably got the impression that the Starbrite rented largely to crazy people or criminals. But that really isn't an accurate picture. I thought you should know about some of the other folks who lived there while Franklin was running things.

Before Inita Mann and Fonda Dix came to the Starbrite, the Pender family lived in Number 1 and 2 for eight months while waiting for their house to be rebuilt after a fire gutted it. With the sorry amount their insurance company paid them for living expenses, the motel was all they could afford, but it was a safe place for them to stay while they tried to pull their lives back together.

Mr. and Mrs. Pender lived in Number 1 and their two kids stayed next door in Number 2. For the first time in many years, a Quincy County School District bus stopped at the Starbrite, taking the Pender young'uns to Youngstown Elementary. To help keep all the members of the Pender household together, Franklin bent his rule regarding pets so that their dog, Mollie, could be with the family, as long as she left Star alone.

Mr. Collins began living in Number 4, next door to Lashaya Bryan beginning in the late fall of 1983. Like Lashaya, he had been referred to Franklin by Reverend Carter and was a member of the Youngstown AME Church. Unlike Lashaya, Mr. Collins was a quiet, pleasant person who was perfectly content with what the Starbrite offered. He was certainly one of Franklin and Mr. B's favorite tenants.

Mr. Collins had been drafted in 1942 and trained at Fort Bragg before shipping out to Europe during World War II. With the Army still segregated in those days, he was assigned to a transportation unit and spent most of the war driving trucks from supply depots to the front lines and wounded soldiers back from there to field hospitals. While he didn't talk much about the war, Franklin knew that he'd been wounded in action and had received a Purple Heart.

Having grown up near Youngstown, Mr. Collins returned there after the war. With his experience driving trucks, he was hired as a bus driver and worked for the Quincy County School District from 1946 until he retired after 37 years to live off his savings and Social Security. So far as Franklin knew, he'd never been married, though there were rumors that he was quite the ladies' man back in the day. While he was working, he lived in a small shotgun house, east of the C&O Railroad tracks, that he rented by the month.

Wanting to reduce his expenses, he sold his furniture and moved into the Starbrite not long after Franklin began renting by the week. Franklin would see him every Saturday, when he paid his rent, and on Sunday mornings when he drove his '62 Chevy to church.

With the exception of a roof leak, he never complained about anything during his stay at the Starbrite and often provided help in calming down Lashaya when she tried raisin' hell. Franklin had always hoped that the two of them would become a couple, even though he liked Mr. Collins a bunch.

It was Mr. B who probably knew him best and certainly considered him to be a friend. Together, they'd drive down to the branch library in Wake Forest and exchange books every week. Mr. Collins was a dedicated history buff who, when asked, could tell you just about anything you'd ever want to know relating to U.S. history, from the time of the Indians to the current day. On the few occasions when he and Franklin got into discussions, he was amazed by Mr. Collin's wealth of knowledge.

"He should have been a teacher," Franklin told Lisa Ann after one such conversation.

Mr. Collins was one of the last tenants to leave the Starbrite. He'd gotten his old Chevy tuned up, put on new tires and brakes, packed up his belongings and handed his key to Franklin.

"Where are you headed to?" Franklin asked.

"I 'spect the time has come for this old man to see more of the country that I've been readin' about all these years. I'm gonna start by drivin' U.S. 1 north until it ends and then turn around and go south all the way to Key West," he said with a big grin. "When I get done with that, I'm gonna drive west and follow Route 66 from Chicago to California. This is a mighty big country and there's a lot of history to see."

"How about that!" Franklin said, shaking Mr. Collins hand. "It sure has been a pleasure getting' to know you, sir."

"The pleasure has been all mine, Mr. Delworth," he said before closing his car door and turning north on U.S. 1, toward Henderson.

Cal Jenkins was a Vietnam War veteran who had never been able to adjust back to civilian life after his discharge from the Army in 1969. With the help of a disability check, he was able to live in Number 7 at the Starbrite for twenty months, from January of '84 until August of '86. That was the longest he'd stayed anywhere since getting out of the service. Some of the tenants complained when he woke up in the night, screaming, but most knew his situation and let him be.

From time to time he'd get a job, but none of 'em ever seemed to stick for one reason or another. He liked the Starbrite, since it wasn't but a 40 minute drive to the VA Hospital in Durham where he went every week or two. He and Mr. B seemed to be kindred souls, sometimes just sitting together outside Cal's room and listening to him talk about the things that were troubling his mind.

On a hot, humid Saturday afternoon in the middle of August, he walked over to the office and handed Franklin the key to his room, leaving without sayin' a word to anybody as to where he was headed. A week later, his sister called the Starbrite to check on him, since he'd missed his regular appointment at the VA Hospital.

Franklin told her about how he'd left, and she didn't seem surprised in the least.

Elva Beasley lived in Number 8 at the Starbrite from November 1983 through March of 1987. She and her husband had farmed 160 acres north of Youngstown for the better part of fifty years.

When he passed away, Elva's kids convinced her to sell the property and move into town. She'd have probably lived in an apartment or small house, but neither were available that fall. Having been friends of Eustace and Willa Mae, Elva felt good about staying at the Starbrite for a month or two, until she could find someplace that better fit her needs. The longer she stayed the more she liked being able to get out and walk to church or to the IGA. She also appreciated that Franklin checked-up on her every few days. He even allowed her to install a telephone in her room, so's that she could speak to her kids and grandkids.

When a one bedroom house on Maple Street came up for rent, Elva went over and looked at it. Deciding that she didn't want to have a lawn to care for and given the number of noisy kids in the neighborhood, she stayed put at the Starbrite.

It was only after she fell and broke her hip that she had to move into a nursing home. She only lasted another three months after that.

Folks at the Starbrite who knew and loved that kindly old lady attended her funeral. Her children were amazed by all the friends she'd made during her three-and-a half years of living in Number 8.

Irene Morgan taught first grade at Youngstown Elementary School and lived in Number 10 from the fall of 1986 through the end of 1987. That was the room that Eddie Franchetti had used briefly. Irene was in her 50's and had never been married. Living on a teacher's salary, she'd always shared apartments or houses with roommates, but decided to try having a place just to herself for a while.

After over a year at the Starbrite, she realized she'd made a mistake and moved back in with a woman she'd shared a house with for five years. As it turned out, they were a couple, but even back then folks generally didn't discuss that stuff in Youngstown, since it wasn't none of their business.

Lashaya Bryan's daughter and son-in-law drove over from Greensboro a few weeks before the Starbrite closed, helped her pack her things and took her home to live with them in a basement apartment of their house that they'd had built just for her. Franklin had bet that Reverend Carter had laid some serious guilt on her daughter for all that to happen.

Sitting in the back seat of her daughter's car as they headed out, Lashaya rolled down her window.

"Slumlord!" she hollered to Franklin.

He just smiled back at her.

"I really need to pray for Lashaya's daughter," he said to Lisa Ann. "Often," he added.

You already know how Marcus Cooper came to live in Number 6 starting in March of 1984. What you don't know is that he continued to stay for four years and was one of the last tenants to leave.

Marcus became yet another member of the Cambers extended family. He was a regular at Brenda's supper table and often had an off-duty beer with Franklin. Are Dee may have been the Police Chief in Youngstown and Marcus' boss, but their relationship went much deeper. Are Dee was his mentor, teacher and a substitute daddy to him. To the depths of his soul, Marcus was committed to never let down Are Dee and to always have his back.

Marcus even took a bullet for him when they were responding to a domestic dispute on the east side of Youngstown in the summer of 1986. Breaking up a fight between a husband and wife, the woman pulled a gun to shoot her husband. Marcus could see that Are Dee was in the line of fire and knocked him out of danger, taking a grazing wound to his own shoulder. In all likelihood he saved Are Dee's life that night. Marcus never even thought twice about it.

During the closed-door portion of the December 1987 Village Council Meeting, Are Dee announced that he'd be retiring in March. Making his recommendations to the Council about promoting Marcus and hiring two additional officers to support him, Are Dee had gone to great lengths to have all the facts and figures that supported his plan to expand the department so's they could meet the continuing growth of the village.

He also detailed the performance of Officer Cooper, including his military record, the achievements he'd made on the Youngstown Police Department and how he'd taken classes with the Highway Patrol to further his law enforcement training. What surprised Are Dee was the silence in the room after he went over everything. Looking around the table at men he'd known all his life, he asked, "What's botherin' you? His age?"

Nobody in the room said a word. Then it hit him like a ton of bricks as looked into the eyes of each of the seven white Council members.

"I think I understand now," Are Dee said. "Boys, I've served this community since 1957, between my time on the Sheriff's Department and as your Police Chief. Up until tonight I've always been proud to be part of Youngstown."

"All y'all go to church every Sunday, saying all the right words, claiming that y'all changed with the times, pretending that things are different than they used to be, but they're still just the same, ain't they? Tell me that's not what this is all about?!" You could have heard a pin drop in the room.

He pulled the badge off his uniform and slid it across the table to Mayor Weber.

"You can take that badge and shove it, 'cause I don't ever want to be associated with none of you's, ever again."

As he pushed back his chair to leave, Mayor Weber said, "Before anybody makes a decision that that's not in the best interests of the citizens we all represent, can we take a vote on Are Dee's recommendations? Are Dee, can you please step outside?"

Looking at his friend of well over thirty years, Mayor Weber quietly said, "Please just give us five minutes. Please."

While Are Dee was standing outside the Village Hall, he debated whether or not he even wanted to hear the outcome of the vote. He didn't have long to wait, as Mayor Weber asked him to come back in.

"Are Dee, on a four-to-three vote the Village Council has accepted your retirement plan as well as your recommendation that Marcus Cooper replace you as Chief of Police, with the stipulation that you stay on the job until the end of March to see that the transition is properly implemented."

Lookin' around the room, he found the three Council members that couldn't make eye contact with him. He knew and so did they.

Takin' back his badge, all he said was, "I'll do my part."

Marcus never knew about what went on that night, only that the Village Council had accepted Are Dee's recommendations and that he was going to be the new Police Chief in Youngstown. Are Dee never spoke a word of any of it to Brenda or anybody else, neither.

On Thursday, March 31st, 1988, Are Dee handed his badge to Marcus and gave him the kind of hug that a proud daddy gives their son.

"It's all yours now, Chief," he said to Marcus.

Marcus probably would have said something back, but the huge lump in his throat stopped him. He moved out of the Starbrite the next week, not wanting to be the last one to go.

Mr. B had left the previous Saturday, handing Franklin a note saying there was no point in having a maintenance man when the motel was about to be torn down. Franklin couldn't argue with his logic.

Mr. B had lived at the Starbrite for over four years. With the exception of his first month, he'd traded his services as a handyman for his rent. It had been an arrangement that benefited both him and Franklin.

No matter what the problem, no matter what time of the day or night, the Starbrite tenants knew that Mr. B was the man who could unclog the drain, patch the roof or breathe life back into a dead air conditioner.

In all that time, Franklin felt like he had barely gotten to know him. Sure, they'd meet every Saturday and Mr. B would give him a list of everything that had broken and gotten fixed, Franklin would pay him back for any materials and they often had a beer together, but beyond that there was hardly much of a relationship. It's tough having a heart-to-heart conversation with someone who chooses to be mute. One thing was for sure, Mr. B always had Franklin's best interests at heart and he appreciated that.

Like some of the other Starbrite folks, Mr. B had attended Brenda and Are Dee's Thanksgiving dinners. Franklin would see him sitting in a pew at the back of the Free Will Evangelic Fundamentalist Church on Christmas Eve or Easter Sunday, but he otherwise didn't attend the regular services. Are Dee said it right, some people just want to be left to deal with their own stuff.

Almost from the start of his time at the Starbrite, Franklin observed that Mr. B was quite a night-owl, keeping the light on in his room until two or three in the morning and tapping out Morse code messages to all points on the compass or maybe just to a few lonely folks like himself.

After Mr. B had packed up his belongings and loaded them into his Pinto, he came into the office to wave good-bye.

"There's no way that I can adequately thank you for keeping this old place together, Mr. B. You gave it your all every week and I'm very grateful. I don't know where your travels will take you next, but I hope this helps in getting you there," Franklin said, handing him a Hallmark envelope.

Mr. B opened it up and found a beautiful thank-you card signed by Franklin and Lisa Ann along with a pre-paid VISA card in the amount of $500.

"Thank you, Franklin," Mr. B said.

"You are very welcome," Franklin responded and shook his hand. Much to his surprise, Mr. B gave him a hug before walking out the office door.

Star the cat was sitting on the hood of Mr. B's Pinto when he came out to the parking lot. Star knew that something was up, when he'd seen Mr. B packing his stuff and loading it into the car.

Mr. B made one small motion of his hand and then opened the car door, inviting Star to come along with him. Star never hesitated for a second and shot in, going straight to his regular spot on the passenger's seat.

With a small puff of blue smoke, they pulled the Pinto out of the Starbrite parking lot and headed south on U.S. 1, toward Raleigh and unknown points beyond.

On the back of his room key, he'd placed a small piece of paper with the words "left you something in my room."

Intrigued, Franklin walked down to Number 12 and opened the door. On the bed were two white boxes each containing a seven-inch reel of audio recording tape. Written on the first box were the letters WH, followed by OO and RMN 6/18/72. The second box had the same series of letters, but was dated a day later. Are Dee was sitting on his front porch when Franklin walked over with the two boxes of tape in his hand.

"What do you make of the coding on these boxes?" he asked as he handed them to Are Dee.

Are Dee studied the boxes for nearly a minute before bustin' out in a big smile.

"White House, Oval Office, Richard M. Nixon," he said. "The Watergate break-in happened on June 17th of '72. Who do we know who owns a reel to reel tape recorder?" he asked.

Some folks invest in stocks, Franklin Delworth invested in people. By converting the Starbrite Motel into weekly rentals, whether by intention or otherwise, he created a place where folks who needed a cheap place to live could stay, be safe and be accepted. It didn't matter what issues they had, nobody made judgements about them at the Starbrite.

People may say that it was an island for misfits, but they'd be dead wrong. It was a quiet spot by the side of U.S. 1 for folks to rest and regroup on their journey through life. No doubt, the road was rougher for some than for others, but that didn't matter near so much when they were guests at the Starbrite Motel.

Chapter 18 – April 7, 1988

Brenda had driven her car the short distance over to the Starbrite and had parked in front of Franklin's house. She turned off the motor, opened the trunk and sat there quietly.

"I feel like the executioner's assistant," she had told Are Dee earlier. "I should have never agreed to take Lisa Ann out to the airport. I just hope Franklin understands."

"He does, Brenda. I talked with him last night and he agreed with Lisa Ann that it would be better for 'em both to say their good-bye's here instead in front of a bunch of strangers. You just need to pay attention to the road and not start blubbering," Are Dee said.

"The hearts of two people who I love dearly are achin' and there's not a danged thing we can do about it."

"She'll only be gone for two years, it's not like they're breakin' up. They'll write and talk by phone. How does that old saying go, 'absence makes the heart grow fonder.' They'll get through this, if it's meant to be."

"There's another old saying, 'out of sight, out of mind.' I only hope that isn't what happens," Brenda said.

As she sat in the car and waited for Lisa Ann, she could hear every tick of her watch.

"I wanted to be here with you when they tear down the motel. Will you be alright?" Lisa Ann asked.

"I think so," Franklin answered. "It'll be like going to Eustace's funeral, burying a loved one. I stayed at the cemetery until they covered him up with dirt. I 'spect this will be a lot the same."

Lisa Ann started to cry, "I really wanted to be with you, Franklin. I am so sorry. Will you try to call me when it's over?"

Franklin didn't answer her question.

"Brenda's out front. You know we've got to leave soon," Lisa Ann said. She reached down and pulled the engagement ring off her left hand, holding in her right hand for a few seconds before she pressed it into the palm of Franklin's hand.

"Why?" was all he could ask.

"If you still feel the same way about us when I get back, I'll put it back on and wear if for the rest of my life, I swear. But if you feel differently while I'm gone, I can't....I won't hold you back," she said with tears flowing down her cheeks.

"Do you think you mean so little to me that I wouldn't wait for you?" Franklin shook his head sadly. "Or is it that you want to be free of me? You need to look me in the eye and tell me the truth, Lisa Ann. We owe the truth to each other."

"I love you, Franklin. I always will. Don't you ever doubt that for a second," she said as she kissed him.

"I love you, too," he said, holdin' on to her tight until she had to break away.

"The time will go quickly," she said, trying to be positive, "and we'll have the rest of our lives together."

"You don't have to go," he said.

When she turned to walk out the door, he followed behind her carrying her two suitcases. She got in the passenger seat of Brenda's car as he closed the trunk.

"Lisa Ann, are you alright?" she asked.

Lisa Ann shook her head from side to side, crying. "Go, please," she said, "go now."

As Brenda pulled out on to U.S. 1, Franklin just stood there watching her drive south toward Raleigh and the airport. Seeing Brenda leave, Are Dee walked over to Franklin's house and let himself in.

"You want to talk, son? I'm a pretty good listener," Are Dee said to Franklin.

Franklin turned away so that Are Dee wouldn't see that he was crying.

At the Raleigh-Durham airport, Lisa Ann boarded the Global Airways flight that would take her to Atlanta, where she'd change planes and fly to Los Angles. From there, she'd take an international flight on to Beijing. It would be a twenty-seven hour trip.

Sitting alone in a row of three seats, near the middle of the plane, Lisa Ann leaned against the window, thinking for the two-hundredth time that morning that she was making the biggest mistake of her life. The previous night with Franklin had been sleepless for her. Cuddled together in their usual spooning position, she could hear his rhythmic breathing and wondered if they'd ever spend another night together.

"This is where I belong," she told herself over and over, yet the opportunity Jack Esterhouse had created for her was something that she couldn't ignore. In the end, she'd justified her decision to accept based on it only being only for two years. She was angry at herself for bending to the temptation and risking everything that she and Franklin had built together and the happiness that had changed her in a thousand different, better ways. Lost in her thoughts, she was reminded to fasten her seat belt. The plane was about to land in Atlanta.

With a nudge from Brenda, Richard Lee came over to the house to check on Franklin early that afternoon. He was making the best small talk he could, given the circumstances.

"So tomorrow's the big day," he said. "They're really gonna knock it down?"

"That's the plan," Franklin responded. "I've got another week before movers come. The new house will be ready by then. They're goin' use this as a temporary field office for a couple of months before it goes, too."

Struggling to think of something else to say to Franklin, he asked, "Did you remember to dig up the time capsule?"

Franklin tried to focus on the question.

As kids they'd made a time capsule in the summer of 1971 when they were both twelve. They'd included a copy of the Quincy County Weekly Tribune, a cassette tape with music and a newscast they'd recorded off the radio, a half-dozen of their duplicate baseball cards and a letter to whoever opened the time capsule telling 'em about who had made it. The original plan was to bury the capsule until the year 2000, but when they showed the wooden box to Uncle Eustace, he said that moisture would seep inside and ruin the contents. He had a better idea of where the time capsule should go, where it would be safe and dry, he told Franklin.

"It never got put in the ground. I'd gotten food poisoning from some bad egg salad at the church picnic and was sick in bed. Uncle Eustace said he'd take care of puttin' it in a safe place for us," Franklin said.

"Do you remember where?" Richard Lee asked.

"I remember that he told me at the time, but I was so sick I guess I've forgotten," Franklin said.

"Maybe somebody will find in the year 2000, even if it isn't us."

"Maybe so," said Franklin.

When Lisa Ann got to the gate for her Los Angles flight, she was surprised to find that she'd been upgraded to First Class.

"Row 8," the Gate Agent said, "Seat B on the aisle, just ahead of the bulkhead that separates Coach from First Class."

When she got there, she was amazed to see Jack Esterhouse already enjoying a pre-flight cocktail and seated next to her by the window.

"Since the trip is so long, I thought you'd be more comfortable up here," he said. "On the leg to Beijing, we'll be in Business Class," he added as she sat down. "Relax," he said, "we've still got 26 hours to go."

Lisa Ann's former roommate, Marie McKay was one of the eight attendants on the ATL to LAX early afternoon flight and was working the rear Coach Section of the plane. Scanning the passenger manifest, she saw a name that looked familiar.

"There are a lot of Prescott's, Lisa A, in the world," she thought to herself, "and the one I know probably wouldn't be flying First Class." None-the-less, she planned to walk up and see, once they were in-flight and things slowed down some.

At the suggestion of Mr. Esterhouse, "Call me Jack," he said, Lisa Ann ordered a Bloody Mary and settled back into the comfortable First Class seat. A lunch was served an hour into the flight, but Lisa Ann had no appetite and barely touched her food.

"Take your time," Jack said to himself, "there's no need to hurry."

When the flight attendant came by two hours into their journey, Jack ordered his fourth drink.

"Make it a double," he said, his voice having gotten progressively louder with the last two cocktails.

They were a little more than half-way to Los Angles, when Jack leaned over to Lisa Ann. "We probably should talk about the arrangements once we get to Beijing," he said. "As you know, things are a lot different over there. Your apartment is located in the same building as mine, just one floor down," he explained.

Lisa Ann was barely listening.

"We'll be working very closely together during the quarters of the year when I'm in China. Day and night; intimately," he said, loud enough that the people in 7A and 7B heard him.

"Exactly what do you mean, Mr. Esterhouse?" she asked, more than a little concerned by his last sentence.

"Please, it's Jack from now on, except when we're in the office. Chinese executives have much different relationships with their administrative assistants than do their U.S. counterparts. When a Chinese executive is working on a major project, it's often for 24 hours a day. His administrative assistant is expected to be available to him. Over there, it's not at all uncommon for them to travel together, often sharing the same hotel suite. When the chemistry is right, sometimes there's even a physical relationship as well as a business one, helping the executive to relieve stress and helping his assistant to grow her career. It's all just part of the package."

"And they think that's acceptable?" she asked.

"Things are different over there, Lisa. That's why I choose you for this assignment. With your beauty and intelligence, I thought you'd adjust well to the new circumstances and opportunities and be ready for a significant promotion once you get back to the states."

"Are you saying that you expect me to be your mistress as well as your administrative assistant?" she asked.

"That's a harsh way to put it. I'm just saying that we'll both need to adjust to the new culture and standards. I thought you'd understood how things would be from the get-go."

"Mr. Esterhouse, are you familiar with the term 'quid pro quo sexual harassment' and the legal consequences attached to it?"

"Did you study law during your stint in secretarial school?" he asked sarcastically.

Jack didn't realize it, but between his growing anger and intoxication, the level of his voice had gotten even louder.

"If you're threatening me, I wish you luck. We'll be in China and you won't have a godd*mned leg to stand on. Grow up Lisa! This is how business is conducted, here or there. Give it a chance, you may find me a far more enjoyable fu*k than that backwoods hick you've been dating. A more mature man like myself can please you in ways you've never dreamed of and pave a career path for you all the way to the top."

After lunch had been served in Coach, Marie had walked up to First Class to see if the Lisa Prescott in seat 8B was indeed her friend. Unfastening the curtain that separated the two sections, so that she could go through, she'd not only recognized her former roommate's voice but also overheard more than enough of the conversation between Jack and Lisa to know that her friend needed some support.

Coming through to First Class and leaning over the back of Lisa Ann's seat, Marie said, "If you need a witness, I'll be glad to testify against this dirt-bag," She it said loudly enough for Jack and several other passengers to hear her.

"Why don't you go mind your own fuc*ing business!" Jack snarled loudly at Marie.

The lady seated directly in front of Lisa Ann in seat 7B stood up almost immediately and stepped into the aisle.

"I'm Ehuang Chin, Director of the Sino-American Trading Alliance," she said as she handed Lisa Ann one of her business cards. "I want to assure you that what this disgusting pig has described is not, in any way, how executives in my country treat their assistants. I have a daughter who is about your age, young lady," she said as she looked daggers at Jack, "and I also would be willing to serve as a witness on your behalf." Focusing directly on him, she added, "Your behavior is disgraceful, sir. Shame on you! Shame!"

Several of the other First Class passengers, having heard the drama playing out, applauded Miz Chin after she finished deriding Jack.

"Lisa there's plenty of empty seats in Coach, if you'd like to move back," Marie said.

As Lisa Ann was getting up to move to another seat, she tossed her second untouched Bloody Mary directly into Jack's lap.

"Sorry, Jack. That must be a result of a cultural difference," she said

The head flight attendant saw and heard most of what had happened. She approached Jack and said, "Mr. Esterhouse, I'm going to notify the captain of your unacceptable behavior. If we have any more problems with you, Airport Security will be waiting the moment we land in Los Angles."

"Esterhouse?" Ms. Chin asked. "You're the Jack Esterhouse of Woo-Esterhouse?"

Jack nodded his head up and down.

"Dong Long Woo is one of the founding members of our alliance. He is a man who sets a strong example for treating his employees with courtesy and respect. I'm sure he'll be quite interested in what I've observed. I shall call him the moment I get to Beijing tomorrow."

I've always heard that you meet some real fine people when you fly in First Class. With the exception of Jack, that was certainly the case on the ATL to LAX flight. The head flight attendant could tell you for sure, since she asked each one 'em what they'd seen and heard. She even got their names and phone numbers to give to Lisa Ann before she left the plane. Wasn't that nice of her?

Franklin tried to sleep that night, but it was impossible without Lisa Ann next to him. He wanted to reach over and cuddle up to her, but he figured that she was halfway to China by then. After trying to sleep for over two hours, he finally turned on the lights and went out into the living room. Sitting alone, he slowly replayed his life at the Starbrite from age four to the present. Like the engineer he was, he methodically organized his memories, going through them one year at a time, briefly reliving the good and bad moments in his life, occasionally slipping into thoughts of the past three years with Lisa Ann. It was sometime after 3:00 a.m., when he was going through 1971, that he remembered where Uncle Eustace had placed the time capsule. After thinking about it, he threw on some clothes, grabbed a flashlight and walked over to the Starbrite.

The electricity had been turned off a few days earlier. The furniture had been removed and donated. Even the plumbing fixtures had been taken out, all in preparation for the bulldozer that would arrive that morning to level the motel. With all the doors unlocked, he walked into Number 1, a dark, empty room, lit up only by his flashlight.

"What on God's green earth are you doin' out here in the middle of the night?" Are Dee asked, standing in his pajamas and slippers, scaring the daylights out of Franklin.

"I could ask you the same question," he said.

"I couldn't sleep worth a darn, just thinking about them knocking down this old place and doing the same to our house in a couple of weeks. I was sittin' out on the front porch when I saw your lights come on a couple of hours ago. I was thinking about coming over, but figured you might need some space. When you came out, I decided to walk over. So what are you doing out here?"

"It's crazy. This afternoon, Richard Lee asked me about a time capsule he and I made when we were kids. I'd been sick at the time and couldn't remember where Uncle Eustace had put it. Then it dawned on me tonight. He was installing the new dropped ceilings in each room. He told me he'd put it up there. I just can't remember which room, so I figured I'd start with Number 1."

"Since neither of us is gonna get any sleep tonight, let's get a pole and start knocking out ceiling panels," Are Dee said.

Franklin went back to his house and retrieved an old rake.

"Is that the best you've got?" Are Dee asked.

"It's the one Mr. B used on the parking lot. Everything else is packed up for the move."

"It'll have to do," Are Dee said. "You want to do the pokin' or the flashlight holdin'?"

Slowly, they moved from room to room, knocking out ceiling panels and finding a few interesting things along the way. Number 2 yielded nothing but dust. In Number 3, they discovered that someone had hidden several recent copies of Penthouse magazine in the ceiling.

"Richard Lee's old room," Franklin said.

"Now, there's a surprise," Are Dee responded.

When they got to Number 5, Lashaya Bryan's former room, and pushed up a ceiling panel, at least a dozen empty wine bottles rained down on the concrete floor, shattering when they hit.

"Lashaya lived here for nearly 5 years," Franklin said. "I never once saw her bring in a bottle of wine. And I sure never saw her dispose of any empties."

"There's a reason, Mr. Genius Engineer," said Are Dee laughing so hard he could barely catch his breath. "She was stuffin' 'em up your

236

ceiling. Lord, it's a wonder that it didn't collapse with all that weight and kill her!"

Are Dee and Franklin both started laughing hard. Moving carefully to avoid all the broken glass, it took 'em about five more minutes to move the rest of the panels, with the same thing happening when they pushed up on each one.

While they was still working in Lashaya's old room, Marcus pulled up in his cruiser with the blue lights rotating.

Getting out, with the spotlight pointed into Number 5, he said, "I got a complaint about two drunks bustin' windows and carryin' on. Now that I see the situation, I got to ask both of you if you've been drinking."

"Go about your business Officer Cooper. I've got this situation under control," Are Dee said, still laughing.

"Are Dee, I have to respectfully remind you that you're now retired and that I'm the Chief of Police in Youngstown, so you can't order me around like that anymore," Marcus said. "Besides, you're not in uniform," he added, looking at Are Dee's pajamas.

"Excuse me, Officer Cooper?! May I remind you who hired you in the first place and who went to the Village Council to recommend that you get promoted upon my retirement?"

"We all know that you did, Are Dee and I am forever grateful. Now quit giving me a hard time and tell me what's goin' on."

After Franklin explained what had just occurred in Number 5, Marcus started laughing nearly as hard as they had.

"I lived next door to that nasty old woman all that time and could never understand how she could keep singin' the same hymn over and over for hours. At least I know now. As a respectful request, could the two of you try to behave yourselves for the rest of the night so that I don't get any more complaints?"

237

"You ain't going to stay while we go through the rest of the rooms?" Are Dee asked. "We may find Jimmy Hoffa."

"No can do. I've got a town to keep safe," Marcus said flashing his teeth with a big grin.

"By the way, who called in the complaint?" Are Dee asked.

"Brenda."

"Figures," Are Dee said.

By the time they were done with Number 8, both Are Dee and Franklin were wearing down. It was nearly 4:00 in the morning and neither of them had gotten any sleep that night.

"Look, there's only four more rooms to go. There's 'bout enough moonlight left that I can take Number 9 and 10. You take the flashlight and rake and go through 11 and 12. I'll grab one of these panels to poke-up the ceiling tiles in the other rooms. It shouldn't take us more than another ten or fifteen minutes," Franklin said to Are Dee.

"Good idea," said Are Dee as he headed into Number 11.

The only thing Franklin found in Number 9 was an unopened package of Twinkies. From the 29-cent price tag, he figured they'd been there since the ceiling was installed. He took them over to show to Are Dee who was just finishing with Number 11.

"Dang if they don't still look edible," he said. "I'll give you a dollar to take a bite out one of 'um."

"I'll give you five, if you do it," said Franklin.

"See how you are, trying to kill me off before I ever get to live in my new house."

Heading back into Number 10, Franklin poked up a ceiling panel near the center of the room.

"Are Dee, come here," he said, just loud enough for him to hear.

"No need, Franklin. I just found the time capsule."

"Bring the flashlight and rake. I really need you to come now."

Figuring that Franklin had seen a snake or a rat, Are Dee came right over, carrying the time capsule. What had dropped to the floor of Number 10 was a large quantity of bundles; twenty, fifty and hundred dollar bills. Neither Franklin nor Are Dee could believe their eyes.

Seeing all that money, Are Dee let out a low, slow whistle.

"Lordy, Lordy, Franklin Delworth what have you just found? Take the rake and let's drop the rest of them panels."

"Are Dee, there must be over a hundred thousand dollars here!"

"I'd say a whole bunch more than that. Go grab a couple of trash bags. We'll take the money to your house and see what we're dealing with."

Are Dee asked Franklin to close the curtains, so that nobody could see inside. While Franklin brewed a pot of strong coffee, Are Dee went home and quickly got dressed. He was surprised to find that Brenda was taking a shower, but didn't stay long enough to ask why she was up so early.

"I did a quick estimate," Franklin said. "I think there's someplace close to seven hundred thousand dollars here. Do you think it's real?"

"Are you askin' me if we're hallucinating or if the money is counterfeit, Franklin?"

"Either. Both."

"Based on the stacks I've looked at, the money is real enough and we're both stone sober, so far as I know," Are Dee said. "You do realize that Number 10 was where that Franchetti guy stayed."

"I know that, but I also remember Aunt Willa Mae telling me that someday I'd find a pot of gold that she and Eustace had left for me. I always thought she was kidding. Now, I'm not so sure."

"Franklin, I don't know as I ever told you the full story, but Eddie Franchetti worked for the New Jersey mob. The Camden police said that the word on the street was that he'd stole a large sum of money and was hiding out here when we arrested him for drunk driving. His uncle came down and bailed him out of the Quincy County Jail a couple of days after we nailed him."

"Once they headed back north, Franchetti was never seen again. The uncle said that they stopped for gas and Eddie asked to use the men's room. His uncle said that Eddie never came back to the car and that he couldn't find him. The FBI figured that he never made it even as far as the gas station. People in the mob don't take too kindly to folks stealing from them, especially when they're kin. The best guess is that he's at the bottom of Chesapeake Bay."

"Marcus and me had searched the room and confiscated his stuff as possible evidence. I don't recollect that either of us checked the drop ceiling. That was sloppy work on our part."

"So, whose money is it?"

"Let's assume that Willa Mae and Eustace saved all their lives and like a lot of folks who lived through the Great Depression, didn't have much trust in banks. Where would they have kept their money safe?"

"Probably not in the ceiling of Number 10," Franklin said. "Maybe in the crawl space under the house, but not where a renter could get at it."

"Now that I'm retired, there's no conflict of interest for giving you legal advice."

"Would that ever have stopped you before?"

"No, but work with me for a minute. If you was to go flashing around this kind of cash, word will get out and who knows what contacts may have been made with those folks in New Jersey, even these years later. If you deposit more than $10,000 cash in a bank, they're obligated to ask you where it come from and report it to the Feds."

"Are you sayin' I should keep the cash?"

"Let's think this through. Do you remember how big the mortgage is on the new church building?"

"It is $595,000. It about scared the pastor to death when the Board signed the papers."

"So what do you think would happen if a box were to show up with the exact amount of money to pay-off the mortgage and with a note from an anonymous donor asking that no one ever be told about where it come from?"

"The pastor would deposit the money at the bank and they'd have to report it?"

"Churches aren't subject to the same rules as private citizens. The preacher could walk into the bank with cash, pay off the mortgage and nobody could question where it come from. That's assuming you don't want to keep it?"

"I wouldn't feel right about keepin' it, given that it may have been stolen, even if it was from a bunch of gangsters."

"Another option would be for you to drive up to New Jersey and return it to them fellers, assuming it's theirs."

"That's not gonna happen," Franklin said. "What about what's left over after the mortgage gets paid off?"

"You could slowly deposit into a few banks, say three or four thousand dollars at a time and do some good for yourself with the money. No matter what you decide to do, you know I'll help you as best I can."

Franklin picked up several stacks of hundred dollar bills and pushed 'em over to Are Dee. "If you're going to live on Lake Gaston, we're gonna to need a good bass boat."

"Franklin, you just handed me enough money to dang near buy a yacht."

"I'm gonna grab an empty movin' box. You willin' to lend me a hand counting out $595,000 and sneaking it into the church?"

"Legally, that would make me an accomplice," Are Dee said.

"How about that?!" Franklin said proudly.

"I'll bring my truck around."

By 7:00 that morning, their work had been completed and the money delivered. Franklin had scooped up the left-over cash and placed it in three empty shoe boxes that he stored at the bottom of his closet.

"I figure we ought to walk across the street and get us a steak and eggs breakfast. I'll even buy," Are Dee said.

The new pastor of the just-completed Youngstown Free Will Evangelic Fundamentalist Church arrived at his office at 8:30 that morning, wanting to work on his sermon for the building dedication coming up on Sunday. Having recently graduated from his two-years of training at the Free Will Evangelic Fundamentalist Seminary in Asheboro and taking his first assignment after becoming ordained, he needed some inspiration for the upcoming service.

As he walked into the sanctuary for a moment of prayer and quiet contemplation, he saw a cardboard box sitting at the pulpit. Thinking that one of the construction workers had left it there, he decided to check it out. Much to his surprise, he found a white piece of paper attached to the top of the box, with his name, Pastor Xavier Carlyle on it.

Dear Pastor Carlyle,

I have been a member of this congregation for many years and have carried this sin in my heart for that entire time.

When I was a child, my family was dirt poor. So poor that my parents couldn't afford Christmas presents for none of us kids. I was six the first time we attended Christmas Eve services. With the church lit only by candlelight, when the collection plate came by, I reached in and stole a quarter. Even at that age, I knew I was doin' wrong, but Satan and the desire for a sack full of candy had overtook me.

I felt so guilty about stealing from the Baby Jesus and so sickened by my own greed and so afraid for my eternal soul that I tossed the quarter in the creek on Christmas morning. I promised Jesus that someday, I'd fully atone for my sin. Today is that day.

Inside this box, you'll find enough money to pay-off the mortgage on the church building, so that our congregation will never have to worry about it again and I"ll know that what I've earned throughout my life will be used for the glory of God.

All I ask is that no one is ever told about where or why my donation was made. I am certain you'll honor my request. I can now go to my grave knowing that I made things right with the Lord.

A humble servant of Christ

Are Dee had carefully penned the note, figuring correctly that new preacher would never recognize his handwriting. Franklin read it before they taped the page to the box and was duly impressed.

"Where did you come up with that idea?" he asked.

"When you've heard as many confessions as I have, it's not hard to find an excuse for almost anything," Are Dee said.

The note most certainly changed the needed inspiration for the preacher's upcoming Sunday sermon.

Franklin and Are Dee had no more than finished their breakfast and walked back across U.S. 1 when a large truck with a trailered bulldozer showed up and unloaded in the Starbrite parking lot.

"It'll be OK, Franklin," Are Dee said, patting him on the shoulder.

Once the bulldozer started, the noise was so loud you could hardly hear yourself think. Wall by wall, the Starbrite was slowly being knocked down. It was darned near overwhelming for poor Franklin. A bunch of Youngstown neighbors had come over to see the building being demolished. Brenda walked over from her house and joined Are Dee, Robert Dee, Faith and Richard Lee, all of 'em standing near Franklin to offer their support.

The only thing that distracted Franklin was seeing Brenda looking over her shoulder at her house. He figured that was because it would soon suffer the same fate as the Starbrite.

While he was watching Number 4 being flattened, Lisa Ann walked up beside him.

"Can I have my ring back now?" she yelled, trying to be heard above all the noise, getting his attention.

Franklin nearly fainted. He grabbed ahold of Lisa Ann and wouldn't let go until she started pushing him back, trying to get some wind back into her lungs.

With Brenda holding on to Are Dee and dabbing her eyes, Lisa Ann led Franklin over to his house, where they could hear each other.

"Before I ever got to Los Angles, I realized that I was heading in the wrong direction. It's a long story, but I'm pretty sure I cost us both our jobs. You were absolutely right about that a**hole, Jack Esterhouse! Anyway, I took the red-eye back to Atlanta and called Brenda from there. She picked me up at the Raleigh airport this morning. There's this Youngstown hayseed who I can't get out of my head. I love you so much," she said as she started to cry, "I'm sorry for all I put you through, Franklin, but you're stuck with me now!"

"Forever?" asked Franklin.

"Yup, forever, maybe even longer," Lisa Ann said. "To Hell with Beijing and Jack Esterhouse!" she added.

"Fu*k 'em!" Franklin said.

"Franklin!" Lisa Ann said. "Such language!"

Chapter 19 – The Aftermath

As you probably already figured, Jack had Lisa Ann fired immediately.

Since Franklin was still employed at Woo-Esterhouse, at least for the time being, she begged him to stay clear of the poop-storm and asked her daddy to help instead. A week later, Norman and Phyllis both flew down to assist their daughter. Norman wanted to personally beat Jack Esterhouse to death with a piece of lead pipe and Phyllis was more than willing to help him. Instead, the Prescott's opened their checkbook and the hired Thornton Girard, one of the toughest and most respected attorneys in Raleigh, who quickly deposed both Marie McKay and Ehuang Chin under oath and took statements from a bunch of the other folks who were flying in First Class that day.

He presented the evidence of Jack's naughty behavior to the Woo-Esterhouse legal eagles as well as Take-It-Back's personal attorney, at a meeting held in the Executive Boardroom and informed them of his intent to file a very public, million dollar lawsuit that afternoon if they didn't offer up a reasonable settlement for Lisa Ann by the end of the meeting.

Jack's attorney claimed that since his client was intoxicated at the time, the quid pro quo sexual harassment claim wouldn't hold water. Thornton let out a good laugh when he heard that nonsense.

"You can tell that crap to a jury or the TV news crew that's settin' up in front of your building and see if anyone is gullible enough to actually believe it," Mr. Girard said. "Either way, Woo-Esterhouse gets tagged for having an individual like Jack as your President of U.S. Operations. In 30 minutes, I'm either gonna walk out of here with a deal in my hands or announce the lawsuit in-time to make their six o'clock newscast. I'm working with a P.R. firm that's already written the press release and I will personally see that it hits the wire services before the stock market closes this afternoon. The clock is running, boys."

"Can you give us a few minutes?" the lead Woo-Esterhouse lawyer asked.

Since the company was about to make a large stock offering and since their C.E.O. hated negative publicity, a confidential, no admission of fault, out-of-court settlement in the amount of $500,000 was offered twenty minutes later, which Mr. Girard accepted on Lisa Ann's behalf.

On his way out of Woo-Esterhouse, Thornton spoke briefly to the reporter for the local TV station that had set up in front of the building.

"What did you tell your boss?" he asked.

"I said that we needed to shoot some background footage for an upcoming story on Woo-Esterhouse. He said to go ahead as long as we didn't spend more than a half-hour to get it."

"Thanks, Art! I owe you one, big time," Mr. Girard said. "Your next DWI defense is on the house," he added, smiling.

Shortly after receiving her settlement money, Lisa Ann contacted the elderly couple who owned the Linville cabin and they agreed to sell it to her and Franklin.

Funny thing, when the layoffs began in the R&D department at Woo-Esterhouse that summer, Franklin's name somehow made it to the top of the list and he was given a skimpy parting package along with a reminder of his two-year non-compete agreement. He had to hire a lawyer, a much cheaper one than Lisa Ann's, to get the promised royalties on the products made using his patent, but did prevail in the matter. (In other words, he won. Sorry, I just had to get one more of 'em in before the end of the story.)

Dong Long Woo, a man of the highest moral standards, felt that Jack Esterhouse had totally disgraced the entire organization and brought great shame to his company. Jack was sent home within a week of arriving in Beijing, flying in Coach this time. Waiting for the right moment, the announcement of Jack's retirement from Woo-Esterhouse was made in August, just after the company's disappointing second quarter results became public. The blame for their poor showing landed directly on the outgoing President of U.S. Operations.

Franklin and Lisa Ann were married in the new Youngstown Free Will Evangelic Fundamentalist Church on October 15th, 1988. Apparently, Preacher Carlyle did a good job of hitchin' 'em, 'cause they're still together today.

After he left Woo-Esterhouse, Franklin used his shoe-box money for a down payment on a run-down block of buildings in Franklinville, restoring them to their former glory and keeping one of the storefronts for the offices of Delworth Electrical Engineering. At one time, many, many years ago it had been a Western Auto and even a church. To his credit, Franklin now holds six U.S. Patents on products he designed and is earning royalties from the companies licensed to use his ideas. Lisa Ann works part time for the firm, managing the office and she's still smokin' hot, according to Franklin.

You might be interested in knowing that one afternoon in the summer of 1989, just as the road widening project was wrapping up, Marcus saw an ancient VW van with Oregon plates, pulled off on the southbound shoulder of U.S. 1 near where the Starbrite used to sit. A bearded guy in shabby clothes, who Marcus thought looked a lot like Eddie Franchetti, was standing next to the VW. He had a sad look on his face and just stood there shaking his head. Marcus probably would have stopped, but he was headed for his lunch break.

Youngstown, NC is no longer the wide spot on U.S. 1 where Willa Mae and Eustace grew up. Today it's a thriving city that over 10,000 good people call their home. As Are Dee had predicted, it became one of the Raleigh suburbs and part of a metro area with nearly three million folks.

Today, there's a whole passel of Yankees living in Youngstown and thereabouts. Mostly nice people who wanted to escape the hustle and bustle of big cities to live quieter lives in a place where the streets are safe, the winters are mild, the summers are brutal and spring can be measured by hours. It's a place where the sun shines in the beautiful Carolina Blue sky year 'round and just looking up toward the heavens will make you smile.

If you ever come down our way, I hope you'll spend some time in Youngstown. We've still got a café where you can order biscuits and Red Eye gravy for breakfast and a grocery store that sells salt-cured Country Ham in canvas sacks. There's a lot of nice folks in our town who'll make you feel right at home, including some of our relocated Yankees. Bless their hearts!

Now, I suppose that y'all thought I'd forgotten about the time capsule. You'd be wrong.

Franklin and Lisa Ann kept it on a shelf at their house until just after the stroke of midnight on January 1st, 2000. Sitting comfortably in their living room, sipping champagne, he carefully opened the old wooden box and smiled as he went through the contents, all of it memories of his childhood. It was only when he got to the bottom that he stopped in his tracks. There was an envelope with Willa Mae's handwriting, addressed to him.

Dearest Franklin,

By the year 2000, I 'spect that me and Eustace will be long gone, but hopefully not forgotten. Before he puts your time capsule in the ceiling, I've asked him to let me add something to it.

I've wanted to give this to you many times, but thought that it might mean more to you as a grown man than it would now.

I told you that someday you'd find a pot of gold at the Starbrite. Well here it is. The only gold that ever meant a dang to us. Now it's yours.

Love,
Willa Mae

Underneath Willa Mae's envelope was a small package wrapped in brown grocery bag paper that Franklin peeled back carefully. Inside was an antique, gold-leaf picture frame that held a five by seven inch photo of Franklin's momma with him in her arms, his daddy, Eustace and Willa Mae, all standing together in front of the Starbrite Motel.

Willa Mae had told the truth. Franklin was holding a piece of precious gold from the Starbrite Motel that meant the world to him. The world.

Taking Lisa Ann outside to have a look at the cloudless, moonlit sky in the first hour of the new millennium, Franklin quietly spoke the words that Willa Mae had taught him as a child, "Star light, star-bright first star I see tonight, wish I may, wish I might have the wish I wish tonight."

"What did you wish for?" Lisa Ann asked.

Saying nothing, Franklin just smiled and gave her a kiss.

Y'all can blow your nose, wipe your eyes one last time and put the tissues away, 'cause we're done with the story.

Made in the USA
Columbia, SC
30 July 2019